AMERIKKKAN JUSTUS

By: DaLena Slayton

AMERICAN
JUSTICE

By: Dalena Slayton

Table of Contents

PART 1

Prologue

Sentencing

"Justice or JustUS?" —D. Slate

"Fifteen years." The judge slammed her gavel on the bench. It was the sound of judgment. At first, her face looked rigid and cold. But when her voice blared out my sentence, it seemed like saying the words made her warmer. It was like saying the words made her happy.

I looked around the courtroom, noticing for the first time that there were no windows on any of the white walls. I felt the air leave my lungs, and I began to suck for air like a fish out of water. Fifteen years. The words echoed in my head and consumed my thoughts.

I stared blankly at the judge. Her chapped lips moved with a vengeance. I tried to translate her words, but they seemed foreign. I couldn't focus. The only words that registered in my brain were—"Fifteen years."

I turned to my attorney, seeking confirmation of what I'd heard. My eyes begged for a different translation; maybe I misunderstood what she said between the legal mumbo jumbo. I wanted him to explain away the words "fifteen" and "years." I waited, expecting him to ask the judge for clarification but he didn't. I nudged him with my elbow hinting that he should ask the judge for leniency or sympathy or something. He said nothing. He didn't have to; I saw in his posture what I had heard from the judge's lips: fifteen years.

His hands rested on the cherry wood table in front of us, and his head hung low. He avoided my gaze. I needed him to see me because maybe then he'd somehow hear the words I wanted to say but could not; my voice was muted. Instead, he held his head down, shaking it silently in his own state of disbelief, as if it were he who'd had just been sentenced to fifteen years.

I nudged him again, harder this time, and waited for him to look up; he had to look up. That's how this worked. I had seen it happen on T.V many times. I didn't know the timing of the things that were supposed to happen, but I knew that there were some words that my lawyer was supposed to say, and they weren't coming out of his mouth. Had he forgotten his script? I nudged him again, hard, and managed to find my voice, "isn't this the part where you are supposed to object or something?" Still, no words. The room grew silent. I could feel calloused eyes burning through my back.

The judge was looking at me as if she were waiting for me to speak. I wanted to talk. I tried to speak, but when I tried to move my mouth, no words came out. I willed an apology for everything I had ever done. Nothing. I tried to muster up tears of remorse, or any tears that would make the judge revoke the sentence. They, too, failed me.

The room remained quiet along with me. I listened hard, hoping to hear something that meant her "fifteen years" was a mistake or that she had changed her mind. My ears felt numb, and my thoughts grew louder. My head was pounding so hard that sweat droplets dripped from my temples and slid down my face until they collided with my tears.

"Why?" busted through my lips, angrily.

The pounding in my head eased as my thoughts rushed to my mouth, desperate for freedom. I attempted to cover my mouth after my outburst. Instead, I found myself reaching toward the judge. I wanted a hug. A hug could save me. If she understood that I was reaching for a hug from a mother who could no longer hug me back, from a father who could never love a "me," and from a system that claimed to be blind, even though the gavel rang differently when it sensed color, then sympathy would change the sentence.

The judge's face did not rest, her lips did not curve upward, and her arms did not reach for me. Her pores seemed to emit the scent of rejection and recognized the "got you" in her eyes, which seemed to boast of her satisfaction with what her sentence achieved. It was that look which sent me into a frenzy.

"You cannot be serious. This ain't real. Wake me up, man!" I screamed.

"Order."

"Mam, I mean, your honor, I mean, hey man, not me. I am a good man. I don't deserve that. Fifteen years? Mam, did you say fif, fifth, fifteen?"

"Order," she continued to shout over my hysterics.

But there was no order, and there would be no order. There was no organization, no rhymes, nor reasons. There were only fifteen years.

Order required me to be silent and void of emotion while the gavel demanded my obedience and my freedom. The system for which order and the gavel spoke demanded my life. The system did not care for the truth; she just wanted my silence.

The judge called for the bailiff and gave a slight nod in my direction. Her commands didn't seem to require words, only punctuation of stiff nods and the slam of her gavel.

The bailiff began to make his way to me, slave-like in his obedience. I stared at the bailiff as hard as I could, looking for the puppet strings affixed to him. The shackles shook against his hips as he reached for them. They were not silent. Each clank barked out a moment in history, leading to this moment when they would secure my return to a state with which my ancestors were familiar. Enslaved. Jim Crowed. Incarcerated. Cages all; different forms.

My mind raced as tears slid down my face. *A black bailiff. Of course, they'd make a black man carry out the orders.* I could picture him, brown like me, striding across a well-kept and fruitful plantation built on the backs of our brothers, his assigned whip ready to deliver a lash that some half illiterate master had ordered because he was too lazy or cowardly to issue the strike himself.

The bailiff grabbed the shackles and unclasped them from his buckle. His expression said, "I am just following orders."

In my mind, I questioned his willingness to comply. *Did he know there was a thin line between "justice and just US?"* I glanced up at the judge and saw the smile beaming across her face. *Fuck it.* I looked back at the bailiff. *Fucking puppet.*

~ ~ ~

I had understood life until this point. I had been sold on the American dream even though I had never actually lived it. I never reached an open hand for reparations or complained about what I thought someone owed me. I hadn't sat on my mother's couch waiting for the mailman to deliver my 40 acres and a mule. When the world threw dirt in my face, I wiped it off and kept pushing. When my wits were at their ends, I developed new wits.

Of course, there were times when I was angry at the world. But instead of pouting, I got on my feet and made my inconveniences work for me the best I knew how. Whenever my hustle was outdone, I didn't throw a fit; I hustled harder. I took the risks no one else would take, and I gave the benefit of the doubt to others even though no one ever found the time to give the same to me. I followed directions. I stood quietly when I was told, I ran when I was told, and I fought back when I was told. I followed the rules so much that I didn't even become a man until I was told. As cruel as the world had been to me, I didn't let it harden my heart. I made it my mission to take care of anyone needing attention.

I tried my best not to excuse my life with excuses. I was a man, and I figured out how to be one on my own. Until this moment, I thought I had everything figured out. Now, I was questioning everything. I realized that I should have been questioning everything all along. I had always thought of myself as a quick learner, but as it turned out, I didn't learn things nearly quickly enough.

I told myself that I would exceed my mother's expectation after watching her give all her time to a job that couldn't pay her enough to afford anything outside of the slums. So, I worked. I chose ambition over reality and statistics. All that "land of the free" shit was bullshit. I survived the tragedies of my life and made a strength out of the stereotypes that were meant to hold me down. I pushed forward when I had no reason to push forward other than the world's narrative of false hope about a reality that wasn't being offered to an average nigga. I put my best foot forward, and despite the average nigga shit that kept jumping in my path, I kept my stride. When most people would have broken in half, I held it together and kept running for my slice of "white-only pie."

I couldn't shake the sound of the judge's voice. Her voice, lifeless through the whole trial, was implicative of my fate. The jury of my peers mimicked the judge; lifeless. Damn the education system for not teaching me the proper definition of peers. I guess I missed the moment when I, a young black man in my 20's, looked like or was considered a peer to a bunch of middle-aged, backwoods, swamp fed, hillbilly bred white boys, and overly conservative elderly white women.

I was declared "guilty" before I ever stepped foot in that courtroom. For the first time, I accepted that. I should have realized my guilt when the District attorney and my hired lawyer exchanged an unnecessary handshake before my lawyer suddenly resigned from my case because of a "family emergency." When what could have been a simple request for a reset date became a request for me to find new representation at the last minute, I should have known. I should have accepted that I was already guilty when the public defender called me Marcus instead of Rilei; I probably could have saved the whole room time if I had noticed that the judge didn't even bother to look at me during the entire trial.

It made sense now. Why bother to know my name and why bother to search my face, or learn about my character, when you already knew I was guilty? The more I thought about it, the stupider I felt for even attempting to defend myself. I felt crazy for thinking that I could be found not guilty when everyone in the courtroom knew I was guilty but me.

Most people think as I thought. Most people convince themselves that they are in control of their own destinies. Most people, however, never stepped foot in the courtroom on trumped-up charges, with some bullshit required minimum sentence. Most people have not been in my situation.

There's a pre-conceived notion of law and order that says if you do the crime, you do the time. I had broken many laws, but the crime that I was given time for was not mine. No one cared to prove my guilt. I was facing the type of situation niggas talked about, but I never took seriously. My situation was the kind you complain about when you're in it while those who are outside your position swear you are exaggerating. We've been brainwashed to believe in the idea of innocent until proven guilty. That's probably why I wasn't afraid of my case going to trial even though I was never offered a plea deal. It took me a while, but I figured out that they didn't need to deal with me. They didn't need my plea; to them, I was already guilty. It was up to me to prove my innocence.

The jury and judge only saw a drug-dealing criminal trying to squeeze his way through the system, an influential black man. They didn't see a man with potential. They witnessed a black man who was climbing above their maximum allowed level for a "successful nigga." Above all, they saw a "nigga" who was doing it not strictly by tearing down his own people but through the veins and nostrils of theirs. Suddenly, the real crime, real evidence, and real justice weren't important; "JustUS" was.

Chapter 1

Foundation

"What do you see in a man if not all the things that it took to make a man?"—D. Slate

While peering down at the computer screen, she read the details of my identity. Clad in her blue justice suit and shiny badge, she slid the electronic finger pad toward me.

"Rilei Connel Easton, 25 years old, born December 12th, 1992, birthplace Akron, Ohio, is this correct?"

I verified my identity while I stared back and forth between her and the finger pad. Her face wore wrinkles, and her eyes looked heavy. I assumed she must be nearing the end of her shift because of the way she rushed through processing. Who knows? Maybe she was just tired of booking "niggas."

The familiarity of the booking process shocked me. It felt like déjà vu. It didn't feel like it was my first time being input into the system. The more I thought about it, the more I realized that I had been prepped for this moment from the time I entered Children's Protective Services. It was nice to know that the booking process was streamlined for comfort and convenience. I didn't feel out of place at all.

~ ~ ~

I was born in 1992 on the west side of Akron, Ohio. I never had a father, but I had a mother, and she was beautiful. She had mocha brown skin, soft hazel eyes, and long silky hair that curled at the slightest touch of water. Her smile was wide and warm, and she always smelled like cocoa butter lotion and vanilla.

I was her twin in male form although I was lighter in complexion. My eyes were hazel like hers, and my curls were just as playful. I was small in stature, but my mother always said that I had an athletic build. It made me feel better to believe her because kids my age were almost always larger than me. I did have some features that I couldn't find on my mother. Those features sometimes raised my curiosity about my father, but never long enough to miss his presence. I looked enough like my mother to pretend my father away.

My mother was my hero. It was her and me against anyone and everyone if need be. My grandparents always told her that I was spoiled, and she needed to let me go out and be a boy, but she kept me close. When my grandfather tried to rough house with me, my mother would get irritated and cause a scene.

"He's not a thug. He is not aggressive. He is a scholar," Mama would yell at him.

"A gay scholar."

"No, Daddy, not gay; he's just a scholar and a decent boy," Mama would reply.

It never bothered me to play with my grandfather, but I pretended it did because I knew it bothered Mama.

Mama preferred the gentler side of the world, and she swore by education.

I remember sitting up late with her and playing with her hair as she read me bedtime stories. Every morning before school, she told me she loved me more than anything in the world, and then sent me off telling me to be great and learn something that wasn't in the books that were shown, but rather in the books that were hidden. "Learn something that can't be taught," she said.

"What mysteries did you solve today," she asked me every evening. Through her eyes, I could tell that she was genuinely curious. Each day after school, she asked me what I was taught and what I had learned. That was our "thing." I was supposed to find the forbidden knowledge. My job was to challenge what I was taught by finding information that no one offered me.

My mother worked hard, sometimes so hard that she would come home and cry from pure exhaustion. She never let me see her, but I heard her in the bathroom when all else was silent. As hard as she worked, she never allowed her time with me to falter. Whatever time she spent working to keep me fed didn't take from the time she had reserved to spend with me. She was never too busy or too overworked to check in on my mysteries or to remind me that she loved me. We never missed story time, movie night, or free days at the museums. I wondered how she did it all and still wore a smile, but the answer wasn't in any book, so I figured she was a superhero.

She taught me how to read at three and pushed against all the school regulations for me to start school when I was 4. Due to the school board requirements, I wasn't supposed to start until I was five, but my mother felt that was holding me back. She argued with the Board of Education and begged them to let me test for early admission. I don't know how she got it done, but she got me in. She pushed education on me in a way that made it seem as though it wasn't an option. Even when I was too young to understand, she found a way to make me challenge conventional beliefs. She would ask me why something was the way it was. When I answered, she would ask me, "but how do you know?"

My mother and I lived with my grandparents in my younger years. She found out she was pregnant with me when she was 17; I was born right after she turned 18. She was a senior in high school and had a slew of college scholarship offers flying in. My father was never there. I didn't question his absence like most young boys did because I never had a need to. I was loved, and I knew I was loved. When I turned 4, before school started, my mother moved us out of my grandparents' house into our first apartment. It was a small 2-bedroom apartment on the east side of town. It wasn't much, but she was proud, and I was happy. At that time, I thought we had it all.

The apartment was, looking back on it, a box. It had stairs, but it was still tiny. We entered through the kitchen and walked straight through to the living room. There was a living room door, but we never used it. The stairs were also in the living room. At the top of the stairs were two bedrooms and a bathroom. My bedroom was in back on the left-hand side. Mama's bedroom was at the top of the stairs, and the bathroom was between.

My mother never made excuses for why she couldn't do something, and she always made sure she had what she needed to take care of me. Even though my mother had me at a young age, my grandparents were proud of her because she didn't let being a young mother stop her from being a good mother. They were so pleased with her that when she moved, they purchased her dishes, a living room set, my bedroom set, and her bed. Once they were finally able to convince her to accept it all, our small box began to feel more like our cozy castle.

The best part of all of this was that all Mama's furniture was paid for. That was a big deal in the neighborhood because Rent-A-Center was infamous in our apartment complex. The few friends I had lived in the same complex as me. I often visited their apartments and noticed that furniture that had been there the previous day was gone. Once, I went to my friend Dante's house. The television and the couches that I had sat on two days earlier were gone. No one ever seemed ashamed because repossession was expected. In fact, sometimes it became a guessing game of whose house Rent-A-Center was going to get next. Parents in the neighborhood had a system where they'd call each other when they saw the trucks coming down the street. The idea was to warn whoever's home was the likely target so they could pretend not to be home. Otherwise, someone was bound to lose a TV, couch, or dining room table.

I loved our place because nothing ever changed. I came home to the same furniture, the same TV, and the same mother asking the same questions, "What mystery did you solve today?" We may not have lived in the best neighborhood, but it felt like the best. Despite the things going on outside, inside was steady. I never questioned my safety or felt worried. On the contrary, I always felt safe and unbothered.

Chapter 2

Woodchips and Dirt

"Many people may know you, but few will understand you." —Unknown

Dante was my best friend. I hung out with him more than any other kid. We had the same classrooms and teachers from kindergarten through the 4th grade. Dante was a frail and skinny white kid with blue eyes and blond hair. He wore his hair like a stereotypical white boy with bangs that covered his forehead. His clothes and shoes were always too big for him, which left him open for all types of insult. He resembled your average school shooter now that I think about it. But that wasn't him, he was much more than what met the eye. Unfortunately, kindergarten students only related to what met their eyes and that did not work in Dante's favor

I was the only kid who didn't tease him for his unkempt style. In our first year of school, we were assigned seats next to each other. Mrs. Bryce, our kindergarten teacher, arranged the class seats in groups of four. Four students shared a table for the school year unless there was a problem or disagreement. And Dante, he was a problem; a walking disagreement.

The first day of kindergarten, students filed in the classroom and took seats wherever we could find them. Initially, Dante sat at a table filled with white kids. I assume that it must have been in his comfort zone because they were all white. There was nothing else that he shared with the kids at his chosen table. The problem was the kids at his table insulted him worse than the kids he was trying to avoid by sitting with the white kids. His tablemates teased him about the way he smelled and the way he looked.

A blond girl named Halie told him that he was a "gangly looking feller" and set the whole class laughing. No one knew what it meant, but everyone knew it was an insult and that it sounded funny.

I was intrigued by the word "gangly" and couldn't wait to find out what it meant. The word was exceptional for a kindergartner, and it played in my mind all day. I used it several ways so that I wouldn't forget to find out what it meant later. While I counted to thirty with the other kids, I inserted gangly between twenty-nine and thirty. When we sat on the carpet for reading circle, I made it a point call the carpet and the book gangly. The story was gangly, the teacher was gangly, and I was going to take my gangly behind home and find out what "gangly" meant. Until then, everything would be gangly.

Halie teased Dante more than she teased any other kid and often used her exceptional vocabulary to do so. Unlike others, I did not believe it was because she had a secret crush on him. Halie's secret crush was on Daniel, who also sat at their table. Jessica, the four-eyed monster, sat at their table as well, and she and Halie were best friends. Dante sat right next to the four-eyed monster, but Halie saved all her insults for Dante. It was as if she were blind to Jessica's peculiar, less than human features. Between lessons, when the teacher was not paying attention, Halie made fun of Dante to draw laughs from the rest of the class. Through her comedic efforts, I learned some of my best vocabulary words in kindergarten. Because of her various descriptions of Dante, I advanced from calling kids bucktooth and four-eyes to more sophisticated insults like: gangly, homely, destitute, idiotic, and my favorite, queer.

I wondered where Halie came from and how she learned big vocabulary words like that. She seemed too elite to be attending the same school as me. My impression was confirmed when her father brought cupcakes to the class for her birthday. After seeing her father, everything became clear.

I assumed she learned words from her father, who probably shouted them to lonely people begging for food on corners. My mother had told me about those kinds of people. They were the type who turned their noses up and had secret hate for everyone who wasn't like them. Mama said to stay away from them and their money because there was a trick to the riches. "Nothing but smoke and mirrors. They aren't happy, baby," Mama would say. Mama hadn't forbidden me to learn and use their vocabulary, though.

I chose to learn the meaning of every word Halie said. I thought to myself, if a man like her father says these words and looks how he looks, then I too, should know these words. I thought they were powerful words for the rich, or at least for the people who could afford to use them at someone else's expense. I called them power words.

I remember the day the word "queer" became the center of my power word obsessions. Halie was coloring as the class usually did before the first bell rang. She noticed Dante looking at her picture instead of coloring his own, and she attempted to cover the picture. Dante must have been in a bad mood, or the power word must have been more powerful than the others because when Halie said to Dante: "Don't look at me. That's why you're a queer" Dante reacted for the first time ever.

"Halie," he had said with a strange calm, "if you don't leave me alone, I am going to staple your eyes and your mouth shut. Then...," he paused with a sinister smile, " then I am going to set your hair on...."

Every student in the class stopped talking and sat with their mouths gaping open. The strange silence in the class drew Mrs. Bryce's attention. Next thing I knew, Mrs. Bryce was walking him out of the classroom. I didn't see Dante until three days later. When he returned to class, he had been assigned the seat next to me.

After his suspension, which had been his first, Dante was always getting in trouble. He was involved in everything from disrupting class to fighting. I understood Dante in some weird sort of way. When he first was assigned to my table, I was the one who broke the silence. I greeted him and let him know he had a friend in me. Although I sometimes laughed when Halie picked with him, I also felt sorry for him because he was always the subject of a sad story or joke.

Talking to Dante made me realize how misunderstood he was. He got teased for things he couldn't control. His mother was a heroin addict. She had been a heavy user since Dante's father passed away; he was killed a few weeks before kindergarten started. His father was one of the men killed in a widely publicized quadruple homicide that happened on the west side of town.

Dante hadn't had any new shoes or clothes since his father died. The clothes he wore were rugged and torn, too big, or hand-me-downs from older cousins who were almost twice his size.

Despite Dante's misfortune, whenever he wasn't being picked on, he always had a smile and a joke to offer. No one else knew that side of Dante because no one, including his mother, seemed to pay him any attention. Not many people took the time to sit and talk to him, but I did.

In class, I talked to him when we were supposed to be reading, doing classwork, or just being silent. Dante's life was fascinating to me. He got to walk home from school, and I always had to get rides; he got to have school lunch, and I had a packed lunch; and, best of all, he got to leave class early some days and get snacks while he spoke to the counselor and watched movies in her office. I had to stay in class.

The more we talked about his life, the closer we became. I envied a lot of what I thought were his freedoms. He was different from me, and I understood that, where I had consistency and love, he had constant change and hostility. I eventually started to feel like, in a way, Dante was my brother, and I had to look out for him. Finding out that we lived in the same apartments sealed the deal, and we became best friends.

Much of kindergarten year, outside of school, consisted of Dante sleeping over at my house. I could say the same for much of the summer. Dante was a year older than me. That didn't matter much because no one could tell by looking at us or hearing us speak. I was structured and well-prepared for school. I was always on time. In fact, I was always there before the bell rang for breakfast, thanks to my mother. Dante could barely make it to school at all, thanks to his mother.

Being friends with Dante helped me learn that age didn't measure anything more years spent on earth. As proof, Dante's age did not make him more rational than me; I was more rational. I was also more intelligent than Dante in many ways. Dante understood life better than me. He had better survival instincts, but age was not the reason for that. His lack of a mother was. He handled disappointment better than I did because he had met disappointment several times, and I had never even been in the same vicinity of disappointment. Nothing seemed to shock Dante. It was as if he expected adversity and welcomed whatever was the worse that life had to offer.

I remember a time my mom was late to pick me up from school, and I nearly lost my mind. I got upset and worried because she wasn't where she was supposed to be when I had gotten out of school. I never once questioned the reason why she wasn't there, and I didn't care why. All I knew and cared about was that she was not there. I was upset because it was a change in our schedule that I wasn't used to. I could normally set the clock by our daily routines, and she had altered them without talking to me.

I was at the point of hysterics when Dante looked at me with quizzical eyes and said, "Rilei, are you crying? Don't be a queer."

Dante had no understanding of my fear, and he had no knowledge of the definition of queer. I knew he had only used it because Hailie had said it to him. I told him so as well. He merely laughed me off and suggested that we walk home instead.

I was hesitant about walking. Mama had never allowed me to walk before. Dante sat on the brick wall that surrounded the school and stared at me. I felt his eyes burning into the side of my face while he waited on me to decide. It wasn't as easy for me to just decide to walk as he wanted it to be. I was being introduced to disappointment and peer pressure at the same time, and it was overwhelming.

Dante, while growing tired of waiting, looked to me, and said, "you know why Halie called me a queer?"

I told him no and continued to focus on the road where my mother's car should have been. He sat in silence. When I realized he had not explained why Halie called him my favorite power word, I looked over at him and asked, "Why?"

I waited for what felt like forever for him to tell me. He finally spoke while twiddling his thumbs. His face flushed red, and he said, "My mom calls me a queer all the time."

I looked at him with my jaws dropped. I had looked in my mother's dictionary for the word the first time I heard it after finding that it was not in my small children's dictionary. To my surprise, the word had only meant strange or odd when I read it in Mama's dictionary, but it meant something totally different when I told Mama to stop being queer.

She was folding the laundry and singing at the top of her lungs. She was sillier than usual, and I wanted to show her what I had learned: "queer." So, I used the word to describe what she was doing, and she nearly had a cow trying to get over to the couch to smack my lips. Mama explained to me later that although what I had seen in the dictionary was true, the word was more often used in a derogatory manner to describe those with "different" sexual preferences. I didn't understand anything she said so she said, "it is a mean and hurtful thing to say, so don't say it."

I loved Mama, and I always listened to her, but I also loved that word. It was my power word, and I couldn't let it go. Instead, I promised myself I would never use it around Mama. Besides, school was filled with mean and hurtful words. But that was school, I never imagined that hurtful and mean words were said at kids' homes as well. I always thought of being at home as being in your safe space.

I picked up my jaw and allowed Dante to finish the story. There was no way he could know what queer really meant because the real meaning wasn't even in the adults' dictionary. I patted Dante's shoulder while he stared into the sidewalk. Our feet dangled from the brick wall, and we sat in silence for a moment. Dante suddenly picked up where he left off and told me that his mom told him that she was going to staple his lips together and burn him alive if he kept whining like some little queer.

Dante said it all so matter-of-factly that I wondered if he really understood what she was saying. I felt bad for Dante at that moment, but I didn't know what I could do. So, I did the only thing he requested of me, I grabbed my book bag and pushed myself off the wall. I turned to Dante and told him, "she didn't use the word right anyway, let's walk."

I had never walked home before, but I put on my brave face. My mother made it a point to take me and pick me up from school every day. Our rides to school were filled with so much conversation that I never thought to look at the directions that we were traveling, so I wasn't even sure I knew the way home from school. But, not wanting to seem like a baby or like a whining queer, I stupidly snatched up my backpack and allowed Dante to carry me on his journey. I agreed to walk as a comfort to Dante, and that's exactly what we did. We walked. And walked. And walked.

The walk seemed longer than I thought it should have been. We turned corner after corner, and at times I would have sworn we were walking in circles and turning the same corners. I was terrified that we had gotten lost. I started to have random thoughts of never returning home, and my mom never being able to find me.

As the first teardrop began to slip from my eyes, my mom pulled around the corner, screaming out my name. Between her high-pitched screams and the shakiness in her voice, I was able to make out her saying, "get your ass in this car right now."

It was the first time I was ever "not" where my mom expected me to be. It was my first time going against what I knew was right. She didn't scold me because she could see it in my eyes that I was traumatized enough. The tears in my eyes were indicative of the fear I felt walking with Dante and feeling lost. I thought to myself at that moment, "so this is a disappointment, may we never meet again."

When I reunited with my mother, I was ecstatic. It was a joy beyond measure strapping my seatbelt across my chest. I wore a smile more joyous than a kid in a candy store.

I needed my mother. I feared the unknown. Dante didn't. I was in shock at the way he hopped in the car so casually, as if my mother pulling up when she did wasn't our saving grace. Dante was brave, or maybe I was just cowardly. With tears in her eyes, and relief in her voice, she apologized, explaining that her doctor appointment had ran later than expected. I wanted to be angry, but there was no denying the feeling that overcame me when my mother showed up, pure joy. That was Teigen, my mother, and she always showed up for me.

~ ~ ~

All the encounters we had as young kids were mostly accredited to Dante. My first-time skipping school was because of Dante; my first time getting an in-school suspension—Dante; and my first fight — Dante.

It was our first-grade year, and we had finally made it to the playground after a morning filled with a spelling test and math problems. Dante had decided that he had a tough morning and was tired of all the kids hogging the swing time.

Once we were out the doors and, on the playground, Dante took off toward the swings that were already filled with other kids. There were six swings in total, and they were all filled. The first three were filled with Halie from kindergarten, Jessica, and some awkward white kid who had red welts all over his face.

The last three swings were occupied by Daniel from kindergarten, another white kid who looked like Pinocchio would if he were a real boy and Joey. Joey was the black kid. The only black kid on the swings. Dante walked up to Joey and told him that he was tired of waiting, and he wanted the swings to be empty before he came back.

I sat back wondering if Dante expected Joey not only to get off the swings but also to round up everyone else and get them off the swings as well. I wasn't sure what Dante's intentions were, but I minded my business on the lumber surrounding the slide area. I could tell when Dante looked over at me that something was going on and I hoped that he could tell by looking at me that I preferred no part of it.

Joey was a big black kid. He was like one of me and two of Dante combined. His cheeks were like a squirrel's when they were filled with nuts, and his hands were two times bigger than my own. He was the only kid who didn't need a stool to write on the chalkboard. When he walked, even though there was a waddle that caused snickers, there was thunder in each footstep that made sure the snickers were inaudible.

Everyone knew Joey as the gentle giant. He was the type of kid who you don't bother, and he doesn't bother you. Joey was also the kind of kid that if you did bother, you ran before he could bother you. Daniel was the test dummy. He had tried to use one of Halie's insults on Joey earlier in our first-grade year, and Joey's large hand made a home around Daniel's small neck. It took two teachers to pry Joey's hands away, and three days suspension to calm Joey down.

Dante was just as frail as he was when we first met, but for some reason, his heart had quadrupled in size since his encounter with Halie in kindergarten. I still feared for Dante after he had spoken to Joey in that manner. But again, maybe I was cowardly, and maybe Dante was brave.

After giving Joey his orders, Dante had walked back to where I sat on the lumber and grabbed my hand. I tried to resist because I didn't fully understand what he had gotten us into. I didn't really want to swing anyway; I preferred the slides much more. I tried to firm up my muscles and keep myself from being pulled up. I kept trying to tell Dante that the slides were ready for the taking. Dante didn't care. He yanked me up from the ground mouthing fanatically, "fat Joey better be off them swings."

While heading back to the swings with me in tow, he bent down and picked up a handful of gravel and woodchips. Dante marched back to the swing where the gentle giant still sat looking perplexed about his and Dante's encounter minutes earlier. Dante gave Joey a sinister once over. I hadn't seen that same look since Halie had called him a queer, and here I was witnessing it again. I panicked.

I glanced at Dante's face to see if I could sense what he was thinking, but all I could gather from his face was that the situation was about to go from bad to worse.

Dante looked Joey up and down with an expression that broadcasted his irritation. Next thing I know wood chips and dirt had taken flight. Dante hurled some at Joey swinging erratically. Joey fell backward off the swing with Dante landing on top of him. I wasn't sure what my role was supposed to be while Dante fought for his life, so I did the only thing I felt safe doing. I grabbed a hand full of woodchips and dirt and sat on the swing in case Dante needed more of his concoction.

A crowd had begun forming. Dante paused in the middle of his fight after noticing that he was drawing attention. He jumped up and ran over to the swing next to the one that Joey had been warned to leave and told me to hurry up and swing with him. I dropped my woodchips and dirt concoction and complied with his demands. I kicked off the ground hard to get a good push. In mid-rhythm, I felt a jerk. I looked back to find that our first-grade teacher, Mr. Tuotomy, had grabbed the chains of our swing, freezing us in mid-flight.

Grabbing us by the ears, Mr. Tuotomy marched us into the school building and straight to the principal's office. It was an abnormally long walk to the office. On the way there, I thought about what my mother would do when she found out about my fight. Mama was not one for aggressive behavior, and for some reason, I could only imagine her attacking me aggressively when she found out that I had displayed aggression on the playground. I began to regret grabbing the woodchips and helping Dante fight.

I was dripping sweat and tears on the walk to the office. Dante was grinning. I could tell that he was more relaxed than I was. I didn't understand how Dante's panic button worked, or if he even had a panic button. I grew irritated that he could be so calm when I was so worried that my life as I knew it was about to change.

When we arrived in the office, the principal called Dante first. After speaking with Dante, the principal sent the hall runner to retrieve Joey from class. He then requested that the school secretary write an incident report for Dante and me. When Joey arrived in the office, Principle Sparsely sent Dante and me back to class.

I was beyond confused about what was going on, but I wasn't going to ask any questions and stir up unnecessary debris from the situation. Relieved that my mother wasn't going to be disturbed with the details of my good day gone bad, I smiled at Dante, thankful for whatever he had said.

Curiosity troubled me the rest of the day until I finally had the opportunity to ask Dante what had happened. Dante and I sat on the familiar brick wall while waiting on my mother to pick us up. I poked at Dante until he confessed what he had said to get us off the hood.

Dante enjoyed seeing me squirm with curiosity. He knew I wanted to know everything so that I had no idea what he had said gave him a rise. After watching me twitch and ignoring my constant pokes in his side, he smiled crookedly and said, "No way was Sparsely going to believe I did all that to Joey; Joey is huge." I agreed with him. Joey was big, but everyone knew that Joey wasn't one to cause problems. Joey just wanted to be left alone. Even Principal Sparsely knew Joey was a good kid because whenever there was an award, Joey was a winner. The kid was practically a saint when left alone. Aside from all of Joey's character facts, Mr. Tuotomy had seen everything.

"Mr. Tuotomy seen the whole thing," I reminded Dante of what he had apparently forgotten. Dante laughed and assured me that Mr. Tuotomy hadn't seen anything. I knew that was not true because Joey had been on the ground, and Dante and I had been on the swings. I wanted to challenge Dante's statement, but I was not going to rack my brain to figure out what Dante said or how Dante's story could even be believable. Instead, I was just thankful that the principal did not call my mom.

My entire first-grade school year was comprised of repetitions of that day, but with different people. Dante became increasingly destructive with each passing day. And I involuntarily became his minion.

It was my job to counter what Dante was doing to others while giving him the illusion that I was doing his foul deeds with him. When he bullied someone, I would come right behind him and offer my apologies. When he stole something, I would go back and put my own of whatever he took to replace it. My mom had to buy me five boxes of crayons that year because I was continually giving kids crayons after Dante took theirs.

Like I said, I understood Dante. I knew he needed attention. When Dante stayed overnight at my place, he was always on his best behavior. He loved my mom, and my mom grew to love him. Dante never cursed or flirted with an insult at my house. His aggressive behavior was put away, and he was a tender child when he was around my mom. He'd volunteer to help clean and cook. He ate his vegetables without having to be asked twice and volunteered to put the dishes up after we ate. On weekends, we played video games during the day and read bedtime stories with my mom at night. He would get as excited as I did, if not more, when it came to night-time stories.

When it was just Dante and me, Dante was a different person. He wasn't the kid who beat up fat Joey, nor was he the bully at school. Dante was just Dante when he was at my house. The Dante that stayed at my house wouldn't hurt a fly, but that wasn't the Dante who I went to school with. My life seemed to be the life that Dante needed and in which he could have thrived. My life, as it was created by my mom, gave Dante his "calm." But my life was my life. Dante's life was his, and it was hell.

Chapter 3

H is for Helena

"To love a drug addict is to run out of tears."
—Sandy Swenson

By the time we were in third grade, our lives had changed, Dante's especially. Helena's heroin problem consumed her after Ralph passed away, and she was unable to hold her life together. Bills piled up and the little furniture she did have started to disappear. Rent-a-Center wasn't the culprit this time.

Dante still smiled and joked as usual, but his jokes became darker, and his smile looked more like a grimace. Dante no longer referred to his mother as Mom; instead, he referred to her as Helena.

In kindergarten, Dante drew pictures for his mom, but when other kids talked about their parents' reactions to their art, Dante was silent. Most kids were proud and bragged about their moms and dads. Not so with Dante.

Helena was beautiful. She was thin, and her body was athletic like my mom always told me mine was. Her addict ways did not change her happy smile, and when she laughed, you could see a whisper of freckles spread across her cheeks and nose. She was mostly pale except when emotion overcame her. Her eyes were blue and shaped like almonds. When I first met her, she had dark and flowing hair. She wore her hair in a ponytail, but the few times I saw it down convinced me that she was my vanilla beauty. Was.

Over the years, heroin turned that flowy hair into stringy, oily, strands. It made her beautiful almond-shaped blue eyes dark. Moreover, it changed her from being Dante's mom to being just Helena.

I could see the mother in her fading away every time I saw Dante. He was a direct reflection of Helena's ability to mother. Helena was smart. She was not as sharp as my mom, but I knew she was smart because she had many books. My mama always said that a person who reads a lot knows a lot. I never saw her read the books, but I knew they weren't around for nothing.

There were times when we were at Dante's apartment, and Helena would go upstairs for hours. We smelled the traveling aroma of her addiction, but she stayed out of sight. It embarrassed Dante that I was there while his mother used, so I pretended that I thought she was up there reading. We never tiptoed into her business as most children do with their parents. Dante was uninterested in her ways; therefore, we stayed downstairs and watched the roaches crawl as we joked about whatever happened at school that day. We were respectful of Helena's privacy, and although I was curious about what Helena did upstairs, I was considerate of Dante's feelings.

When my mother's shifts changed at her job, I walked home from school with Dante. By then, my mother knew and loved Dante as if he was her surrogate son. On school days, I stayed at Dante's apartment until my mother got home from work. He only lived a few doors down, and he wanted the company. My mom disapproved of me going to his house, but I always made it home before she found out I was there.

With Helena's addiction getting the best of her, she would leave for days at a time with no word or warning to Dante. She never left food in the house, and the lights or hot water were cut off on more than one occasion. After school, Dante and I rushed to his house, hoping he could catch his mother before she left. Most of the time we were too late, but on a few occasions, we caught her before she made it out the door.

Those times were painful to watch because Dante tried to talk and tell Helena everything under the sun, but she heard nothing. He gave her pictures that he had made, and she used them as placemats for her drugs, so she didn't lose any of the contents in the carpet.

One time, Dante gave her a Mother's Day card that he had made in class. She didn't bother to open and read it. Instead, she rolled it up, lit it on the stove, and used it to light her cigarette.

Dante had intentionally gotten detention that day so he could stay in during recess. He had spent all our recess stealing other kids' crayons to get the right colors for Helena's Mother's Day card, and it became a makeshift lighter.

It was hard to watch Dante beg for Helena's attention. I was relieved when she was already gone before we would get to his house. It was easier to deal with Dante's disappointment than it was to deal with his pain. He was upset because he never knew when she was going to come home, but at least I didn't have to watch him beg for her love if she'd already left the house.

Sometimes, Dante would stay at my house on school nights, but most of the time, I went home alone from his house. Dante hated being at home, but he stayed home and waited for Helena to come back. Every day he was there took more out of him. Helena's drug problem was eating away at Dante, and it showed.

One day, while walking home from school, Dante and I saw a small table outside one of the dumpsters near the apartments. He motioned to me to help him grab it. Dante was convinced that if he brought home some furniture that didn't belong to Rent-A-Center, Helena would be proud. I knew she wouldn't care, but it made Dante feel good, so I helped him carry the table to his apartment.

It was an old and raggedy table made of wood. There were warps in the wood from water damage and some areas where the wood was peeled. The table was a splinter trap. It was filthy, and it belonged at the dumpster. I wanted to tell Dante it was a waste of effort, but before I said a word, he said, "Now she can use this instead of my cards, she will love this.

I chose to say nothing and went to grab something from the kitchen to clean the table. The water had been shut off, so we ran to my apartment to get a cup of water to clean the table.

We spent several minutes scrubbing the grime off the table and several more trying to straighten up the rest of the apartment so the table would stand out. Once we were through, we laid back on the floor, marveling at our work.

We were in mid-conversation talking about how Halie had gotten into it with a new girl at school named Jasmine. Jasmine had punched Halie in the nose for using one of her father's power words. After all these years, Dante still hated Halie and was excited that someone finally "got her." I, on the other hand, hoped that it would not stop Halie from introducing me to more power words.

As we were talking, Helena burst into the living room and dropped a bag on the table. Not recognizing we were in the room or noticing that there was a table to spill her things on, she fumbled with the bag and pulled out its contents. Frustrated, she grabbed the bag and flipped it over several times. Items fell out missing the table, and I noticed a small baggy dropped out.

Her eyes glowed as she ripped open the small baggy and grabbed a spoon that had fallen to the floor. I became more interested in what she was doing versus the roach that I had secretly named Ted. I watched her intensely from the corner to which Dante and I had retreated when she busted in the door. She dumped whatever was in the baggy onto the spoon, still not bothering to look up. She tossed the empty baggy across the floor, reached for a pink lighter, and held it under the spoon. And still, not a glance in our direction.

I could smell the familiar aroma as it wrestled the hairs in my nose. I watched while she put the lighter down and reached for a needle. She didn't know we were watching as she sucked up whatever was on the spoon into her needle. She grabbed an elastic band and fidgeted with it to get it around her arm. She struggled for a few seconds, and only when she got tired did, she finally look up. Her eyes searched the room as if she were missing something. They landed when she found it.

"Dante, baby, come over here please."

Dante looked at me as he got up and dragged his feet over to his mother with slight hesitation. "Dante, Baby, you look so much like your father. Now be a good boy, tie this here round my arm, won't you?"

Dante said nothing, he just looked. I, still curious, hung in the back next to Ted, who must have been curious as well because he was watching as intently as I was as Dante tied the band around his mother's arm and stood looking at her with tears gathering in his eyes. She smiled at him and blew him a kiss.

I watched Helena as she tapped on her arm and inserted the needle, knowing that Dante was watching as well. I looked over at him and saw him falling to his knees as he observed the last bit of liquid drain into her arm. I thought about the times I had seen my grandfather inject himself with insulin. I thought to myself, "Helena must have diabetes." I knew there was more to it, and I knew that she didn't really have diabetes, but it seemed to be the most convenient explanation and the only thing I could think of to pacify Dante's truth.

Helena exhaled with relief and nodded at Dante. He stood, his face blank, not saying anything. She reached up and held his chin lightly in her hand. Then she whispered to him that she was never supposed to have been a mother. She started to nod off but managed to say to Dante: "I am not equipped for this. I don't have enough love left for you."

Dante knelt, trying to ease her head to the ground as she nodded. There weren't any beds in his house, but there were couch pillows in the closet underneath the stairs. Dante and I had stashed a few pillows under his staircase weeks ago when one of the neighbors got rid of their old sofa. Initially, we had planned to bring the sofa in too, but before we could get to it, a truck came by and staked its claim.

Dante ran to the staircase to grab a couch pillow to put under Helena's head. She was vulnerable, and he sensed it. He took advantage of the opportunity to see his mother's sensitive side and care for her as if it would prove him worthy of her love. It was as if he hadn't heard what she had said so clearly: she did not have enough love for him.

Dante moved mechanically trying to comfort his mother. I felt tears start to dance in my eyes. I felt the hopelessness that Dante should have been feeling but apparently was not.

"I love you, Ma," he said as he straightened her hair against the pillow. Helena appeared to have drifted off to sleep. Perhaps she was dreaming a good dream because a smile spread across her face. Dante beamed with joy when he saw her smile. Then, Helena spoke. She replied, "You know nothing about love. You don't love me, and I don't love you." She looked at him without a trace of emotion in her eyes and pointed at the needle she had just used to administer her "insulin."

Dante looked over his shoulder where the needle lay on the carpet. I thought I saw a tear fall from his eye. He handed Helena the needle and watched as she undid the band from her arm.

"Here, tie this tighter around my arm, won't you?" She paused, "then leave."

Dante did as he was told. After tying the knot, Dante turned to me, "Come on, Rilei, let's go." He didn't wait for me to respond, but walked to the door, opened it, and left. I followed.

We walked around the complex in silence for what felt like hours. It seemed like the whole world had delivered quietness and then stopped moving. Everything, even the sky, looked grim. It was as though every facet of life knew what had happened in Dante's apartment. Everyone except for me that is; I was lost.

"Hey, you know my grandfather used insulin?" I asked Dante. I had smelled the aroma before, and I knew what caused it although I wished I didn't know. I had never seen Helena using heroin; I'd only smelled it. I was not sure of what it all meant. I preferred the story that it was insulin because then I could pretend that Helena was sick. Dante pretended that Helena loved him even though she told him that she did not. So, I figured that pretending was the "go to" option in this situation.

Dante stopped in mid-gait and stared at me blankly.

"Yo, Rilei, you really gotta grow the fuck up."

I paused. I knew that Dante was upset. I knew he had been quiet since we left the apartment, but I needed to know more, and the silence was killing me. So, I pushed.

"I don't know man, but what's up, tell me." If Dante had told me that Helena was using drugs, I might have eased his stress with my insulin solution. Instead, he told me I needed to grow up. His attack on me was odd since he wouldn't take his mother at her word when she said she did not love him. I didn't need to grow up. My mother didn't want me to grow up. Dante needed to grow up. He needed to understand what was going on with his mother so he wouldn't waste his energy dragging in more raggedy tables or busted up couch pillows.

I wanted to know what was going on. Watching Helena inject herself had my head in a frenzy. The intellectual side of me knew Dante's mother used drugs. However, the child in me thought that drugs were only smoked. I had never actually seen Helena use drugs before, nor anyone else; but I had heard people in my neighborhood make statements such as "she smoking that shit," or "he smoke dope." Naturally, those types of statements led me to believe that drugs were something that had to be smoked.

Dante looked at me again, slumped his head, and quietly said: "She's a fucking Junkie."

Dante stopped walking and sat on the curb. He picked up the nearest pebble and tossed it into the street. I could tell Dante had many thoughts brewing and spinning in that head of his. He always flushed red when his mind was racing. He never held back too long, but it did take some prodding to get him to speak sometimes. I did what I always did to prod him to speak. I asked, "Why you say that?" I sat back and waited for the silence to break.

"Fuck, man, she doesn't even care anymore. I can't believe that junkie bitch asked me to tie that. And I... I tied it. I am your fucking kid, man. If my dad knew..."

Dante fell silent as he reflected on his father. "I used to get mad when I heard my aunt and uncle would call her a junkie. My cousins teased me and said I had to wear their clothes cause she's a junkie. I didn't believe them. I told them she ain't out here with all these other guys when we walking home so how much of a junkie could she be? She doesn't look like them. They look like junkies. She doesn't even have no money to be a junkie. Where would she get the money? It's nothing in the house. I asked Ma about the drugs before, and she told me they were things to help her relieve the pain. Everyone has pain sometimes. That don't make her no junkie. I was stupid."

Dante's face went from red to pale. His eyes were not blue anymore. They were dark.

"I believed her. Now, whenever they come around if they come around at all, all I hear about is how she stole this or that, and how she is not allowed back over my aunt's house because she stole her T.V., and Rilei, there has not been a T.V. at the house in forever. I put things in that house. If she was going to steal a T.V., she could have at least brought it to the house and let me watch it."

I looked at Dante and nodded, but I didn't speak because I wanted him to keep going.

"Even now, I have to wear clothes that are too big, and she never says anything about it. I look a wreck, and she doesn't even notice. My hair keeps getting matted in the back, and she won't comb it. My aunt used to comb it for me. My aunt used to bring over Chris' old clothes and homemade candies, but now she won't even come to visit me. My uncle doesn't come by anymore. He used to take me to get my hair cut. He used to tell me stories about my dad. He said we were going to keep the memory alive. But no. Where are they all now? Gone because of her. And it's just her and me. Half the time she gone, and it's just me. And she has the nerve to say she doesn't have enough love left for me."

I saw the tears forming in Dante's eyes as he talked. I had wondered if he had picked up on Helena's statement but assumed he hadn't because he had carried on as if he had not heard it.

I knew that Dante's mother did not have any brothers or sisters, so I figured he was talking about his Dad's brother and sister. I recalled how kids teased Dante in kindergarten about how he dressed. I also when Dante sneaked homemade chocolates to school and shared them with me while we colored. It was all starting to make sense.

Dante told me how his mother had not bought groceries or cooked in months. He talked about how she had started bringing men to the house that he had never met only to disappear off into her room with them. The more he talked, the angrier he became

33

"The only time she speaks to me now is when she wants me to call my grandparents for lunch money. I don't even use lunch money. Nobody comes to visit us anymore, and it's because of her. I haven't seen her smile before tonight, and she wasn't even smiling at me. I am so stupid. What reason does she have to smile at me? She doesn't even notice I am here. My father would've..."

Dante stopped talking and wiped another teardrop out of his eyes.

I never talked to Dante about his father. It was a topic that was best left alone. Plus, it's not like the word came up since I didn't have a father of my own to talk about.

I waited patiently to see if we were finally going to explore the life of Ralph. It wasn't. Dante stood and kicked at the dust and rocks beneath his feet.

"Fuck it all, junkie bitch," he said as he turned and headed in the direction of my apartment. I watched as he stomped toward my place. I knew Dante's style of dress was unique, but I had never paid much attention to it before now. His pants hung below his waist even though they were folded over multiple times. As he walked, he had to keep pulling them up. His shoes clunked behind him. I could see the heels of his feet peeking above the rim of his shoes each time he took a step. His t-shirt was the only thing that halfway fit him. It would have looked better if it were too big too because it might have covered the parts of his behind that his pants didn't.

I wanted to say something to Dante. I didn't want him to storm off feeling as lost as I felt. I could only imagine that if I felt lost, he had to be feeling ten times worse in some way or another. I ran to catch up with him to share my revelation and cheer him up.

When we got to my door, Dante looked around. His eyes searched up and down the road, and tears started streaming down his face. It was the first time I had seen Dante cry. I had a strange urge to hug him, but I knew that he needed to have that moment alone.

I walked to my door, unlocked it, and went inside. I made sure to leave it cracked so Dante would feel welcome or, even better, at home.

My mom must have heard me enter the house. She was something special. Although I said nothing, she knew everything. She walked up behind me and placed her hands on my shoulders. She told me, speaking softly but with certainty, "all mysteries can't be solved. Many can be investigated, but not all can be solved."

I understood what she was trying to say. I wanted to fix Dante's issues. I had watched him break and rebuild himself so many times that I just wanted him to have what I had. I wanted to share my mom with him and let him know what it felt like to have a mother love you back. I wanted him to have the things I had. I had hope, love, patience, and haircuts. I had my mother. Even though Dante had a lot of burdens, no one could carry them better than Teigen; but Dante wanted Helena.

My mom and I sat on the couch for what seemed like an hour waiting for Dante to come inside. When he finally walked in the door, he smiled and said: "Hey Ms. Teigen," nonchalantly as if it was just a regular day. It was as though if he hadn't been outside for an hour crying. It was as if he had made peace with his world and was his happy self again.

He walked to the couch, hugged my mom, and asked if he could stay the night even though he knew she would say yes. Usually, he didn't ask. There wasn't a need. This time I think he needed confirmation that there was a place for him. He needed to hear my mom affirm that he was welcome because everything in his world said he wasn't. My mom often understood things without anyone having to explain them. I think she felt that Dante needed something different that night and she didn't hesitate to give him what he needed.

Mama got up and put her hands on Dante's cheeks. She stared into his eyes. For a minute, I thought I saw Mama's eyes begin to water. Just as I was inching closer to get a better view, she bent over and embraced Dante, whispering, "Yes, you can spend the night son. I love you." Dante's face lit up. He nodded at my mom and wiped his eyes. He leaned into her hug while remaining silent.

I sat on the couch and watched quietly, careful not to make any sound to draw attention to me and taint the moment. I wondered how long he would hold on to my mother. I had hoped that he would not try to bury all his years of pain and turmoil in my mother's chest, but I knew that he needed somewhere to let them rest. I also knew that if anyone could handle his feelings, it was my mother. Mama pulled back from him, looked him in the face again, and then looked at me. She smiled and said, "all right now, you boys gone head and go eat then take it to bed. School is in the morning, and everyone is getting up early because I am dropping you all off."

She walked over to the kitchen then quickly turned around and said, "oh yeah, I almost forgot, report cards are coming out soon, and I want to see both of you guys report cards." Dante's face lit up again. I think it was at the thought of someone asking about his report card because I knew that Dante grades were nothing to light up about.

Mama had a way of doing that. She knew how to take a tragic moment and turn it into something beautiful. She had ways of making the world seem bright even when the sun couldn't.

She knew what Dante needed. There were many times that I would see my mother stand in the doorway of my bedroom and whisper. I would lie still and pretend to have my eyes closed while I listened to her chant softly into the night and ask for countless blessings over my life.

This night was no different except she chanted with more conviction than I ever heard her use before. Her whispers were more audible and more aggressive. It felt more powerful than at any time before. Her request for blessings wasn't for me that night; they were for Dante.

Several weeks had passed since Dante left after the scene at Helena's apartment. Things carried on as usual to some extent. Dante had managed to accumulate so many clothes at my house that I had to make room in my closet for him. My mom started letting us walk to school so that she could go in to work earlier and get overtime. She was fine with us walking because we were together. She also needed the overtime hours because she felt responsible for taking care of Dante. She packed us a lunch every day and made breakfast every morning to make up for no longer being able to give me a ride to school. It wasn't really about the ride for me, though; it was about the conversations Mama, and I got to have during the ride.

I was used to packed lunches, but the breakfast was new for me. Mama was usually adamant about having me to school on time in the morning to have breakfast. Things were different with Dante around. With him around, we would have breakfast and our morning conversations together at the table.

My mother got carried away with trying to be the perfect mother for Dante and me. I often felt that she was only obligated to me and that she would wear herself too thin trying to over please Dante. Dante was my best friend, but he was used to having nothing, so I felt the little Mama did for him should have been plenty.

Mama pointed out to Dante and me an apple and banana bowl that she had set out on the table. She would say a healthy snack costs less in the long run. I loved bananas and apples just as much as the next kid, but Mama used to have a snack sack that was filled with cookies and quarter juices for me to pick at my whim. I approached Mama about her antics and tried to explain to her that she didn't have to change too much because anything was an upgrade from Helena for Dante.

I made the remark to comfort Mama and assure her that she didn't have to change from being the Mama I knew and loved. Mama didn't take it the same way. She went on a tirade about how it is a blessing to be able to give to the less fortunate, and humility was an important character trait that was not to be forgotten. "Give from the heart Rilei, a lot of people give for alternative reasons, and they mean no one any good, but you give from the heart, and there is no room for ill intent or jealousy." Mama had a way of reminding me what Dante meant to me as a friend and keeping me grounded. I knew that my mother was trying to change Dante's life for the positive, and I knew Dante needed it.

Aside from eating breakfast and gobbling up "healthy snacks" together, she made sure we ate dinner together so that she could ask us about our day and what we had learned. She reserved the question about "mysteries solved" for me though. She knew how to keep our special things special without making Dante feel left out.

Months had passed since Dante had seen his mother. Helena never bothered to call or stop by to see where he was or make sure he was ok. Every now and again, I would catch Dante sitting outside, staring in the direction of his apartment. I knew he was looking to see if his mother would come out or go in. It had to hurt to be gone and not have your mother ask about where you were.

Dante would go home sometimes, but by the end of the day, he would be back at our place, eating dinner with us. Mama would try to make it so that Dante didn't need to go back to Helena's for anything. She would use whatever extra money she had to buy Dante clothes and shoes that fit him and school supplies. Mama even bought Dante an air mattress with his own comforter set. I knew she was trying to be what she thought Dante needed. I think she was exactly what Dante needed; however, he needed it from Helena.

Chapter 4

Teigen

"Only the dead have seen the end of war." — Plato

Several times, I wondered about the life my mother would have had without me. I asked her what she was like as a kid, what she liked to play, whom she played with, or if she played at all.

She was always full of smiles, but I never understood what brought so much joy into her life aside from me. My grandmother and grandfather were gone, and my mother had no brothers or sisters. She had only one friend that ever came around and no boyfriend or husband. She never went out on dates and she never "hung" out. She only worked and returned home to me.

I knew that I brought her joy because she always said how proud she was of me and how I was the "silver lining" in the clouds after the storm. My mother always told me that she never wanted more children. She said there could never be another me and she was lucky to have gotten all she could have ever wanted the first time.

I knew it wasn't true. Mama had wanted more children, just like I knew she wanted a husband. I had heard her tell someone over the phone that it would be nice to have such a life. I had even heard her crying late at night sometimes, and I knew that she was crying for the things she wished she had. I may have been her silver lining, but she still wanted a rainbow.

The only visitor and friend who came over to our place was my god-mother Lacey. Lacey was always laughing, smiling, and telling Mama about the men she had previously encountered. Her stories were always entertaining and full of details.

Lacey would sometimes try to get my mother to go out on some of her escapades, or at least to meet one of her friends, but Mama always turned down the offer. Mama would say, "You know my situation, and Rilei needs me home. I already work too much."

I didn't need her home like she thought I did. I just wanted her to be happy. I tried to set her up with a guy of my own, my gym teacher. He was my favorite teacher, and he would refer to me as son whenever we were in gym class. I used to wonder what it would be like to have him as a father.

I tried to talk to Mama about him and get her to visit him at parent-teacher conferences, but Mama never showed interest in anything other than my grades. At one of the parent-teacher conferences, I blurted out that Mama was single, and she liked to cook dinner; but Mama would never follow up on my efforts and would go right back to asking how I was doing in class.

Sometimes, when Lacey visited, she brought Dante and I candy or toys. She did not have any kids, but she was kind enough, and she kept Mama entertained when she was around. It was not enough because Mama was still lonely. She never said as much, but I could feel that in her.

In most ways, Lacey was different from Mama. All she talked about were dates she had been on and what man was going to pay which bill. Her commentary was so out-of-pocket sometimes that Mama would send Dante and me away while they talked. I didn't understand why Mama was friends with her because they were so different, but when I asked, Mama said to me, "what about Dante and you?"

Mama explained to me that she and Lacey had been best friends since childhood, much like Dante and me. I imagined the type of friendship Dante and I had, and I pictured Lacey and Mama having the same friendship. Dante needed a friend, and I was available, so I wondered if that was how it was for Mama with Lacey too; after all, Lacey did look like the kind of person who could have been teased as a child.

Lacey looked like Mama in the way her hair coiled atop her head, and her eyes were also hazel; however, she was darker than Mama and carried more weight. Even though she had many men to share stories about, she also seemed lonely.

Lacey dressed in tight clothing that hugged every realistic and imaginable curve that she had or thought she had. Her stomach always poked out over her pants, and it reminded me of the banana nut muffins from the school cafeteria. Lacey's teeth were not like Mama's either. They were crooked and crowded, and Mama said that it could be the reason for Lacey's bad breath when I asked her about some of the unpleasant odors that Lacey passed down.

Despite Lacey's physical disasters, she was kind. Mama said Lacey had her back in the worst of times and never let anyone bring her down. They were friends because Lacey needed understanding and friends who did not judge, like Dante. And, like me, Mama was available.

Months passed, and it became a common thing for Dante to sometimes sit at Helena's to see if she would show up. For months, he seemed satisfied just being in Mama's and my presence. Eventually, Dante's staring up the street turned into his walking up the street. Walking up the street eventually led to Dante waiting at Helena's. He never said much, but Mama and I could tell that Helena was not coming to check on him and he was not seeing that her absence was taking a toll on him.

Things around me had started to change. Mama started losing weight, and she went through various mood shifts. Lacey's presence around the house increased as Mama's weight decreased. Dante seemed to stay away more with each mood swing Mama had. It seemed like the dynamic was beginning to change from Mama, Dante, and me to Mama, Lacey, and me. Mama wasn't fighting to keep Dante from trying to find Helena as much anymore, and Lacey wasn't coming over for just gossip and laughs anymore.

Things had become so different that whenever Lacey came over, there was a more tense and somber feeling in the air. With Dante being in and out, the mood of the house bothered me. Mama told me that Lacey was coming over to help cook and clean because she was too tired to do it herself, but I felt that there was more to it.

I knew that Mama has psoriasis, but aside from irritation, I had never seen her affected by it. I remember when she found out she had it; she became depressed and upset. She had started wrapping herself with bandages, and at first, had stopped giving me and allowing me to give her hugs. I didn't understand it, but I tried. It was unlike her to go to the doctor unless it was necessary, but she was going more frequently and for reasons that she never usually went. I was worried about her, but overall, I knew she was ok.

One Saturday night in the middle of January, Mama sat beside me on the couch while Lacey pretended to be cleaning in the dining room. I could tell by the inconsistency in her footsteps that she was listening as Mama and I sat together.

Mama sat silently beside me, staring at the side of my face while I watched my favorite episode of Doug. I could feel her eyes burning into my cheeks, but I was so wrapped up in the episode that I did not bother to look up. Her eyes did not let up, but continued to search my side profile until I eventually looked up at her and asked, "What's up, Mama?"

She glared at me, and I knew a conversation was swirling in her head. Her hazel eyes softened into a warm brown as a tear escaped the corner of her eye. The vibe she gave off shook me so much that I sat upright and faced her. Her lips parted and hung open for moments before she finally spoke.

"Rilei, you should always know everything there is to know about the people you love. What you don't know, you should ask. You should always be interested in knowing the truth of things, not rumors."

I twisted my face up with a look of confusion. I felt the presence of family secrets and hidden truth lurking around, but I didn't know what secrets and truths there could be when I already knew everything there was to know about my mother.

Unsure of what this conversation would reveal, I turned to face my mother and looked her in her eyes with my most convincing face and said, "I already know everything about you, Mama." I projected as much confidence as I could to convince her that this was true.

Mama hesitated as she shifted, nervously, "No baby," she said, "but you will."

We sat on the couch as Mama fidgeted and recounted the story of her life. I listened as she sequenced events and watched as they begin to play in front of me as if I was watching a movie.

She told me about how she grew up happy but poor on the west side of town in some projects. Her parents were sticklers for routine and strict, so she sneaked out every night to hang out with one of her best childhood friends, Lacey. Lacey was older than Mama by a year, but she still saw Mama as her best friend.

They met in elementary school when Mama was in the 4th grade, and Lacey was in the 5th. They spent their elementary years doing childish things as children would do.

Mama recounted every event from sock hops to debutante balls as I listened quietly, happy that I was finally hearing my mama's childhood story. Mama spoke with excitement as she told about the times they snuck out during middle school to attend house parties and get into other shenanigans.

She talked about one time when they had to sneak in my grandparent's room through their bedroom window while they were asleep. Their goal was to steal 2 dollars out of some money jar to pay for a bus to go to a house party. Mama laughed as she explained how my grandparents kept a dollar jar for bets; swear words and odd money.

"Odd money," I thought to myself.

As if she could read my mind, she replied, "Yes, honey, odd money. Your grandma had a thing about odd numbers; she was very superstitious back in the day. If she ever had an odd amount of bills or money, she would take away a dollar to make it even. The odd dollar would go into the money jar."

Mama paused for a moment to look over at Lacey in the dining room. Lacey was sitting at this point and smiling back at Mama while nodding for her to continue.

"Lacey and I were fumbling outside of the window. She was trying to give me a lift…," Mama's voice trailed off as the scenes of her life began to play in front of me once again.

As she spoke in the background, I closed my eyes to see Lacey lifting Mama into the bedroom window of my grandparents.

Mama fell into the bedroom, almost waking them with the thud from her landing. When Mama got to her feet, she crept over to her parents' bed and removed the money jar from the headboard shelves. She was nervous, and her heart was beating so loudly that it seemed her father would hear it and wake up.

What only took minutes to do felt like hours as her palms begin to sweat with fear. She was worried that the jar would slip from her hands, so she wiped her palms on the covers and continued to remove the jar.

Once she had the jar cleared from over the bed, she ran to the window and threw the jar out so that her parents wouldn't hear any clinking from the change inside. She didn't think her parents would notice the missing jar before she had time to put it back. So, she quickly shut the bedroom window, ran out of her parents' room, and straight through the front door.

I could see what she described as she spoke. I could see her running to the back of their apartment unit and picking up the jar from where she had thrown it out the window.

Mama chuckled a little and continued with her story, and I kept with my narrated movie.

I could see Mama motioning for Lacey to come on as she ran and stood behind a big tree that shaded the play area behind Mama's apartment unit.

Lacey and Mama sat there while Mama grabbed four wrinkled dollars from the jar and crammed them into the back pockets of her jeans. Mama darted across the yard and placed the jar on the back porch near the trash can.

Mama figured that if she were unable to return the jar when she got home, she would just pretend that she did not know what happened to the jar.

With the four dollars secured in her back pocket, Mama and Lacey headed to the house party that was being held by a popular classmate. By the time they got to their destination, everyone else seemed to be heading out. Mama had noticed someone she knew leaving the party and asked him where everyone was going.

"Tony was his name," Mama said in a matter-of-fact tone as she continued.

Tony told them that the parents of Melissa, the girl who was hosting the party, had gotten into it really bad and everyone got kicked out.

Tony loved having the 411, so he went into detail about how Melissa's mom had come downstairs to find Melissa's father ducked off in a secluded corner, touching one of the girls. He said that Melissa's mom was screaming and calling the father all types of names while she smacked him over the head. Tony laughed while he told them about Melissa's dad trying to restrain her before getting frustrated and attacking her. Tony said Melissa started crying and screaming for everyone to get out as if it were their fault. Tony sighed and said, "yeah, so the party is over."

As Mama told her story, Lacey sat in the dining room, laughing. Mama let out a few chuckles and placed her hand on top of my head.

"I couldn't believe that after all that hard work we didn't even get to party." Mama laughed harder, followed by a cough. The cough startled her and sent her back into her story.

Lacey and Mama looked at each other and shrugged their shoulders. Frustrated, Lacey, and Mama returned home. Mama went to the back porch to retrieve the money jar. Once she had the money jar secured, she signaled to Lacey to come over so that they could climb back into the house through her bedroom window. As Lacey knelt to give Mama a lift into her bedroom, Mama noticed that her bedroom lights were on. She was sure that she had cut them off before she left. She tapped Lacey's arm, signaling to lower her back to the ground. Once on the ground, she looked at Lacey and said, "We might as well knock on the front door."

Mama said she was punished for weeks after she was caught sneaking out. She was given extra chores, no allowance, and made to tutor the next-door neighbor's badly-behaved kid.

Mama said her parents were so upset that she had to start going to church on Wednesdays for Bible study and Grandma made her stay for all three services on Sunday because she was convinced that the devil had snuck inside of her.

Mama said that none of this bothered her because the drama surrounding Melissa's dad at school was enough to keep her mind entertained even though she was in trouble at home.

Chapter 5

"In the opinion of the court, the legislation and histories of the times, and the language used in the Declaration of Independence, show, that neither the class of persons who had been imported as slaves, nor their descendants, whether they had become free or not, were then acknowledged as a part of the people, nor intended to be included in the general words used in that memorable instrument...They had for more than a century before been regarded as beings of an inferior order, and altogether

Unfit to Associate with the White Race,

either in social or political relations; and so far inferior, that they had no rights which the white man was bound to respect; and that the negro might justly and lawfully be reduced to slavery for his benefit."

—Roger Taney, 1857

Melissa was popular. She had blonde hair and blue eyes. From how Mama described her, she was every bit of money from the way she dressed to the way she carried herself. She wasn't extraordinarily beautiful, but people treated her as if she was because they knew her father had money. She wore all the designer clothes of Mama's time and clearly had the lavish lifestyle that every kid from the ghetto dreamed about.

Melissa was usually cheery and happy, but sometimes Mama and Lacey would catch her in the bathroom, crying and cutting herself. No one ever questioned it; no one ever asked anything about Melissa's life or her problems because everyone was busy kissing her behind. They ignored her awkward long sleeves in the summer and quiet cries for help because no one wanted to bring up the obvious and ruin their chance to be close to her and her father's money. Let my mother tell it.

Mama grew up in a time where everyone knew everything about everybody. But people were great at covering up and even better at pretending to mind their own business. Spreading gossip was the city's favorite pastime, yet, smiles and façades were how people got by.

Melissa's dad came to the school often, but never to visit or pick up Melissa. Her dad was tall and slightly muscular. He also had blue eyes, but his hair was dark brown, and his skin was not as pale as Melissa's and her mother's. He had stubble trailing down his face that connected to a short-grown beard, and his facial features were chiseled and strong. He was the average height of a male with more than average muscles. He was handsome for any race, and any standard and Mama said all the girls cooed over him.

"He was well-spoken with perfect teeth, and a Barry Manilow voice and everyone called him Mike, even Melissa," Mama recounted his flawless traits cynically.

Melissa's mom was Morgan. Morgan and Mike had been married for years, but they never got along. Mike was abusive, and he would often beat on Morgan. Sometimes, if he were really agitated, he would beat Melissa.

Melissa would come to school wearing sunglasses in the middle of the winter sometimes, and everyone knew why, but no one dared ask. She was the only kid that wore tons of makeup in middle school, and because her skin was so pale, a bruise on her could be spotted easily. The teachers, the counselors, and the Principal knew; everyone knew, and everyone minded their business. Especially the school since Mike was one of the biggest donors to the board of education's fundraisers.

Melissa and her mother were wealthy because of Mike. His parents left him a lot of money, and they were very prominent in the city. Melissa's grandfather owned land in the south that had been passed down to the first-born son since slave days. He found out that his property was oil-rich underneath and he had been swimming in cash ever since. His name was on a will to inherit his father's land once he passed, and as a surprise bonus, there were returns on investments his father had that Mike didn't expect.

Mike had his hands in local and state politics and would invest in political campaigns while making friends with people in high places. He looked like a saint donating to all the local kid charities and schools and giving poor children scholarships to private schools. Mama said that was how she and Lacey got into their private high school.

In the eighth-grade, Mama wrote a winning essay that would pay her first year of tuition to the city's best private school. Mama was smart, and because her GPA was always a 4.0, her subsequent years were sponsored by different academic scholarships. Lacey got in because her mother qualified for the low-income scholarship that paid for Lacey's tuition if her GPA stayed above 3.0.

Everyone who did not live in Mike's house and did not have the pleasure of fully knowing Mike, loved Mike. He spent a lot of time in the projects claiming he was rebuilding the lost character of the hood. My mother said that he must have only found the lost character in the young girls of the hood because that's where he focused most of his attention.

"When Lacey and I made it to high school, everything was smooth sailing. I became good friends with Melissa because I decided not to mind my business one day while she hid in the bathroom," my mother said as she adjusted her herself on the couch.

"Yep, I decided to be the one to ask her one day if she was ok. That was the start of our friendship, and from there, I introduced her to Lacey. Ever since then, it was us three, thick as thieves. We did everything together. We would stay the night at either my or Lacey's house on the weekend and Morgan would take us shopping or on girls' trips on our spring breaks." Mama smiled as she continued her memories.

"Once, Morgan took us to the mountains in Colorado to go skiing. I could not believe they let me go, but I was so happy when they said I could go that I didn't think much more of it. I packed my bags a month early and could not wait."

Mama paused, then glared at the ceiling and said, "Yep, so many trips. So many good times. So many good memories." Mama hesitated. She looked me in my eyes and said, "but not all good memories, Rilei." Suddenly tension filled the room. Mama's eyes begin to water, and her skin flushed.

I felt an urge to say something, but I couldn't speak. Suddenly, everything around me felt dark, and my body felt heavy perched on the couch as if I were cemented to the cushions.

"Rilei," she began, "listen carefully. I will answer questions tonight, but after that, we will move on. We will forgive and forget. I love you, and I know that you love me. I am telling you this because it is time. I want you to know everything about me, just like I want you to grow up and know everything about yourself. We can't allow other people to fill our minds with rumors about ourselves. This is our canvas; we can't let people go painting their picture on OUR canvas. Do you understand?"

I nodded silently, allowing my eyes to wander up and down her face.

"Rilei, this is only the right time because I don't know how much more time…, I just don't want you to hurt. I want you to understand that I love you with everything left in me and from the time I…; let me start over Rilei. Please listen closely."

I did. I heard the tears in her throat. I heard the deep swallows and the hesitation in her voice. I felt the burn in my nostrils. I felt the tears hanging behind my eyes, but I fought them back. I closed my eyes so that I could tune the world out and hear only my mother.

~ ~ ~

"It was Christmas break, my senior year. I begged your grandparents to let me travel to Hawaii with Melissa and Lacey. Lacey's parents had already okayed her to go. I was just waiting. Your grandparents were so adamant about me spending Christmas at home, but this trip would have been fully paid for at no cost to them since Mike was paying. Morgan had left him our sophomore year when the suspicions of him cheating on her were at an all-time high. Mike had been trying to win her back and prove himself a changed man, and this was his apology gift to Morgan and Melissa for being such a shithole of a person."

Mama chuckled to herself as she continued, "he was so good at just shelling out money. Morgan took him back, of course. She couldn't keep up her old lifestyle the way she wanted to without him. And Melissa, well she accepted the trip under the condition that Lacey and I could come along. She just figured she would ride the charity wave for as long as he allowed. She thought he owed her at least that much.

After spending weeks begging my parents to let me go, they finally relented and decided I could go. Of course, your grandmother bugged the hell out of Morgan to gather all the details. Lacey, Melissa, and I were all supposed to share a room, and Morgan was supposed to have an adjacent room. The trip was only to be a week-long, so I would be able to spend the second half of Christmas break at home with my parents to bring in the new year.

After the details were gathered, I was cleared and on my way to Hawaii. I was so excited to be 17 and going to Hawaii. I just knew that I was all of that," she giggled and continued, *"we boarded the plane, and I felt no fear, only excitement. Lacey, Melissa, and I all sat next to each other on the plane. Morgan sat on the aisle seat across from us, and we were all filled with joy and smiles from ear to ear.*

Then, he boarded the plane. He smiled over at us and took his seat next to Morgan. I remember looking at Melissa and asking, 'what is he doing here.' All she could do was shrug her shoulders. Morgan never let out this detail of the trip. Everyone looked disappointed at the fact that he was coming except for Morgan.

Although we were all disappointed, I was the only one who was sick from his presence. I just had this feeling, and I wanted to go home. But I stayed."

Lacey shifted in the dining room chair. I had forgotten she was there listening, even sniffling. I grew nervous, but I closed my eyes as my mother's words begin to play in front of my eyes. I listened to her story unfold, and I drowned myself in her voice.

"When we landed, he wasted no time. He complimented all of us, but only grabbed my bags. I tried to play it cool and justify it being because my bags were seemingly larger than everyone else's.

When we checked into the hotel room, the lady at the desk handed out 5 room keys. Thinking nothing of it, I asked Mike for my bags so I could head to the room. I do not know why I still thought we were all in the same room. Mike told me that he was going to be bringing all the bags up to the rooms. Then he smirked and said, 'don't you worry your pretty little head about these bags.'

I saw him reach over and grab Lacey's and Melissa's bags, so I felt at ease. Once we got on the elevator, we started searching for our room numbers so we would know what floor to go to. That's when I noticed that we all had our own rooms and we were on different floors. I tried not to make a big deal out of it and just appreciate the fact that I was even invited to come along, but I felt uneasy.

I decided to go to Melissa's room with her for a while until I could convince myself to feel more at ease. While I sat in Melissa's room, Mike came by to drop off Melissa's bags. He noticed me in there and said 'Oh, I got everyone their own rooms; I figured that privacy might be a factor with you teenaged girls, and of course I have my own room, cause, well you all know Morgan.'

His explanation made me more nervous, and I felt even more uneasy, but I ignored it; never ignore your gut. He told me to come on and let him take my bags to drop my room. I made Melissa come with us. We dropped the bags off, and then all met up for dinner in the lobby.

The next couple of days were fun. I had begun to get comfortable with Mike being around. He wasn't so creepy. He was actually nice to all of us. That helped. That put me at ease. It was Friday night; we were due to leave that Saturday morning. I had fallen in love with Hawaii and the beaches. I didn't want to leave. Lacey and I decided we would sleep in Melissa's room that night since it was our last. We just wanted to sit and talk about the *trip and everything that we did. Mike had intervened and told everyone to make sure they slept in their own rooms that night because we needed to make sure the rooms were together and that we did not leave anything. It didn't make sense to us, but we agreed to it," Mama said as she got still and her voice lowered. At this point, Lacey's head was pointing toward the ground, and I could tell that she didn't want to make eye contact with either me or Mama.*

Mama's eyes went into a deep stare. She started to talk with her face, blank, and void of emotion. Her eyes appeared motionless, and her body stiffened as if she were having an out of body experience.

"I tried to leave. I was laying in the bed, trying to sleep. It just didn't feel right. I wanted to go lay with Lacey. I got out of the bed and started putting all my things near the door so that I could roll them to Lacey's room. I figured it wouldn't be a problem if I had all my things together and was ready when they were. Once my bags were by the door, I left the room to grab the luggage carrier that was kept down the hall. I was walking back with the carrier, and I slid my key to open the door."

Her eyes begin to water profusely. I could hear Lacey in the background sobbing. I reached up to wipe the tears from her eyes, and she grabbed my hand and stopped me. "Rilei," she said, "don't do that, just listen and promise not to hate me afterward." She continued talking.

"I slid the key, I pushed the door open, I turned back to wheel the carrier into the room. As I let the door close behind me, he appeared. He stood there, at my

door, just standing. I told him I was just going to wheel my things down to Lacey's room. He looked at me and asked if I wanted him to do it. He said he was just checking on us all, just trying to make sure we were ready. I told him everything was ok, but he just stood there. His eyes begin to search over my body. I felt like a lamb away from her flock. He got closer to me and slid the collar of my pajama top slightly off my shoulder. I should have screamed, but I couldn't. I was frozen. He touched my face. He told me that my skin was beautiful, and he preferred his coffee black.

I couldn't move Rilei. In my head, I was fighting him. In my head, I was screaming. I thought everyone could hear the chaos in my head, but no one came," she paused. "He kissed me and placed his hands on my hips." Mama had begun to mimic the encounter. I felt my eyes watering, but trying to keep in my tears, I kept listening.

"He guided me back to the bed, and once the mattress hit the back of my knees, my body fell onto it. It was as if my mind and spirit vacated my body. I don't mean to make this complicated, but it was the first time I saw my body as a vessel. I was not inside of my own self. I kept yelling at myself to get up and fight, but my body wouldn't respond. I could not hear me yelling at me. I just wanted him to stop, but my voice was not there. He kissed all over my body, and I just laid there as if I were dead.

I watched him. I watched him enter me in a way that made me understand that nothing in life was free. I watched him treat my body in ways that made me question if God really created me. He squeezed my thighs as if he wanted his fingers to penetrate to the bone, and *he pushed inside me, trying to crack whatever was left of my soul. Rilei, I don't want to scare you honey, but he killed me. He killed the "me" that I had hopes of being. He penetrated all my dreams and broke them down from the inside. He fiddled with every belief I had. My life, as I knew it fell from my eyes in the form of tears as he mixed them with his perverted pleasure-filled sweat."*

Mama's volume had increased, and what sounded like sadness, began to sound like anger and pain.

"Every drop of sweat that touched my body stung as it landed, but still, I could not scream out. He violated me for what seemed to be forever before I was finally able to convince my body to allow my mouth to say stop. When the words finally rang out, I felt some type of power, and it seemed as if I re-entered my body. I started flailing and trying to kick him off me. He laughed and told me that black girls never seem to know their place," Mama said, mimicking his voice.

"Each and every thrust he taunted me with swish sounds meant to imitate a lashing from a master to his disobedient slave. I gave up Rilei, I stopped fighting him. I just wanted to be obedient so that it could be over," she cried hysterically as her hands collapsed upon her face.

~ ~ ~

I didn't know what to say. My eyes were swollen with tears of anger and confusion. I was slightly infuriated with her because I did not know what I was supposed to do with this story. I did not get what I was supposed to learn from it, and I did not know how to take away her pain. This did not compare to the small bruises and bumps that I needed her to kiss or bandage for me. She was laying a burden on me that I couldn't put a band-aid on and expect for her to just "feel better."

I started to cry more. I wanted to hug her and make it all go away. There were so many thoughts that crossed my mind. I thought about why she would want to tell her 8-year-old son this. I wanted to say to her that I was the wrong person to say this too. I wanted to tell her that there was not anything I could do about it. I wanted to ask her if she ever told grandpa, or if she ever called the police. I wanted to ask what happened next, and if he were still alive and if so, why? I wanted her to lean over and cry on my shoulders, forget about it all, and just pretend it never happened. I wanted her to smile. I wanted to erase this story from her memory. Instead, I stayed silent.

"I learned a lot that night, and three things happened that changed my life forever. Rilei, you are not fatherless, and despite anything else, you are the best part of me. I am sick, and I do not know how much longer I will be around to keep you.

I want you to know everything because one day you will be a man, and I need you to be a different man than him. I know that there are parts of him in you that I will not be able to do away with. Sometimes they make it hard for me to look at you, but never hard to love you.

I need you to understand there are things in life that may be hard to deal with, but you love them regardless. Like Dante and Helena. Please, I may be hard for you to look at now, but please love me still. I want the rest of my time here on this earth to be free, free from these memories, and from the secrets. Every day you grow, you become more of a man...,"

"Is he still alive? Mike, is he still alive, and does he know that I am his son?" I interrupted her because the question would not stop burning in my brain.

She attempted to answer me without answering my question. My mind was only set on hearing whether he knew that I was his son.

"Does. He. Know. That. I. Am. His. Son?"

"He knows that you exist Rilei, but there was no invitation for him to be your father," she said, frustrated. "That does not matter, what matters is I am dying from a disease that man gave me. With that night came a curse, and you are the only silver lining from the storm that is my life. You are the only thing to come from it that kept me sane afterward. I know this is a lot, but I need you to love me, and I need us to get through this."

I grew quiet and got up. Looking back at her, I said, "Mystery solved, huh." Not waiting on a reply, I walked over to the stairs and placed my hands on the banister. I looked at her once more, her face looked weary as if she aged 30 years in the last hour. Her eyes were bloodshot, and her skin appeared clammy. Her hair was pulled up into a messy bun, and for the first time, I was able to see the wrinkles on her forehead. She looked much older than 26. She looked much older than yesterday, and for the first time, I could not find her beauty.

"You should go to sleep and get some rest, Mama. I love you," I said to her as I walked up the stairs. I could not bear to keep looking at her in that state. I must have tripped up every step; my feet were so heavy. I felt heavy with the weight of her past, and I didn't know how to distribute it evenly. I didn't know what to do with the information. I could not figure out how to walk with the weight of all she'd told me, so I sat on the top step and cried.

As the tears streamed down my cheeks and onto the carpeted floors, I kept thinking of my mom. I pictured her fading out of the hallways as she walked out of her room kind of like what happens in movies when someone passes away. I pictured her old with gray hair, smiling from ear to ear as she always did when she saw me, and that too faded. Then I pictured what I thought Mike was like. I pictured him laughing. I pictured him sweating. It was more than I could take. I grabbed my shoe and threw it off into the air where his image stood, and I screamed.

His image remained there, still laughing, still sweating. I grabbed my other shoe. This time I threw it harder. Before the shoe could land, I was on my feet charging towards the sound of the laughter. Once I made it to the end of the hall, the sound looped, and his laughter rose. I couldn't get the sound out of my head. I smacked my head repeatedly, trying to knock it out of my mind. I banged my head against the wall, hoping that the wall would be strong enough to remove his laugh. I banged, and I banged until soft hands grabbed my head and turned me around.

There she was, Mama, always there for me. She fell to her knees, sobbing uncontrollably. I wanted to be there for her, but all I could ask her was, "why?"

If I heard everything correctly, my mom was leaving me. If I understood everything right, not only would I not have a mother, but I would not have a father. If everything were correct, then my mother would be dying while the laughter lived.

"Why?" I managed to ask her again. "Why are you leaving me?" It was the only thing I cared to know. It took her a while to explain to me in a manner that I could understand. After it was all said and done, I figured out that she was dying of AIDS. She said it became full-blown because she could never afford proper treatment for HIV, and it progressed.

She told me that when she found out, she was pregnant; she hid the pregnancy for as long as she could. She went months without any type of prenatal care and never bothered to get checked for sexually transmitted diseases. Her biggest fear was my grandparents finding out the truth of how she had gotten pregnant.

She talked about how she maintained her friendship with Melissa so that she could stay informed about Mike. Her school counselor name was Mr. Doty. Several times in her early pregnancy, she spoke with Mr. Doty, hinting to him that she had been raped. At first, Mr. Doty was interested and wanted to report her case, but once she told Mr. Doty who she was accusing, he reneged and called her a liar. He then suggested that she tell her parents and tell the truth about being promiscuous.

My mom was hopeless after Mr. Doty refused to believe her and kept her secret to herself.

At the end of her eight months, her stomach became too large to hide, and she knew she had to tell my grandparents. Instead of telling them the truth, she told them that she had become pregnant at some house party by some guy she hooked up with. My grandparents forgave her, and even with their disappointment, they helped her find a doctor so that she could receive prenatal care.

Mama started to have complications with her pregnancy shortly after she visited the Doctor for the first time. She went into labor at 38 weeks, and she had to have an emergency C-section. Not long after she delivered me, she found out she was HIV positive.

At that moment, she told my grandparents the truth about everything. She felt like she was suffering an unjust death sentence because of her silence, so she started speaking the truth.

"I thought that if I told the truth, it would go away. I thought that everything would just rewind if I told the truth," she explained.

She said nothing ever happened for her case. My grandfather was livid. He wanted blood. My grandmother bugged the police day and night. They tried not to express how angry they were around my mother, careful not to upset my mother more than she already was.

My mama had told me that I was her peace token, her silver lining after the storm. She latched on to me the way she did because I was the only beautiful thing that she felt she had left.

Mike was never prosecuted. My grandmother filed charges, but the DA never followed up. The investigation was weak at best, and no one sought to make a reality of the claim that he raped my mother, not even with me as evidence.

Most people shunned her and laughed at the idea that such an elite man would have raped *a child, let alone the black child of a lower-class family. They made a mockery of Mama's family referring to them as ingrates and as entitled second rate citizens. They scoffed at Mama and criticized her for having the audacity to accuse the man who allowed her to attend private school, of fathering her bastard child.

Without formal charges being filed by the DA's office, Mike was never made to answer for his crime. No one ever thought to test my DNA, and my mother made it clear to me, that even if they had tested it, she would have never let them near me.

My mother suffered alone and in silence. Everyone who cared about her was scared to bring it up for fear that it would torment her more. Lacey stayed by her side, but eventually, she just wanted to do normal high school kid things, and my mother had a baby. They remained best friends, and my mother named her my god-mom.

Melissa cut the friendship off when my mother went public after my birth. Melissa told her she was a liar and that her father would never touch a child, let alone a black child, in that manner. Melissa was embarrassed by the chatter at school. She knew that it could be true; in fact, she knew it was true.

Her mother and father had been working on their relationship at the time of the Hawaii trip, and since they got back together, Melissa had been living the high life. Mike was buying her everything and sending her wherever she wanted to go. She knew he was still a perverted man, but she didn't want to trade in her mother's new-found happiness, nor her own spoiled habits. It was easier to just make a liar out of Mama.

Mama said it was easier on Melissa to make her out to be a hoe rather than confront the rumors with the truth. Mama said she didn't know who Melissa was anymore, but Melissa made sure the entire senior class knew who my mother was. Mama said that, after the rumors started flying, it was as if the entire senior class had never really known her at all.

With the support of my grandparents, my mother graduated. Despite the torment she faced, she still went to school, and she even graduated at the top of her class. Mama was offered scholarships to several colleges, but she turned them down to raise me. My grandparents helped a lot, but she took on the primary responsibilities that came with being a parent.

After graduation, Mama picked up two jobs to help support herself and me. She went to work and came home to me with no free time between. Mama turned down every opportunity presented to her as far as dating. She told me she had already weathered the storm of men and got her silver lining from surviving.

There were times when familiar faces would challenge and remind her of her past, and Mama would break down. Mama confided in my grandmother about these times, and my grandmother would tell her, "don't' let nobody tell you who Teigen is. Far as they are concerned, Teigen is a mystery, and those who are worthy will be the ones to solve it. Other than that, let the foolish repeat what the fools teach."

From that conversation forward, Mama would tell those who spoke as if they knew her that she was a mystery. I finally understood why Mama always challenged me to solve mysteries instead of just listening to others.

Chapter 6

4:04

"Every silver lining has a cloud." —Mary Kay Ash

My grandmother died when I turned six. My grandfather died of a broken heart only a year later. My mama was an only child, and all she had left were Lacey and me.

Here I was, eight-years-old, turning nine in a few weeks, and my mother was dying. I was in the fourth grade, and the Christmas break was nearing. Usually, the house would be lit up with lights, wreaths, and mistletoe all over. This year was different. The house was quiet and dark. Mama had been on leave from work because she had been sick. Her skin was darker, and she seemed fragile most of the time. It bothered me, and I would break down in anger just to turn around and smile for her to keep her peace.

As the days passed, she looked sicklier. Some nights I woke up to the sound of her throwing up or coughing up her lungs. Lacey came by every so often, but mom didn't enjoy company much anymore.

Dante still stayed the night most of the time, but sometimes he stayed out all night on the corner with the older kids from the neighborhood. Mama was so disappointed in Dante that she told him if he wasn't in the house by 8:00 on any given night, then he might as well sleep wherever he was. Mama tried to enforce discipline on him, but Dante had completely lost Helena to her addiction, so he was beyond control. Even though Dante loved my mother, he still wanted his own.

Dante started buying his own school clothes and his own shoes. He often had to do favors for the big kids, but they gave him enough money to take care of himself, so he didn't mind. I thought about going out there with him to see if the big kids would let me do favors as well so that I could pay for whatever treatment my mom could not pay for. I figured if I could get enough money in time, I could save her life. As much as I wanted to go out to help make money, I couldn't stand to leave my mom alone.

Dante sometimes put money in a shoebox to save for my mother's treatment, and although neither of us knew how much it would cost to fix my mom, we both knew that we didn't have enough yet. There was not even enough money to tell mom about it, and I knew that I had to keep it a secret because Dante told me that the big kids said that how he got the money was a secret.

It was December 15th, 2001, three days after my birthday that went completely unnoticed, and on one of the nights that Dante didn't stay the night. I sat on my bed, peeking out the window at the corner where Dante hung with the older kids. I watched Dante run to multiple cars and run back. As I was watching out my window, I heard my mother begin to cough. It had become a regular thing, so I focused harder on Dante so that I could drown out the sound of her coughs. I heard Mama get up from the bed, followed by the pitter-patter of her feet hitting the floor as she ran to the bathroom to throw up. I continued to stare out the window, focusing on the corner. I watched Dante run from the car to curb repeatedly.

Minutes passed before I realized that I had not heard any more coughing or vomiting. I got out of the bed and walked over to my mama's bedroom to check on her. After realizing that she was not in there, I made my way to the bathroom. She laid sprawled out across the tile floor near the toilet. All I saw was blood, and I panicked. I ran downstairs to grab the house phone and dialed 9-1-1.

Upon seeing the ambulance arrive at the apartment, Dante came back. I was directing the paramedics to the bathroom when Dante grabbed my hand and pulled me outside. He told me that we had to leave before they sent someone to pick us up. He seemed sure that if we were there much longer, someone would come to pick us up and take us away. I was convinced; Dante and I ran to Helena's and did not stop until we were at his front door. Dante pulled his key out and unlocked the door.

Once we entered the apartment, I realized that much of everything they once had was gone. The table that sat in the middle of the floor was gone. The living room was empty aside from two folded chairs that sat abandoned in the dusty corner. Dante reached over to flip on the light and quickly realized the electricity was out. The only light was from a light post directly across the street.

Dante walked further into the living room towards the kitchen. On the counter, there was a hot dog that looked like it had been sitting there for a few days and a needle. Dante picked up the needle and let out a small chuckle. He twirled it around in his fingers for a minute before he launched it angrily at the wall. Dante walked out of the kitchen and looked at me. "Let's go," he said, "I'll see if Ollie can drop us off at the hospital."

We ran off to the corner to meet the big kids. I did not have time to process what was happening entirely. Everything was happening so fast, too fast in fact. I wasn't even sure if my mother was at the hospital, or to which hospital she had been taken. I thought about seeing her sprawled out on the bathroom floor. I didn't even get to check and see if she were ok, I didn't even get to give her a hug or tell her that I love her. I started hyperventilating. The more I thought about my mother, the harder it became to breathe.

I started to feel angry; I was so angry that I was rushed out of the house, and I was mad that Dante had been the one to rush me. As I continuously replayed the images in my head, my breath became more labored, and my head started to ache with anger. When we finally reached the corner, I felt like I was about to explode. I couldn't hold it in any longer.

"Stop, hold up. Who the fuck is Ollie? And how the hell are we supposed to know which hospital? Why did you pull me out of there like that? We don't even know if she is alive, Dante. There was blood. Real blood. She could be dead. What if she is...," Dante had interrupted me and pointed at Ollie. Ollie walked over to us and looked directly at Dante. Dante started to explain the situation, and then Ollie looked at me.

Ollie was big and dark. He reminded me of the gorillas that I had seen in the Zoo exhibit the year my grandmother died. He looked like he was 800 pounds, and his voice sounded just as heavy. He approached me, and his eyes pierced into my chest. I felt weak and small in his presence, yet, I stood strong because I needed him to get me to my mother.

When he finally addressed me, I felt a chill run through my spine. He asked my name and told me to chill out for a minute while he grabbed his car. Ollie was 18, he was the biggest kid on the corner, and I am assuming the oldest.

Ollie left to get his car and rolled back around the corner in a 1996 Mercury. There was dark tint on each window, making it impossible to see anything on the inside. He beeped his horn signaling for Dante and me to come on. I ran to his car faster than I ran to anything ever before. I popped open the back door and hopped into the car.

Immediately a smell rushed my nose. It was sweet and filled with nature, but it still stunk. I had never smelled anything quite like it. It wasn't as bad as smelling the dumpster near our apartment where people treated the area as much like a urinal as they did a trash bin, yet it still made my stomach curdle.

Dante popped into the front seat and motioned to Ollie that he was ready. Ollie and Dante looked back at me in the back seat where I sat with my seatbelt fastened and my eyes wide.

Ollie let out a slight chuckle as we pulled off. I rolled my window down a little to let the stench out and to ease the conflict in my stomach. I put my face up to the remaining glass and peered out into the night feeling empty.

It seemed like hours passed before we arrived at General Hospital. Mostly everyone went to this hospital, and it was the closest to our apartments. Ollie said that it was most likely where they had taken Mama. He looked back and told me that he was my eighteen-year-old brother, and we were here to see our mother. He asked me my mother's name, and I told him, "Teigen Easton."

I told him her age and her favorite color. I started to tell him about how she laughs and how she was smart. Ollie stopped me mid-rant, "It's cool, Lil dude. We can catch up, and you can talk about her as much as you want, but for now, let me get you in here; just remember I am your big brother. She is our mom. My name is Olson Easton, alright. If those people get involved, it's over for, so make sure you listen alright. You ain't trying to end up in nobody's system."

I nodded in agreement as I popped open my door. I could play the game, but he was not my mother's son, I was, and I knew my mother would never let anyone take me.

We walked up to the emergency desk, and Ollie immediately started to talk. His voice was calm with a hint of worry as he asked about a woman who may have been brought in an hour ago. He told the lady my mother's name as she searched through the records. "Teigen Easton," she said as she glanced up, half-focused on us, half-focused on the computer. Ollie nodded at her to confirm.

"Room 404," she said as she got up and leaned over the counter to point out the directions. "Use the elevators on the right and go to the 4th floor. Follow the signs for the ICU, and she will be in 404." Ollie nodded once again as I took off running down the hall in the direction that she'd pointed.

My heart was beating out of my chest, and my feet were moving faster than my mind could process. All I could hear was the beat of my heart and the sound of my feet running. I reached the elevators at the end of the hall and started tapping the button to call the elevator as fast as I could. The more I pressed the button, the blurrier my vision became as my thoughts escaped my mind in the form of tears.

The elevator chimed its arrival. I entered the elevator and glanced at the keypad for the 4th-floor button. My body froze. I was unable to move. My thoughts had finally caught up with my adrenaline, and I was paralyzed.

I stared at the button that would take me to the 4th floor, tapping it several times with my mind. The elevator doors closed, but the elevator did not move. The elevator and I sat still, both frozen, both fearful of what the 4th floor would offer. It was as if the elevator shared my thoughts, and it too could see that the fourth floor was a floor of despair. So, we sat, unmoved, and silent as our thoughts ran amuck.

"Ding," the elevator chimed as it opened its doors for Dante and Ollie. I felt slightly betrayed that the elevator allowed them to enter our space, but I knew that it would happen. Ollie reached over and pressed the button that would hand-deliver us to the floor that was actively trying to destroy my life. He pushed it so casually. I was angered at how easy it was for him. I was angry that Dante didn't intervene. Dante knew my mother. Dante knew everything, yet he was standing there as if he knew nothing.

"Floor 2."

No flinch. No nothing. No looking around at each other, no looking at me to notice that I noticed them not giving a fuck.

"Floor 3."

No tears, no worries, even though we were a floor away from the end of the world. My mom would have helped Ollie too. With my mom, he would not have to be the big kid on the corner. With my mom, he could solve mysteries. With my mom, he could have packed lunches, he could have daily hugs, he could hear, "I love you." With my mom...

"Floor 4, Ding."

Dante exited first, Ollie second. Easily. Their ease confirmed that they didn't understand what this floor was. I walked off the elevator, courtesy of my feet; but every other part of me stayed with the elevator. I followed Ollie down the halls to the 4th-floor nurses' desk. He began speaking, but I couldn't hear him.

I could hear was her voice, Mama's voice, "Rilei, I'm dying." I could see her face, withering away like a rose that had outlived its season. "Rilei …" I heard her say my name, I felt her hands against my face, and her hug – its warmth, I could feel it. I could feel it all from the hallway. Her body may have been in room 404, but her spirit was with me.

Ollie motioned at Dante and me to follow as he headed down the hall. His walk was more like a run. I took three steps for every step he made. I became agitated at his pace and the fact that he was speeding to my mother's demise.

I was more irritated with Dante. Ollie didn't know what he was doing, but Dante knew. Dante talked to Ollie on the way to the room. It was supposed to be a silent walk, but there he was, talking. I couldn't focus enough to hear the conversation fully, but I was able to catch the word "corner" as it fell from Dante's mouth. I was preparing to tell Dante to shut the fuck up, but as soon as I opened my mouth, we stopped walking.

There it was. Room 404.

Ollie stepped aside, revealing the door to me. The handle stared at me. Dante reached for it, and Ollie quickly smacked his hand down. I was thankful. Finally, it seemed as if Ollie understood what was behind the door for me. Ollie looked at me and said, "take your time, we ain't got nowhere to be."

I wanted to take my time as Ollie suggested. I wanted to sit still for a minute and give myself time to wake up. Everything was happening too fast, and I just needed it to slow down some. I looked around, and there were no tears in Dante's eyes. I needed someone else to share this fear with me. I wanted to know that I wasn't feeling it alone and that it wouldn't only be my loss. I looked up at Ollie and noticed that there was a single tear forming in his left eye, and with that, I reached for the handle and popped open the door.

Bandaged nearly from head to toe, I did not recognize who was laying in the bed. There was so much noise from the machines that my thoughts were forced to be quiet. I felt Ollie's hand cusp my shoulder, and Dante's eyes burn through the side of my face. The room stood still awaiting my reaction, but I did not have a reaction.

I did not know who the hell was laying in that bed. I looked to Ollie and told him that was not my mother laying there. Last I checked, my mother was not a mummy. Ollie looked at me with sorrow and sympathy in his eyes. Dante stayed quiet. I, on the other hand, was ready to go because my mother was not there. I turned to head out of the room when Ollie stretched out his arms and used his giant hands to palm my chest, stopping me in mid-walk.

"Hey, it's gone be alright man."

I didn't understand what he was talking about and could not figure out why he was talking to me.

"I know," I said, trying to resume my exit, "that is not my mom."

At that moment, Dante jumped in front of the door and threw his body against it. He looked me in my eyes, and for the first time, throughout the whole night, since the day we walked out on Helena, tears flooded Dante's eyes. Completely surprised at his sudden show of emotion, I glanced back over at the bed. It was her.

At first, I didn't move. I was trying to make sense of the bandages. I was trying to understand why she was wrapped up like a mummy. I looked at Dante and Ollie for explanations, and when their silence outlasted my patience, I ran to her to free her from the bandages.

Ollie followed me as the machines began to beep erratically. He was yelling something, but I could not understand the words. He wasn't helping. Dante wasn't helping. No one was helping me free her from the bandages. I was alone in saving her, and their tears were for show. I continued to pull on the bandages that were covering her smile, thinking to myself, "who the hell would cover a smile?"

I needed help to free her, and there was none. I understood at that moment, how Mama could feel alone in a room full of people. Just as I was going to ask Ollie for his help, I felt my body being lifted off the ground and the space between the bandages and me increased.

I kicked my feet and swung my arms. I tried to turn my head to see who was holding me back. I saw white coats, and blue scrubs rush over to the bed. Everyone was covered, and all the faces were unidentifiable. I screamed helplessly as I continued to kick and swing my way to freedom. The distance between my mother and me grew until I was looking at the other side of the door to her room.

I turned my head, desperately seeking the identity of the one who stopped me from freeing my mother's smile. I kicked, swung, and turned my head until I got too tired to move. Once my body was exhausted, I allowed my head to slump down into my chest as my eyes rested on the placard, which displayed the room number: 404.

The hallway felt colder this time. I don't remember it ever having felt warm, but I noticed the goosebumps rising on my arms and a strange freezing sensation in my fingertips. I threw my body against the wall and allowed myself to sink into the floor. I was too tired to fight any more and too scared to look up. Two bodies on each side of me sunk to the floor as well. I didn't bother to look up, but I focused my ears while I waited for someone to speak so I could identify who was next to me.

First, it was Dante. His attempt to comfort me was feeble, probably tainted by his interactions with his own mother. For a second, I felt sympathy for Dante, realizing that even though his mother was living, she was dead inside of him. I looked at him in search of the same emptiness that was beginning to fill me. I was convinced that seeing his emptiness would make me feel full again.

Once I met Dante's eyes, I realized our emptiness was different. Our desperation to be filled up on the inside was not the same. His emptiness seemed to be content, evident by the blank look on his face. He had lived with his emptiness for so long that it was as if he never had anything inside, to begin with. My emptiness was not only new, but it was draining. My emptiness was painful because I knew what it felt like when I was whole.

Convinced that Dante's comfort could do nothing for me, I turned to Ollie. There it was again, that single tear in his eye. What was his deal anyway? That tear; was it fresh, or was it the same tear from before? I stared at him for a while, trying to figure out if he just naturally had wet eyes. After staring for what seemed to be hours, the tear began to travel down his cheek following what looked to be a possibly stained trail from the last tear that resided there.

Something about that single tear traveling down Ollie's face made me curious. Questions filled my head faster than I was able to sort them. The longer I sat there, the more questions weighed on my mind. I was afraid I'd let the wrong question slip out so I bit my bottom lip hard as I could, but it didn't stop the questions from formulating in my head. The weight of everything unanswered pressed down on my eyes. My head felt too heavy for my neck, and my neck felt too heavy for my shoulders.

Tears formed at the corner of my eyes once again. I forced my weighted head up so I could see Ollie. I needed to see if that single tear had reformed.

This time, he caught me mid gaze, and he too was biting his lip. When he met my eyes, tears erupted. Not the single tear that he shed a while ago, but a flow of tears. For some reason, the questions begin to settle in my head. They all seemed to come together for me to form one question, "are you alright?"

I wasn't sure how I could ask him that as if that was his mother lying in a room overcrowded with white coats, but I did. Not only did I ask, but I needed the answer. Ollie looked at me with his bottom lip still tucked underneath his teeth. He placed his hand on my head and said, "It never gets easier."

I looked at Ollie again, as if I were seeing him for the first time. Before that moment, he was huge, but now I saw that he was fragile. He was tall with dark curly hair and thick eyebrows to match. He was built like a fully padded football player, and his skin reminded me of my mother's complexion. Ollie's dark brown eyes were most intriguing. It was as if you could look into his insides through his eyes. I was curious. I stared into his eyes long enough to find that Ollie was empty inside. He was empty, empty like I was.

The questions started to flutter around in my head again. I recognized the emptiness in him. I understood why the tears couldn't fall at first and why they lingered at the corners of his eyes. His tears, like mine, were all he had left. It only seemed right that I asked, "Where is your mom?"

The question seemed to bounce off the walls of the hallway and echo beyond. Ollie didn't answer, but I could tell he heard me because of the way his face distorted after the words left my mouth. His silence was not an option for me. After all, we were at the hospital, watching my mother cease to exist. I decided no question was too forward and no question would go unanswered.

I repeated myself using my hand to shake his arm so that I would know he heard me. Even though he snatched his arm out of my reach, his face softened instantly. He must have been able to tell that I needed his story to comfort mine because he looked down at me and told me that he wouldn't let me go to a foster home. There he was, Ollie the gorilla, to Ollie not so bad, to Ollie the Gentle Giant and protector.

Although Ollie didn't answer my question how I expected, he answered it in a way that let me know that he did not have a mother. I wanted to ask why, but just as I started to ask, Mama's door opened. Covered with a plastic smock, gloves, and a mask, the doctor approached us and asked for Olson. I thought about getting up instead of Ollie. I wanted to get up instead of him. I even tried to get up, but I couldn't.

Part of me did not want to hear anything that didn't sound like my mother was coming home, while the other part of me needed to know whatever the doctor knew. I kept thinking of what Ollie said about the foster home. I wasn't sure what a foster home was, but I knew that it wasn't a place where my mama would be. Mama had always been there for me, and I couldn't imagine her not being there. Things had changed so much in the last months, but not her presence and not her love.

Ollie returned to where we had been sitting on the floor. I glanced up to see if his face would reveal what the doctor said to him before his mouth revealed it. I felt like it would be easier to see it, then it would be to hear it, especially because I could feel it in my bones, and I knew what he was going to say.

The problem was that Ollie's face was blank. It told absolutely nothing. I didn't want to hear anything, and even that did not matter because he wasn't saying anything.

I felt the anger rise in me. It rose so fast that before I knew it, I was up and tugging on the handle of Mama's door. Everyone in the room rushed over to me except two men standing directly over Mama. They looked at me while they mouthed something that I couldn't understand.

I continued to watch while the room of white coats made their way to me. I wanted to make sure that Mama was being taken care of. I watched intently hoping that they would remove some of the bandages. "If only I could see her smile," I thought to myself. I was convinced that nothing was over yet and that if they would only remove some of the bandages, Mama would be alright.

With everything moving so fast, I focused on Mama. I imagined her getting back up with her skin glowing and healthy again. I imagined her holding my hand and wiping the tears from my eyes. With my imagination running wild, I saw the two men pulling a sheet up over her head.

My legs felt weak, and my limbs fell numb. My knees buckled, and I sank to the floor. As the sheet settled over her face, in bright red, 4:04am flashed on the digital clock next to Mama's bed.

"Time of Death," the doctor mouthed as I was once again lifted and pulled from the door.

"4:04."

Chapter 7

Domino Effect

"The death of a mother is the first sorrow wept without her." —Author Unknown

Life went downhill after my mother passed. Everything seemed to speed by yet stand still at the same time. There was no direction or guidance after Mama left, and I was lost as a result.

After Mama died, Lacey came by to check on me, but that was it. I thought she would have taken me with her, but no. I guess I was an adult to her.

She did manage to take some of Mama's things, though. She took shoes, clothes, grandma's wedding ring, and the T.V. that was in Mama's bedroom. When she was done taking, the more generous side of her handed me a few dollars and two pictures.

"Lacey, Teigen, Melissa" were scribed on the back of the first picture. On the back of the second picture was written, "Mike and Morgan," and on the bottom "Morehall's Christmas Vacation, Hawaii." She told me that Mama wanted me to know everything and that Mama wanted her to help me get through life, but she couldn't handle looking at me and seeing Mama.

The idea that I reminded so much of Mama made me smile. I wondered how she couldn't stand to be reminded of Mama but could stand to have all of Mama's belongings. Lacey said that was all she could do to help me now.

I wanted Lacey to take me with her. She had promised Mama that she would look out for me and take me with her. I told her that I wouldn't be a bother and that I could help her around the house and get myself ready for school. Lacey did not budge on her decision, however.

"Are you sending me to foster care?" I asked her all that I could think to ask her after she had just raided Mama's things and chose everything she liked while discarding the one thing she didn't want, which was me. I struggled to think of what would be next. She looked at me with tears in her eyes and said no. Lacey said she couldn't keep me, but she would not subject me to the system if she could help it.

"I can't take you with me right now Rilei, but I will be back and forth to keep my eyes on you and to check in on you. Ok?" She stared at me, waiting on me to confirm that I had heard her. "I am going to keep my promise to Teigen, you are my god-son, I just can't take you today. Let me heal, and I will be back. I just can't handle it at this moment," she said.

She said a lot. She said that life was hard enough to get through on her own, and she could not stand knowing that Mama was gone. She said that was her reason why she couldn't take me. She told me Mama had paid the rent up a few months with all the overtime she worked so that she and I could stay in the apartment with no worries and so that she could focus on helping me to get through whatever her death would leave me fighting. She said that Mama did it so that I would be alright.

Lacey said she would be around to check on me every day since I could not come with her. She said that she loved me, and that time would heal all. Truth is, when it came down to it after she finished grabbing what she wanted, she walked out with Mama's things and might as well have said nothing at all. That was the last time I saw her, and those were the last things she said. The last memory she left me with was watching her twitch her hips out the front door carrying Mama's red laced heels with the peep toe and wheeling a suitcase behind her.

Ollie picked up the pieces that Lacey left. I stopped going to school because Ollie and Dante had me convinced that if I went back, CPS would pick me up. I wasn't even sure how CPS would know if I was going to school, but I didn't argue because Ollie seemed to know a lot about CPS and foster care. Besides, Dante had stopped going to school too, and with all the trips we had to make with Ollie, and corners we had to serve, there wasn't time to go to school.

Months had gone by since my mother had passed, and all I had left was Ollie and Dante. We stayed at Mama's apartment until the day we saw a notice on the door to vacate the property. After that, we tried to go to Dante's and stay there, but we found that the locks had changed, and it no longer seemed as if anyone lived there.

We stayed in Ollie's car for what seemed to be forever, but it was probably just a few weeks. It was a cramped space, and my assigned area was the backseat. I was angry at first – always having to ride in the back and now having to sleep in the back, but I soon realized I had the most space to stretch out at nighttime when it was time to sleep or even just relax.

Eventually, Ollie was able to get in touch with a man he called Unc, and Unc let us come to stay with him.

Living with Unc was different, but in the months since my mom had passed, everything was different. I went from eating a full breakfast every day and solving mysteries to eating microwaved ramen and learning how much water and baking soda to use when cooking crack. Unc had told Dante and me when we first moved in that no man lives for free. He made a point out of telling me that life is fucked up. He said he understands that I lost my mother, but I would have to quit with all the sissy shit and earn my way.

In many ways, I admired Unc. It was how I imagined having a father; the only problem was it wasn't like I was his son.

Unc looked out for me, but he made me work for everything I got. He would buy me clothes, but he also kept me up all night cooking and bagging whatever shipments of coke he got in. Dante got the easier jobs; he never had to turn powder into rock. Unc would say that crack was not a white man's drug, so there was no way he was going to let a white man profit from it. I never understood what he meant by that because as far as I could see, we were all profiting from the sales that Dante made.

Unc was philosophical, but not like Mama. He had a lot of things to say that sounded smart until you really listened. After sifting through his words, you would find that you were only left with bullshit.

Unc would make Dante deliver because he said that Dante was invisible out there and if there was a risk to be taken, Dante should be the one to take it. Unc felt like Dante was born privileged and above the law; I figured Unc was ignorant and wondered what he would think if he knew about Helena. If anyone knew anything about Dante, privilege would never be found next to descriptions of him.

Unc looked out for Dante too, but it was different from the way he looked out for Ollie and me. Once, Unc got pulled over for a broken taillight, and a white officer pulled Unc out the car and called for the dogs to search his vehicle. Unc was so mad when he came home that he kicked Dante out of the house. He made Dante sleep outside on the back porch for a few days while he came off his anger. Even though he knew Dante wasn't the reason he got pulled over, Unc said that it made him feel better to have power over at least one of them.

I thought about what my mother told me about Mike and constantly wondered if I was like Dante and if Unc noticed. I realized that I had a white father, but I did not know the first thing about being white. I looked a lot like a lighter-skinned version of my mother. I didn't have mixed features. I didn't look like I was anything other than the regular black kid I always thought I was, and I figured that somehow, that saved me from Unc's aggression.

Aside from the negative things that came from Dante being white, there were positive things that came from Dante being white. Ollie and Dante worked the corners and never got hassled much. Ollie had Dante running while police drove right past them. I think seeing a white kid running drugs was beyond them, so it was much easier to ignore it. Since Dante didn't draw much attention, he was always sent to work the streets. Unc kept me upstairs practicing culinary skills with drugs.

It seemed like we stayed with Unc forever, but it was not long before things went wrong, and Ollie got picked up on a kidnapping charge and drug charge.

Ollie had been riding to Cleveland to pick up a shipment, and on the way back he was pulled over with Dante in the car. It just so happened that Helena had put out a Missing Person notice for Dante.

When Ollie was arrested, they found drugs and two guns in the car; and even though Dante was sitting in the front seat strapped with a seatbelt, and in possession of one of the found guns, Ollie was still charged with kidnapping alongside drug-trafficking charges, child endangerment, and unlawful carry.

Unc and I had gone to the police station after receiving the call from Ollie and finding out what happened. When we arrived, Helena was there sitting on the bench with a cigarette.

I thought to myself that it was a nice change for her to be concerned about Dante's well-being. Surprisingly, she looked normal, even nice. Her hair was pulled up into a neat ponytail, and she was wearing clean sweats with a clean white shirt. Even more surprising, she looked worried.

When she saw me enter the building with Unc, she called out to me as if I were her long-lost puppy. She motioned for me to come over to her while she stared at Unc. Unc's face was frozen, and I could tell he recognized her.

During the exchange of glares, an officer walked out with Dante. When Dante saw Helena, his expression changed from being what seemed to be mad to confused. Dante looked at Unc and me and shrugged. Helena played the role of a loving and concerned mother, kissing all over Dante and checking him for signs of bruising. All I could do was watch.

Unc pulled on my collar to get me to come with him. After assessing the situation, Unc decided that it would be better to leave and come back later. I couldn't go.

As I watched Helena hugging and kissing Dante, I realized how empty I felt. I walked over to Helena and hugged her before I even realized I was moving. I don't know whether it was me walking over to her or me hugging her, but it caused the Officer to look up. When he looked up, so did I, and it was just in time to see Unc leaving the station. Helena told the officer that I was Dante's friend and she would be taking both of us home and just like that we were out the door with Helena.

Dante and I were both confused at what had transpired, but unlike Dante, I was eager. I clung to the motherly vibe that Helena had given out at the station, and every second I witnessed it was a second that I could feel my mama. Helena walked us up to a car with some white man in the driver seat and an odd-looking female with holes in her face who didn't look much older than Ollie in the back seat. On the way to our unknown destination, Dante and I sat quietly in the back, listening to Helena and the man talk.

The more I heard, the more I gathered that nothing had really changed with Helena. It turned out she had gotten notices and a summons to court because Dante had not been in school. CPS had started to investigate her, so she filed a missing report for Dante.

Hearing the story unravel quickly drained me back to feeling empty. I knew then that Helena was still the junkie that Dante accused her of being; even worse, she would never be capable of being a mother.

The next morning just happened to be a Monday and Helena dropped Dante and me off at the front door of our school. Before pulling off, she told Dante, "I don't care what you do; just don't miss school."

I went to school that day. Dante never went again.

Chapter 8

Foster Care

"What's the difference between a house and a home?"
—Anonymous

We both went back to stay at Unc's house. Dante maintained his will to not go back to school. I missed being at school. I wanted to keep going, and I did.

I woke myself every morning to walk to school and back to what was now home – Unc's. Sometimes Dante walked with me, but most of the time he slept in. Many times, I barely got any sleep at night because Unc had a batch of cocaine that needed to be cooked or other random drugs that needed to be broken down, scaled, and bagged.

Unc didn't mind me going to school, and he didn't mind Dante not going. His only concern was that we earned our keep. Dante paid his share by being a scrambler. I paid mine by turning raw cocaine into rock, and I was good at it. If we paid our way, Unc let us do what we wanted. I went to school, Dante hustled.

Somewhere near the end of the school year, I was called into the guidance counselor's office. I had a feeling while walking to the office that I should have turned and left, but I kept walking. When I got to the office, it was filled with not only the guidance counselor and the Principal, but two faces I had never seen.

They introduced themselves, but my thoughts spoke louder than them. I knew without them telling me who they were. Just when everything was going right for me, something had to rock the boat. I spent my whole life being Teigen's child, and just like that, not more than five minutes later, I was a child of the state.

My first encounter with a foster home was hopeful. My foster mother had a few other foster kids, and she was kind to us all.

She was a heavyset black lady with a deep voice and a mustache, but she cooked well, and she helped me with homework. She had affectionately renamed me "Baby." I am not sure if she ever knew my real name or any of the other kids for that matter because she called us all the same thing – Baby. Somehow, we always knew who she was talking to by the way she said, "Baby."

Mrs. Edna, we called her. She was particular about the way we pronounced Mrs. She stressed that a married woman was different than a "miss" or a "misses." I never argued with her, but they were all the same to me, and I couldn't hear the difference even when she tried to break it down phonetically. Besides, I had never met Mrs. Edna's husband, and one of the older foster kids said that Mrs. Edna was a widow. I didn't bother to confirm the story because I knew better than to ask questions about the dead. Mama had taught me well when I had questions about Grandma and Grandpa when they passed away. For some reason, I had suspicions about Mrs.

Edna's widow status and didn't believe it to be true. Mrs. Edna quickly became my mystery.

I heard her speaking on the phone one day in a hushed tone and got the impression that her husband wasn't dead at all. In fact, I figured he must've run off with another woman because when the caseworkers came by, Mrs. Edna claimed that her husband was on a business trip, but I heard her on the phone swearing to the "good lord" that she was going to put a "hurtin'" on him whenever he finally came back around.

Mrs. Edna dramatics made for good entertainment. I never met her Mr. during my stay, but that was alright because I enjoyed Mrs. Edna by herself. She wasn't big on discipline, and she rarely had time to pay attention to all the kids she kept because she spent so much time on the phone in her hushed tones. But, the longer I stayed with Mrs. Edna, the more it became home. Once it became home, I got too comfortable.

One of the older kids Mrs. Edna kept became sick from inhaling paint fumes. Aside from the paint fumes, the kid had bruising. I am not sure where the bruising came from because Mrs. Edna never laid a hand on any of her kids.

CPS investigated her and eventually removed all the kids from her care. I finished my 4th-grade year at the Children's Home.

Next, I was placed with a white family out in Copley, the Uhlers. This foster home consisted of two parents who had biological 15-year-old twin boys, Daniel and Derrick, and a 16-year-old daughter Danielle.

I was put with them at the beginning of the summer, and it was near the end of the summer when I knew that this arrangement would not work either. I never even bothered to learn or use my foster parents' names, I made sure to always refer to them as "fosters" to remind myself not to get close and to remember that it was temporary, even if I had to huff paint to make it so.

Daniel was the oldest of the twins. He was the exact opposite of his younger twin, Derrick. Daniel was rail thin with freckles and red hair. His eyes were green like emeralds. He reminded me of a leprechaun. His small stature, along with his squeaky voice, could easily cause him to be the center of attention for all the wrong reasons. He wore his clothes fitted, and his nails were well manicured like Mama's used to be. Daniel played the violin and read comics, and if the wind blew hard enough, it would carry Daniel, his comics, and the violin away with it. Derrick, taller and bulkier, but identical in the face, played football and bullied me. If the wind blew Derrick's way, it would stop before it reached him and turn around.

Daniel was the only one in the whole family, who was kind to me. It was a relief, for the most part, to have him around because when he wasn't, it seemed that my foster parents were annoyed by my existence. It was hard trying to fit in. Everything I did seemed to irritate my foster mother. I even used my best charm with her, and she was still angered by every breath I took. I learned to avoid everyone's path except Daniel's. Emotions at the house seemed to revolve around my foster mom's, and she never had any positive emotions towards me.

Whenever she cooked, I got fed last if there were enough leftovers. I was responsible for cleaning after dinner, and if that wasn't done, I was punished. My foster father's favorite punishment was to make me kneel in the corner. He would scatter rice in the corner and make me stick my nose in the crease of the wall while planting my knees in the rice. My knees would be so cut up sometimes that it was hard for me to walk afterward.

There were times when my foster mother would say the state did not pay enough for everything she had to do for me. At those times, she fed me cereal or granola bars for dinner. She would send me to bed early because she said that I wouldn't be hungry if I were asleep. Daniel would come into the room with bites of whatever they had for dinner and share it with me. Daniel and I would talk about comics and cars. Sometimes, Daniel left me a few comics to keep me entertained until I fell asleep.

When I first arrived at the foster home, Daniel had given me a picture frame for my room. The picture frame had a family in it that I was sure came with the frame. The only pictures I had of Mama were the ones I had gotten from Lacey before she disappeared. I was unable to get them from Unc's house when I was taken from school. It helped to pretend that it was Mama and me in the picture frame Daniel gave me. It got me through the nights when I felt most alone.

Daniel made the foster situation easier than the rest of my foster family did. I often heard them talking about me, but I ignored it and rejoiced in the fact that I at least had somewhere to stay and one friend in the house, Daniel. He was different. He cared. He talked to me about

Mama as much as I wanted, and he snuck me snacks and juice when the family tried to starve me. He was considerate and fair. He was my only ally in the house until he reached his hands in my pants.

The first time he tried to touch me, I was confused. I grabbed his hand and stared him down until he ran out of the room. I didn't want to make things awkward with the only friend I had in the house, so I kept it to myself and never brought it back up to him.

Keeping quiet about it wasn't enough because not too long after, Daniel came into my room claiming he wanted to give me a comic book and granola bar. Next thing I knew, I was on top of him hitting him with the picture frame he gave me because once again, his hands had wandered below my belt.

I ran away that night, but I didn't go far because I had no clue where I was going. My foster parents ended up riding up behind me and bringing me back. They threatened to press assault charges on me if I didn't apologize to Daniel and promise to keep what had happened to myself. Although I wasn't sure what my foster mother meant by pressing charges or how much trouble would follow, it scared me enough that I kept my mouth shut.

I completed most of my 5th-grade year trying to avoid the perverted twin. He attempted advances on me several times, and I ignored them for fear of whatever assault charges were, but eventually, he went too far.

My foster father was building some contraption in the garage and had ordered me to retrieve a 2X4 located in the shed that sat further back in the yard.

While I was searching for the wood, Daniel came into the shed and shut the door behind him. He wasted no time cornering me. While I bent over to grab the wood, Daniel snuck up on me and swept my legs from underneath. Once I fell to the ground, he quickly flipped me over and put his knee to my chest and his hand to my mouth while he fiddled with his zipper. Unfortunately, for Daniel, the 2x4 was only a reach away, and once I got it in my hand, I blacked out.

I ran away after that, and that time I didn't stop until I was sure I was out of reach. The police picked me up that night after seeing me roaming the streets, and once again, I was back at the children's' home.

Caseworkers and detectives had visited me several times asking about the incident, and although I told them several times what had happened, nothing happened.

I thought that the twin would get in some type of trouble, but no. After being released from the hospital, he received treatment for being privileged and confused about his sexuality in a criticizing and harsh world; meanwhile, the state tried to figure out what kind of criminal charges were appropriate for a 10-year-old with behavior issues. Assault with a deadly weapon was the chosen charge for a mistreated foster child who was being sexually harassed and assaulted.

The original chatter was about whether to try me as an adult. It was said that I had done a number on

Daniel and that the type of behavior I displayed was indicative of a sociopath. Because of my age and the fact that I had no other infractions in school or otherwise, they elected to deal with me in juvenile court.

Regardless of what they claimed, I knew the decision to put my case in juvenile court had something to do with what happened at the foster home. I felt like it was an attempt to avoid bringing up the mistreatment and the perverted twin's antics.

They sentenced me to the juvenile detention center. It was a sentence handed to me as if it were a slap on the wrist, and that slap on the wrist put me in the juvenile detention center for defending myself, while it freed a 15-year-old confused boy who had assaulted me.

Lucky for me, I was still able to go to school even if it was in the detention center. Many people came in and out of the center while I was there. It seemed like I had been in the center forever before I was finally released. In reality, I spent only a year and some months in the center.

I went back to the children's home and back in school before the next foster family came along. The caseworker told me when I was leaving that this foster family dealt with troubled kids so I would be best not to mess it up.

I didn't want to mess it up.

I loved this foster family, and for the first time in a long time, I felt loved. Mr. and Mrs. Donald had been foster parents for a while because Mrs. Donald couldn't have her own kids. She talked about how she had wanted to adopt, but then she decided that helping kids in the system was her calling.

I didn't want to get comfortable with her, but she had a way of convincing me I was home. She took care of me. She brought me school clothes, shoes, and even toys. I had not seen toys since Mama was alive. She enrolled me in a new school and attended conferences and school events.

She paid attention to me. She talked to me a lot about my past and my relationship with Mama. She showed me how to pray and how to cook real meals instead of drugs. She even offered to pay for me to play sports if I wanted. She recognized that I was smart and played into my intelligence by trying to get me into more advanced level classes.

There were other foster kids while I was in her care, but they came and went. I figured that they couldn't appreciate what was right in front of them at the Donald's. They must have never had a Teigen to give them warm embraces, mysteries to solve, and kisses at night. I knew what I had, and it was the closest to what I'd had with Mama in a while, so I stayed.

By the time I made it to the 9th grade, Mrs. Donald had managed to get me into AP classes. Being in high school came with a lot more freedom. I was doing well in school, and Mr. and Mrs. Donald were so proud of me that they signed the permission slip for me to have off-campus lunches.

It was during one of those off-campus lunches that I saw Dante outside of my school. At first, I was not sure it was him, but just like a real best friend would, I quickly recognized his unkempt style. Even when Dante was able to get and choose clothes, he still managed to remain scraggly looking.

I couldn't resist skipping the rest of my classes that day to reunite with him. I called his name from across the street, and when his eyes found me, he looked as if he saw a ghost.

"Rilei, my mans. Damn, I never thought I would see you again. You lookin' like you straight out here. Where you been at?"

We sat in front of the school, catching up and shooting the breeze. He told me about how Ollie was still in prison, but they went to see him when they could. Dante still stayed with Unc, and Unc stayed in the same place he'd been living before I went to foster care. Dante said that after I left, Unc tightened up his grip far as what went on in the house.

"Yeah man, you know how that crazy-ass dude is, man. Still trying to talk 'bout stuff he don't know 'bout, but I just stay out his way and do what I gotta do feel me."

I wanted to go by and see Unc, but I knew that the way Mrs. Donald was, a second late in the house would send off all types of panic alerts in her head. Instead, I let Dante know to meet me the next day after school in the same spot, and I left. After that day, I felt like I had the best of both worlds. I had my foster family, and I had Dante and Unc back.

I never let my interactions with Dante and Unc interfere with going to school, but they did interfere with getting back home in time. Mrs. Donald would get mad and tell me that she wouldn't keep putting up with me coming home late, but she did. I apologized every time, but after seeing how worried Mrs. Donald was, I made up a lie that I was on the Dance committee and explained to her that it was the reason I was always late. Mrs. Donald knew me, and she knew I couldn't dance, nor did I care about a dance, but she believed me anyway because it was easy to do.

I eventually told Mrs. Donald about Dante. I had gotten tired of lying to her, and even more tired of having to make up crazy dance scenarios for dances that were never going to happen. She was upset, but she knew the truth deep down. That's when it confirmed for me how much I really loved Mrs. Donald. Like Mama, she could see through me, all the way down to the best parts even when I showed the worst.

She didn't brush off my information about meeting up with Dante. She inquired more about it. She didn't ask questions to pick and judge like the Uhlers' did when I met them. She asked questions that she was really interested in knowing the answers to while she fed me to the point that I had a full stomach.

I told her everything. I told her how we grew up together, about Dante's mother, and about Ollie and Unc. It felt like I was talking to Mama, and in true "Rilei fashion," I talked so much that she asked to meet him. I was outdone.

I set it up so Dante came home with me after school so that we could play video games and he could have dinner with us. Dante would have never agreed to an outright "Parent Meet and Greet." I knew the best way to lure him in and have him meet Teigen reincarnated was to bribe him through video games.

Mr. Donald didn't like the idea of Dante being around, but Mrs. Donald loved it. She had a heart for kids that she felt she could help. That was the way she reminded me most of Mama. Mr. Donald was different. He loved me like the son he didn't have, but he didn't see much in Dante.

"Trouble, that's what he looks and smells like."

"Matthew, the boy, is Rilei age, how much trouble could he be? He may be troubled, but he is not trouble."

"I wouldn't give a rat's ass if he and Jesus were the same age. I could smell him before he brought his ass in here, and all I smelt was..."

"Trouble, huh. You are something else, Matthew."

It didn't take much to hear their conversation from my bedroom. My bedroom sat right over the kitchen, where Mrs. Donald and Mr. Donald stayed cleaning up after dinner. They were easily heard through the vents, and I wondered how Dante felt. His face showed no emotion, though. It didn't flush red, nor did he seem interested in what was said. He simply chuckled in his sinister way and continued playing the video game.

By the end of the night, regardless of what Mr. Donald had said, Mrs. Donald was trying to convince Dante to move in. Even though Dante refused, he started coming over a lot. It irritated Mr. Donald, but he made do and remained cordial with Dante.

Mrs. Donald made sure he ate whenever he came over and even brought Dante an air mattress to sleep on in case he wanted to stay over. He never said it, but I knew Dante wanted the life I had with the Donald's. Unfortunately, Dante was too used to the life he already had. There would be no hustling and scrambling at the Donald's, and Dante had been hustling and scrambling since before Mama passed. It wasn't like Dante to try to depend on anyone else. I, on the other hand, needed to depend on others. I liked the way it felt.

Dante and I spent the next two years hanging out after school between Unc' and the Donalds.' Unc didn't mind, and he never said much to Dante because Dante was still making money and returning before Unc could worry. Unc held his gripes about Dante being white but also acknowledged Dante for being loyal. Unc claimed that I left him and chose some rigid Uncle Toms instead of him. Even if it annoyed me, I laughed it off and give him credit for being the court's jester. The nigga was comical, after-all.

I cared about Unc, and I was thankful for everything he did for me after losing my mom, but I loved the Donalds. I wanted Unc to feel like I had the same loyalty to him as Dante had. Moreover, I wanted Ollie to be proud of me when he finally came home.

I tried to go by Unc's house often, but when I reached the 11th grade, Mrs. Donald tightened up and put her foot down. She wanted me studying for the S.A.T. and made sure that I was home to do it. Mr. Donald had an old project car, and he told me if I did well on the test, we could fix it up, and he would give it to me. Mr. Donald talked about adopting me legally so that I could benefit from his military benefits. Mrs. Donald said that paper wouldn't make me no more of her son than I already was, but she made sure that I knew that she would be honored if I chose to be adopted.

I would be too. I didn't fully understand the mechanics of adoption, and in my small mind, I battled with rather it would be a betrayal to Mama. Mr. Donald was better than every father I pretended to have when I was younger. Mrs. Donald was the best Teigen reincarnation I could hope for, but they weren't Mama. Even with both, it didn't compare to being Teigen's son. I declined.

With fewer appearances at Unc's came the increase in Dante's appearance at the Donald's. Mrs. Donald never missed an opportunity to try to convince Dante to stay with us. Even though she couldn't convince him, she did persuade him to study for his GED while I studied for the S.A.T. Mr. Donald never took to Dante, but he knew his wife and didn't interfere with her kind nature. He told me, however, to keep my eyes peeled because he sensed something he didn't like in Dante.

Ever since kindergarten, people sensed what they did not like about Dante. No one really knew Dante but me and Mama. I heeded any warning Mr. Donald threw my way, except that one. I knew Dante, and all the world did was turn its back on him. I knew what that felt like when the world took Mama. I wouldn't do that to Dante. I respected Mr. Donald, however, and agreed to disagree.

Mr. Donald had been up for a promotion at work. He had known about it for months before he was finally called to interview for the position. It took a few months, but he finally received an offer as a bank manager position. With the extra income, he decided he wanted to move his family to a nicer house in a better area. Mr. Donald always said he could not stand being in the inner city because of its criminal characteristics. He was overly excited at the opportunity to get out.

The news of the promotion and anticipated move excited Mrs. Donald so much that she was packing before the ink even dried on Mr. Donald's job offer. Once the promotion was finalized, we moved to one of the more valued areas of Akron, Merriman Valley. It was a beautiful house with five bedrooms and two living rooms. Every home on the block was brick with freshly manicured lawns. The driveways were filled with newer cars, and no one was in the streets. There were no corner stores or corner boys. There were no Pontiacs, Cutlasses, or Grand Marquis. Kids rode their bikes down the street in family packs, and it was like nothing I had ever seen before.

Most interesting was that everyone around waved friendly waves with disgusted faces until they saw Dante. Disgusted faces turned into curious faces at the sight of him. Dante had helped us move in. Once he saw the house, that was all it took to convince him to move in too. Oddly enough, he fit into the neighborhood. Poor grammar, high school drop-out, and the best scrambler Unc ever had, yet, he fit into the neighborhood better than the Donalds and me.

Everything was going great. Dante was still between Unc's and the Donald's, but he was primarily at the Donald's. Mrs. Donald tried everything to convince Dante to stop selling drugs and focus on his GED, but Dante loved the hustle much too much by that time. Mrs. Donald was worried that Dante would feel left behind when I went off to school. I had already taken my S.A.T., and we had just gotten the scores back. Not only did I do well, but I scored almost perfect on the math section and exceeded well beyond average on the other sections. Mrs. Donald knew that once I was gone, Dante would leave, and she worried about where he would go. I didn't worry. I knew that if anyone could survive on their own, it was Dante.

True to his word, after my scores came in from the SAT, Mr. Donald whipped out an old Chevy Camaro and told me it was ours to work on and mine to keep. We worked on it every day in the summer. Even Dante got interested. Dante went from only being at the house around dinner and bedtime to being there in the day to help work on the car.

Mr. Donald still didn't like Dante being around, and he didn't trust Dante with me, but he was happy that the car gave Dante something to do besides hanging in the streets. Other than keeping Dante out of the streets, it was also a relief because the neighbors would call the police and complain that people were working on a car in the driveway when they didn't spot Dante. They claimed it was an eyesore, and it was driving down property value. Mr. Donald said that it was him and me that was the eyesore they were complaining about. The police would harass us, but since no laws were broken, nothing would ever happen.

"I earned this just like they earned that; they have some nerve. I don't give a rat's ass what the hell is going on with their property value. I paid my mortgage on the god damned first of the month like them."

That was Mr. Donald's know expression for when he was serious about something. It was always "rat's ass this" or "rat's ass that." All I knew is if he mentioned a rat's ass, then his perspective on a situation was not going to change. So, we continued to work on the car in the driveway despite the interruptions when Dante was absent.

It took months, but by the time 12th grade rolled around, the car was ready to be driven. Dante and I drove to school together every day. Although Dante wouldn't go to school, he would ride with me early in the morning. I dropped him off outside the school and usually caught up with him after. On the days I met with the counselor after school to fill out college applications, Dante went to Unc's house to drop off money and pick up product. Everything seemed to be smooth sailing. Dante and I were finally living our best lives.

Then, as always, when things seemed to settle, someone kicked up dust. CPS launched an investigation of the Donalds, claiming that they misused funds to support their lifestyle. After all the years I had been there because I was only 17, they wanted to remove me from the home.

It all started when Dante had come up short on Unc's money. Dante had been hustling while I was at school one day and had seen Helena. Helena chatted him up good and made him feel like he had a mother. Dante was so caught up in seeing his mom that he damn near melted at the sight of her.

During lunch, he bombarded me asking me for the keys so he could take her to eat. I gave them to him on the condition that he was back after school to pick me up. The final school bell had rung, and Dante was nowhere in sight. I was so angry that I caught the bus to Unc's house, knowing that Dante would be there, and I was right.

I saw my car parked outside in perfect condition. I thought to myself, "this nigga ain't been in no accident and he ain't dead. What the fuck?"

I was so mad that I busted into Unc's ready to snatch my keys and snatch Dante's Adam's Apple from his neck. I instantly calmed when I found Dante curled up on the floor bleeding.

Flashbacks rushed through my mind of seeing my mom in the bathroom bleeding. I called out for Unc to help me, but he wasn't there, so I grabbed Dante and carried him to my car. I searched his pockets for the keys, and once I found them, I sped back to the Donald's.

On the way to the house, Dante told me Unc had jumped on him because he had come up short. He said Helena must have lifted some baggies off him while they were out to lunch and he came to try and explain what had happened to Unc, but Unc didn't understand.

As coincidence would have it, the next-door neighbors were out when we arrived at the house. We had always suspected them of being the ones to call the police, but we never had proof. When the lady from the house next door saw me pulling a beat-up Dante out of the car, her mouth dropped open, and her eyes burned with anger and 'the audacity' into my back.

It seemed like not even a wink later; the police were at our door. Dante refused to file a report, and they eventually left, but I could tell that seeing the Donalds in that house, and Dante all beat up left a bad taste in their mouth. It must have left one in the neighbor's as well because a few days later, CPS showed up talking about child endangerment, and misappropriation of funds.

Just like that, I was removed from another foster home, and this time, I was placed in the Children's home until I aged out. As a result, I spent my 12th-grade year between Children's home and running away to Unc's. I wanted to go back to the Donald's house, but I didn't want to put that type of pressure on them. Mrs. Donald's foster rights were revoked, and she was heartbroken. I couldn't stand to get her in any more trouble than I already had.

Dante returned to Unc's even after everything that had happened because he said it was all he had. Unc forgave Dante and, just like that, it was business as usual. I was back to being Uncs' favorite chef, and Dante was back hustling around the high school.

The day I graduated, I decided that I would get my own place. I was tired of living with Unc. Dante wanted his space too. Although he had gone back to Unc, he never forgave Unc for jumping on him and couldn't wait until he could quit dealing with him.

Dante had been saving up shoebox money just like he did years ago when Mama was sick. He almost had enough for us to get a place when Unc came across Dante's stash. Unc took all the money Dante had saved. He told him that it would pay him back for the time he came up short, then everything would be square.

Dante must've frozen with memories of the last beating that Unc gave him because he said nothing. I, on the other hand, was not frozen, and I was tired of all the setbacks. I started to say something to Unc, but Dante somehow unfroze and threw his hand over my mouth. I let Unc carry on with his ramble.

"White folks gotta pay too. You feel like I did you wrong, but it ain't shit compared to what you did to my people...shit. I beat yo ass 'cause it was a lesson young mothafucka. Y'all beat our asses 'cause y'all was trying to teach a nigga to obey right? Well, obey me, mothafucka. I'm gone tell you what, this lil' money here gone set us right though."

I wanted to pounce. I was sick of his shit. Dante never did anything to him. Unc's version of history was so skewed that I wondered if he ever picked up a book. He had never been whipped or chained, on the open sea, or anything else. All Unc knew was the projects. He talked so much about not letting a white man profit from our people, yet he was out there selling the shit to separate "our people." And, Dante was profiting from it.

Unc had gone from being a full-time dealer to a part-time dealer and a part-time addict. Sometimes I would spend all day cooking, weighing, and bagging only to come back and find half my hard work in Unc's pipe. It got to the point where he was damn near taking my shit directly off the stove.

Unc was vicious when he was high. He didn't have much of a filter sober, but when he was high, the first thought in his head came out of his mouth. He would go off on his rampages, and Dante was usually his victim.

This time, Unc was in rare form.

I arrived to find that Unc had burned through an entire package again. He wanted Dante and me to ride to Cleveland to pick up more, but I decided I wasn't doing it because I was sick of him smoking all the shit. On top of that, he had taken all the money Dante had saved up, but Dante wouldn't let me say shit about it.

Dante and I had told Unc we were gone move out soon and it set Unc off in a way I never saw before. It had to have been that either I made the rock too potent, or he was snorting some other shit now because he started talking too much.

Unc started to tell a story of how back in the day when he was younger, he and two of his friends had gotten word on lick to hit on the west side. Unc said he was boning some "snow bunny" female who put him on the lick because she was tired of her child's father beating on her, and she thought he might be cheating as well.

She gave him the details and an address and convinced him that it would be an easy lick with a decent payoff. Unc and his friends followed up on the tip. When they arrived at their destination, they found that it wasn't what it was promised to be.

Unc talked excitedly about how they entered the house in stealth mode on some video game shit. He said they heard voices coming from downstairs in the basement, so they crept down the stairs to follow the sounds. One of Unc's friend had been clumsy and tripped on something laying on the steps. It gave away their position.

Since they were discovered, Unc grabbed his Glock 19 and charged down the rest of the stairs. Instead of finding what they were told they would find or anything of value, they found four construction workers who had been snorting lines of coke. Unc said he got so aggravated that he started shooting.

After he spent all his bullets, Unc and his friends searched the pockets of the workers. Unc said he noticed that in one of the wallets he found, the guy had a picture of his family. Unc described the picture, and in the middle of the description, Dante looked up. Unc laughed at Dante and said, "They kill one of us, nobody bats an eye, but you get to killing them, and you become the devil himself."

I noticed Dante trying to fight back the tears as Unc continued to drill into Dante with his story.

Unc said that a few months later he noticed the same female on the corner hustling EBT stamps. He was pissed about the lick not turning up how she said but allowed her to make it up through sexual favors.

The more he described the encounters, the more Dante melted into his seat. Unc started talking about how she would leave her kid at home to come to see him and how he would make her do all type of tricks when she was with him. Without saying her name, Unc described the woman in a way that made it evident to Dante and me that he was talking about Helena.

Right when Dante was at his breaking point, Unc caught Dante eyes and said, "yea, she may have been white, but your mother could fuck." He followed up with, "I bet that was probably the last thought that coke head had before he ate that steel. He was probably thinking, damn I gone miss that pussy. Huh Dante, what you think?"

Before Dante could respond to him, I was midway through telling Unc to shut the fuck up. I knew that the story had paralyzed Dante. I had never challenged Unc before, but the fact that he had taken Dante's money and then decided to take Dante's dignity, had got to me.

Unc must have been just as surprised as me when I spoke up because he did "shut the fuck up." He was so quiet that I could hear a fly piss on cotton. His eyes were intense as they stared me down, and his jaw was clenched tightly and quivering.

When he finally came to terms with what I had said, he looked at Dante and said, "so you just gone let him talk to your step-daddy like that?" Dante remained quiet.

Unc turned his aggression toward me and said: "Do I know your mother?" My heart was beating rapidly, and I did not feel the same fear I once felt when I was trying to figure myself out. By the time Unc could fix his lips to say something else, I was already in his face trying to control my fists that had taken a mind of their own.

The more I swung, the more relieved I felt. It was addicting. I finally felt like some of the pressure that was weighing down on my emptiness had been relieved. Every time my fist connected with his flesh, I felt lighter and freer. No one ran over to break this up like they did for Daniel.

I swung for all the times I should have swung on Daniel. I punched at the changing faces; I could see Mrs. Uhler and Mr. and Mrs. Donald's next-door neighbor. I swung for Unc. I was teaching him the lesson he craved. I was giving him the beating his ancestors received that he wanted to relate to so much. I swung until I couldn't anymore, and after I had grown tired of swinging, all that was left was the well-known empty feeling.

I was so tired that I collapsed on the floor against the table that was in front of the couch where Unc sat. I looked up at him and saw nothing but blood.

For some reason, every time I saw blood, it brought me back to my mother laying on that cold bathroom floor.

Unc laid there on the couch completely motionless. It seemed like hours had passed with me on the floor staring up at Unc trying to decide if I was still angry or if I was done. I noticed Dante twitching in my peripheral vision with his face flushed red. When we made eye contact, Dante whipped a small .380 from his waistband and emptied his clip into what was left of Unc.

The sound from the gun blast forced me to get up. All I knew was that we needed to get the money and whatever we had in the apartment out. I didn't have much at Unc's because I kept my things in my car. Dante had a few things, but everything he had, for the most part, was disposable – so we disposed of it. When we were satisfied that we had cleared everything that needed to be cleared, we hopped in my car and left.

I decided to pay a visit to Merriman Valley since we had nowhere else to go. I was surprised to find that with all the sudden change life had offered, Mr. Donald's car was still parked in the driveway. I had not seen the Donalds since I had been removed from their home.

I jumped out of the car and jogged up to the door. I was so anxious to feel a hug from Mrs. Donald and show Mr. Donald how well I had taken care of the car that I had forgotten that there was blood on my shirt. I had forgotten nearly everything that had just transpired because all I could think about was what it would be like to feel loved again.

When the door slung open, Mrs. Donald was standing on the other side with her arms outstretched and a welcoming smile just as I had imagined her. She was so excited to see me that she almost knocked me over in her rush to hug me. I was so wrapped up in the moment that I didn't notice that Mr. Donald had come down the stairs. When he saw it was me at the door, he smiled and nodded. I could tell he was excited to see me, but he was never one to get emotional.

He was walking toward me, and Mrs. Donald was releasing me from her hug when he noticed my blood-stained t-shirt. Mrs. Donald must have caught a vibe from him because she looked down and saw the blood on my shirt as well.

Mrs. Donald frantically searched all over my stomach and back, trying to find the source of the blood while Mr. Donald was making his way to the telephone to call 9-1-1.

It took for me to grab Mrs. Donald by the shoulder and shake her a bit to get her to calm down and to gather Mr. Donald's attention.

When I finally had them calm, I put them at ease with a fictitious story about how the blood came from some petty fight that Dante and I had gotten into with some guys. I knew that they didn't buy the story, but they were so relieved that the blood was not mine that they didn't investigate further.

When everything was settled, I rounded up Dante, and Mrs. Donald ushered us into the kitchen to have reheated lasagna. I wanted to ask them to let Dante and me stay there for a while, but I didn't want to interrupt the harmony at the table. I decided I would wait and ask Mr. Donald after we had eaten.

When the opportunity arrived, I pulled Mr. Donald to the side and made small talk about the car. He had noticed the car pulling up in the driveway when I came, but he was so caught up in seeing the blood on my shirt that he did not mention it. He told me that he was proud of me and how much they had missed me over the past year. I took that as the perfect sign to segue into asking for a place to stay for a while.

Mr. Donald must have sensed it coming because before I could ask – he answered. He said that when I was removed, he suspected it was because of the neighbors. He said he had a theory that they had called CPS after seeing me drag Dante into the house. He told me that they had called the police numerous times with numerous complaints because they didn't approve of them living in the neighborhood and could not understand how they could afford to be there.

Mrs. Donald's foster care privileges had been revoked because she was accused of using the funds to provide her "lavish" lifestyle and her house. They even wanted to press criminal charges for misuse of the money, but when Mr. Donald was able to show income, they just stripped their foster privileges instead.

Once he finished explaining, he told me that Dante and I couldn't stay there because there was constant havoc with the neighbors already and the lifestyle that we were involved in would only give more ammunition for the neighbors to shoot him down.

I could see the hurt in his eyes when he told me that I wasn't welcomed back. I didn't get angry because I understood what he had to lose. I figured that I would be sleeping in my car for a while until Dante and I could figure things out.

I didn't want to go back to sleeping in a car; I just wanted things to work out for once. I was grateful for the times that we had to pile into Ollies Mercury because it taught me that a car roof is better than no roof, even if my Camaro didn't have the same back seat. It's no wonder that I always wanted a front seat back then because it was nowhere near as comfortable as the full back seat.

Mr. Donald told me to sit still for a second while he ran upstairs. I sat still, but my mind raced with thoughts about what would happen next. Unc was dead, and I didn't know what would come from that situation. The fact that I didn't have anywhere to go made me nervous. I had been from pillar to post before, but I had always at least had the Children's Home.

While I sat categorizing my thoughts, Mr. Donald had come back downstairs. He looked at me and said, "Son, I can't let you and Dante stay here, but what I can do is give you this."

Mr. Donald handed me a wad of money and told me that I should use it to find somewhere to stay or rent a room for a while. I tried to give him the money back, but he wouldn't accept it. He said it was the only way he would forgive himself for not letting us stay. I jammed it in my back pocket without counting it and hugged him the way I imagined myself hugging a father. I envisioned him as my father and adopting me. I should have let him adopt me.

Dante and I stayed a while longer before I noticed it was late and signaled for him to come on. I didn't want Mrs. Donald to invite us to stay after the conversation, Mr. Donald, and I had, and I knew she would if we waited any longer. I respected Mr. Donald, and I understood his position. I didn't want to put them in a position that would jeopardize their peace any more than it already had been jeopardized.

I realized that I was a different person than the one Mama raised me to be, and I had to grow up. I finally understood that hugs would come and go, and so would people, but I had to keep pushing regardless because I was never going to get the kind of love that I got from Mama. The unconditional love that Mama gave would have caused her to lose everything she owned to make sure I was okay. That was what separated Mama from the Donalds. I believe they loved me unconditionally, but they could only take calculated risks; meanwhile, Mama would have risked it all.

On the way out, I hugged Mr. and Mrs. Donald and promised to keep in touch, but I knew I wouldn't; I was moving on.

Dante and I got in the car, and I could tell Dante wanted to know what was up. I pulled out of the driveway and started driving without acknowledging Dante's curious eyes. Once we were far enough up the road, I pulled into a vacant parking lot and pulled the money out of my back pocket. After counting it twice, I looked at Dante and said, "that's a stack, what are you trying to do?" Dante looked at me, smirked and said, "We slept in a car before." I understood.

The next day we were busy. We rode past Unc's, and it was taped off as expected. Dante went in through the back anyway. He said there was something in there that would set us straight and whatever it was would be worth the risk of going back onto a crime scene.

When he came back, he was smiling, and I knew he had found whatever he was looking for. The next stop was at the house of some female I had never met. Dante had run in for a few seconds, and before I could appreciate his absence, he was back.

We made a few more stops that were much the same, and once he was through, Dante said: "we're going to Cleveland." I wasn't sure what all the stops were about, but they seemed to have set things in motion. Dante came out of the last house with confidence and a smile. I could tell he had promising information.

I was okay with Dante calling the shots because I wasn't sure how to call them, but I knew I needed to learn. I knew that things had a way of changing when I least expected, and I was tired of being caught with my neck out. I needed to become a survivor like Dante. I didn't have the same connections that Dante had, and I had not been out in the streets as long, but I was smart. I knew that I had to start building my network and learning the outside hustle. I was a master chef already, but I was lost when it came to the street business.

When we pulled into the vacant parking lot that night, Dante had grabbed his box of saved money from under the seat and counted. I watched him repeatedly recount the figures in his head and decided it was the perfect time to interrupt and find out what was up. Dante grew irritated with me for interrupting, but I didn't care. I felt that if it took him that long to count 1200 dollars in his head, then he should have carried himself to school when I did. I had already counted Dante's money twice in my head before he initiated his recount, and I was tired of waiting.

"It's $1200 bro. Put that shit up before you give me a migraine."

Dante explained to me that Unc had a number book in his room and even though he wasn't sure who it was, he was confident that the number of whomever Unc got his supply from was in that book. Dante carried on about all the trips he had taken to Cleveland with Unc to pick up product and the one time he went with Ollie. Dante swore he could work his way in with the "plug" through the person he met up with to get the shipments with Unc.

The idea made me nervous. I wondered if they would ask about Unc and what we would say if they did. When I was out in public, I felt like people could see guilt all over me. It was as if I wore a huge sign on my forehead that said, "I killed him." Dante walked around as if he forgot the sign was on his forehead as well. After all, Dante pulled the trigger. I don't know if Unc was dead before that, but any question of whether he was alive was answered after Dante fired off his .380.

We moved around freely, but I was cautious. No one confessed to knowing anything, and no names were floating around revolving Unc's death, so Dante felt like we were in the clear. I had watched enough crime shows to know that it was only a matter of time before suspicions arose and names were named. Mrs. Donaldson was glued to channels that hosted shows like First 48, Snapped, and any other crime show. I used to watch them with her, and we discussed all the ways that people get caught.

Unfortunately, Dante missed that bonding time and was blissfully unaware of the consequences of what we did. I tried to tell him to chill and sit down for a minute, but he swore that no one would look for Unc or care about what happened to Unc.

"He had no family Rilei; he was just a junkie and a liar. No one cares about those types of people. Stop worrying so much."

Dante was convinced and unremorseful. That was all it took for him to convince me that we were free to move around, but inside, I was still cautious.

Chapter 9

Paola

"I'll spend a lifetime making it right." —Anonymous

We spent the next few years going back and forth to Cleveland picking up all types of shit from some guy who claimed to have the best narcotics on our side of the Mason Dixon. His product was alright, but Dante and I used him because he was cheaper than anyone else. We didn't make a whole lot of money because of his inferior product, but it was enough for us to get by.

Dante and I had found our own apartment, and I was finally getting comfortable. I felt like I was in a place that no one could take from me. I had even started looking into going to college again. I wanted to do something that I knew would have made my mama proud, and even Mrs. Donald.

I missed the feeling of being in the classroom and the small amount of guidance it gave. Mama was always a huge advocate of education. She wanted a college degree for herself but was never able to go. I felt like going to college and becoming something other than what the world turned me into would be the best way to honor her, not the little shit that Dante and I were doing to survive. I also wondered if she would be proud of me for just surviving in general.

There were talks of appeals going around the streets for Ollie, and it seemed like things were going to turn out for him. Dante and I had a plan that when Ollie got out, he was going to take over my place so that I could go to school.

Dante knew that I didn't want to keep up or excel in this lifestyle, and I knew that he did want that for himself. I had agreed to work up our network with him so that when Ollie's appeal came through, they would be able to call shots instead of nickel and diming like it felt we were doing. Not much had changed with the dynamics of how we ran things. I still cooked and bagged, and Dante still ran the product.

Most of the time, customers came to the house to pick up. It wasn't quite curb-service like it was before. I told Dante to quit bringing that shit to the house, but Dante said that curb service attracted more attention than having people come by and visit. I knew that was the 4th-grade education in Dante, so I had started keeping emergency money and product in a storage locker out of the way in Greene. Whenever there was too much traffic at the house, I slept at my storage locker just in case I was right about Dante attracting too much attention.

And I was right.

Not even a month later, Dante was arrested when one of his customers was followed by an overly anxious patrol cop. Dante got put on probation for a year, and after that, he stopped bringing customers to the house.

I wasn't spending much time at the house. Dante still had better street skills, but I couldn't make sense of the way he operated. I wanted to separate myself somewhat so that I didn't get tangled up in Dante's reckless habits. Although he wasn't selling directly from the house anymore, he kept too much product out in the open and allowed too much company. I figured we would be prime targets for a raid, or a stick and I didn't want to be there for either.

I put together whatever needed to be sold and then I'd leave. I spent a lot of time at the library reading and trying to stay out of the way. Dante was running wild and drawing so much attention that the library became my haven. It was quiet there and low key. No one from my "survival world" came to the library.

At the library, I read about anything and everything. I found myself stuck there from open to close. I had never realized before how much I loved to read, but something about reading made me feel like I was back with my mother. I could feel myself solving mysteries when I read, and I got so caught up in the books that I escaped my own reality. I could feel Mama's presence around me whenever I visited the library. I rarely felt it when I was at home, but it was if her spirit lived in the library.

I visited so much that I was on a first-name basis with the librarian's assistant, and I could tell someone where to find a book before she could.

It shocked me the day she made conversation with me. I had been sitting at a table near the front where I always sat when she came over and asked if I wanted to apply for a library card. At first, I told her no without even looking up from my book, but then I caught a whiff of the vanilla scent my mom used to wear when I was younger.

I looked up. It was like it was my first time seeing her. She had long silky curly hair that bounced on her back, smooth milk chocolate skin, and light brown eyes. Her breasts set up firm in the floral blouse she wore, and I could see her waistline disappearing at the seat of her hips where her red skirt hugged her down to her knees.

"On second thought, maybe I do need a library card," I said. She smiled.

I got up and followed her to the desk. My pants sagged as I followed, so my walk turned into a waddle to keep them from coming down. When I got to the counter, I pulled my pants up and started to fold the top down for a better fit. Something about her made me feel a need to have a neater appearance. I tucked my t-shirt into my rolled pants.

As I filled out the form to get a card, she glanced at my newly tailored outfit and let out a chuckle. I smiled at her awkwardly while I unrolled the top of my pants. Trying to cover up my stupid mistake, I said, "just wanted to see if I could make you laugh."

She asked why I visited the library so much. I told her it was to ease my mind, and that reading made me feel like I was learning something again. She seemed intrigued by my simple and shallow answer. We talked more. I opened up to her about my dreams of going to college and leaving the city. She showed interest in me and my dreams. That day we conversed for hours until the library closed.

Every day after that, if the library was open, I was there. She helped me fill out college applications and apply for student grants and loans. When she was busy, I read, and when the library emptied out, I was in her face talking. She told me she had a boyfriend, but in my mind, I was her boyfriend.

I had never had time to pay a female any mind really. There were females here and there, but never any that kept my attention long enough to make me forget about the turmoil in my life. But she could. When I was around her, I didn't feel like myself. I felt there was more to life when she was around, and that was just it. There was more to life when she was around.

It took a while, but I eventually got her number. I still saw her at the library, so I didn't text or call her out of respect for her relationship. She was different than most of the women I had met; something about her reminded me of my mother. She had a way about her that made me feel she could teach me, heal me, and seduce me all at the same time.

I craved her conversation. I stayed at the library just so I could get it without disrupting her personal life. She always kept a straight face with me when she let me know she was unavailable, but I could tell that she wished she was available.

I refrained from reaching out to my library girlfriend outside of the library. At least I did until the night I got home, and Dante tossed me some mail with Florida A&M University's seal on it.

I opened the letter and let Dante read the beginning. Dante did not read well, but through all his phonetics and fumbling across the words, I heard "Accepted," and my fingers started moving mindlessly across my phone as they dialed her number. It surprised me that I knew her number by heart although I had never dialed it or called her before.

A voice sounded through my line, and I instantly started screaming out the news before the line went click. In all my excitement, I didn't realize that it was not her who answered the phone. Once I realized no one was on the line any longer, I texted her. I waited for what seemed like forever, and I didn't get a text back. The news was bursting out of me, but I couldn't reach her. I figured I would just tell her at the library the next day.

I woke up the next morning and headed straight to the library. She wasn't there. I proceeded, as usual, only alone. I began reading some random book off the shelf before I started to miss her presence to the point that I was ready to leave. I decided to go ahead and check out the book and read at home. There was a different vibe without her there.

It seemed as if a few days passed, and she still had not been back to the library. My news of acceptance was growing stale, so I decided to try to call her again. Her voicemail sounded, "You reached Paola, I cannot answer…" and I hung up. I sent another text to see what was up and again, it went unreturned.

I finally asked the lady who was working the counter in her absence about Paola. She told me that she was out sick but should be returning the next day. So, there I was the next day, waiting at the library door an hour before it opened.

When she got out of the car, my heart fluttered, and a smile jumped onto my face. She closed the passenger side door, and the car sped off quickly. I noticed her face as the car splashed water from a puddle on the street onto her tan peacoat. She looked disgruntled but continued walking as she pulled her keys from her purse and made her way to the library doors.

When she caught sight of me, a smile darted across her face. She fixed the smile into a look of indifference before I could let her know that I saw it. She unlocked the library door without looking at me again and walked inside.

I sat there a moment longer trying to think if I had done anything. When I concluded that I had not, I got up and went into the library as well.

I browsed around for a minute while I tried to think about how to approach her. While I was browsing, I happened to come across a book with Florida in the title. I snatched it up and went over to her desk. She still didn't look up. I cleared my voice. She didn't budge. I reached over to tap her, and she glanced up at me just long enough for me to notice the discoloration on her neck.

She didn't have to say much because it didn't take much for me to figure it out. Without saying anything, she showed me her broken phone screen and hinted at the fact that she had received my calls and text.

I apologized and told her that I was only calling to tell her about the acceptance and didn't mean to cause problems. Her eyes leaked tears, and the more she cried, the more I thought of Mama when she told me about Mike.

Every tear she shed sent violent images in my head until I could no longer control my anger. The thought that I caused her pain drove me insane. I had never met a woman abused in this format. I had never seen a woman wear physical abuse and emotional abuse at the same time. I could picture Mama wearing the abuse like Paola; she wore the abuse for years. It killed Mama.

I excused myself for a moment and went into the restroom. I texted Dante letting him know to meet me at the library when it closed and to make sure he came strapped. Dante loved adversity, confrontation, or any sort of drama. I was sure he would be on time.

After he confirmed he'd be there, I went back and sat in my regular spot to read until the library closed. Instead of waiting for her to lock up, I darted out the door to meet Dante. We jumped in my car and pulled to the edge of the parking lot and waited. She finally exited the building holding her tan pea coat in one arm and glancing around cautiously. A car pulled up, and she jumped in. I followed it.

The whole ordeal was quicker than I could account for. I only remember them pulling up at an apartment building and seeing her get out. After that, I don't recall anything other than standing over him with blood all over my t-shirt.

Images of Unc kept flashing through my mind as I contemplated pulling my gun from my waistband. I could feel Dante's hands on my shoulder, trying to pull me back, but my feet wouldn't let me move. I could feel my chest heaving, and I could hear little screams in the background, but I couldn't bring myself to process exactly what was happening.

It wasn't until I felt her hands on my chest, pushing me away that everything started to sound audible. I was able to make out her telling me to hurry up and leave while she pulled my shirt down to hide my gun. I caught a whiff of her vanilla scent and focused on her pea coat that was on the ground. I could tell that she must have dropped everything at a moment's notice to tend to me. A smile landed on my face, and at that moment, the ground released my feet and Dante, and I were back in the car speeding to the house.

Dante questioned me over and over about everything that happened, but I was unable to explain it to him. He wanted to know who Paola was and how I met her. He attempted to lecture me on how we had to stay focused and not cause extra attention. I wasn't in the mood to be lectured, but I knew he was right. I told him about Paola and everything that had happened up to the moment I texted him.

Dante started laughing, and the mood got lighter as he recounted the events that were still foggy in my mind. He began to act out his version of me after I encountered Paola's boyfriend. As soon as I started to engage and laugh off the incident, my phone rang, and it was her.

I took the call to my room. She had never called me before, so I was nervous. I answered the phone, and after a few moments of silence, she started to speak. Her voice was calm as she thanked me for what I did and fell silent. I didn't expect her to call, let alone thank me, but I was relieved to hear her voice. I heard her soft sobs in the background, so I attempted to change the subject. "Hey, I got into FAMU," and there we were, talking again as if we were back in the library.

The conversation lasted for hours while she talked about her dreams and goals. She told me about how her mother, like mine, passed when she was young. She was raised by her father, who moved them to Florida to start over. She talked about how her father brought her over to America from Columbia after her mother died. She said they were trying to get away from her father's previous life. She didn't mention how her mother passed, but she did say that her father was tied into some major drug trade going on in Columbia.

I envied her description of the relationship she and her father shared; even more, I envied the description of her father. He seemed to be the kind of man that I wanted to be. He had money, confidence, and he was well connected. He was a dope boy that got out of the life and was still successful based on what Paola described. He was also a protector, and he knew what to do when it needed to be done. He wasn't timid and impulsive like me.

Paola disagreed.

Paola started talking about what had happened that night and said I reminded her of her father because of how I reacted to the news of someone hitting her. I didn't understand how someone could come from the type of father she had and be with someone who would hit her. I asked her how she ended up in the situation, to begin with. Paola told me how she had ended up in Akron on a scholarship. She said she majored in Criminal Justice because her father wanted her to be a defense attorney. She met Moses while she was at a party with one of her college friends. It wasn't long, according to her, before she figured she was in love. After much convincing; she moved out of the dorms to live with Moses, and from there, everything changed. She didn't admit to being abused upfront. Instead, she talked about how her grades had slipped due to her absences, and she lost her scholarship. Once she lost her scholarship, she was utterly dependent on Moses, and he made sure she knew it.

Moses had a temper, and despite how confident he appeared, he was insecure. It was as if Moses wanted her to wear a hijab and an abaya to make sure she was always completely covered. She said he would sometimes show up at the school unannounced just to see how she handled different men who approached her and to make sure that she wasn't showing any skin.

Paola thought back and spoke about a time that she had left school early because she wasn't feeling well. Moses was into a lot of foul activity, and Paola claimed that when she was home alone, she double locked the doors out of fear.

Usually, Moses was home when she was home, but when he wasn't, she was often doing homework and could get to the door quickly when he arrived.

Except for one time.

Paola came home early, and she had fallen asleep, not realizing that she still had both locks to the apartment door locked. When she woke up, she had over 50 missed calls from Moses and a few threatening text messages. Paola tried to call him back but didn't get an answer. No more than 5 minutes after she hung up, he was banging on the door. He was convinced that she had someone in the apartment because, to him, there was no other reason to lock both locks.

Even though she begged and pleaded with him to hear her out, he decided that kicking her ass would be the only way to make amends. She recounted being hit for the first time. Through tears and a busted lip, she tried to plead her case. After the third or fourth hit, he knocked her to the floor and kicked her everywhere that he could land his boot. When he was finally done, he threw her in their bedroom closet and told her that if she came out, he would kill her.

Paola explained that she couldn't move because a sharp pain was shooting down her sides and across her pelvis. It was to the point that it hurt her even to breathe, let alone to move.

She fell asleep in the closet. When she woke, she said she heard the thud of a hammer banging on or near the closet door. When the banging stopped for more than a few minutes, she said she tried to open the door only to realize she was locked in the closet.

While she told her story, I imagined my mom and Mike for some reason. I felt the anger building up in me, and I knew I didn't want to hear anymore, but I didn't want to interrupt her either. I continued to listen to her tell her story while tears of anger flooded my eyes.

Paola recapped her memories of being left in the closet for what she said felt like days in excruciating pain. When Moses finally let her out, she said her eyes had dark bags around them and bruises covered her from her head to toe. She begged Moses to take her to the hospital because she had been bleeding, but Moses told her she would have to catch the bus because he didn't want to deal with the speculation.

She caught the bus to the hospital as she was told. She found out that she had suffered a miscarriage and that she had 3 broken ribs. She was so upset that she dialed her father, but when she heard his voice, she couldn't stand to tell him what happened. So, she hung up.

Upon returning home from the hospital, Paola said she walked in to find a receipt on the bed with her tuition fully paid and the keys to a new Toyota. Her feelings were conflicted. She didn't know how to feel about the loss of her pregnancy, so she kept it to herself and took her gifts. Moses spent the next few days showering Paola with gifts and expressing regret.

After a few weeks of Moses catering to her, she decided to tell him about the miscarriage. Moses wasn't receptive at all, and instead of believing her, he believed that she had gotten an abortion because she didn't want to have his child. Just like that, she said Moses took away the car and tried to snatch back the paid tuition until he realized he couldn't.

Paola recounted event after event depicting the abuse of her relationship until I had to ask her, "Why did you stay?" She said that, despite how much they had been through, he still paid her way through school, and that meant she never had to confess to her father that she had lost her scholarship. Paola also claimed that she felt he was all she had left of what should have been their child.

"Not many people are going to understand Rilei. I hope that you do not judge me, but in a way, I still consider myself a mother, and he is still, in a way, my child's father. Even without that being a factor, my dad's expectations of me have always been so high that I don't want him to know what happens here. I just want him to be ok and know that I am ok, you know?"

I understood her in a way. I knew the feeling of wanting to meet someone's expectations and wanting everything to just be ok for once.

I asked her how she ended up working in the library. I wanted to change the topic of the conversation. Strangely, she said that she ended up working in the library because, like me, she found peace there.

I could hear the passion in her voice as she spoke.

"While I was an undergrad, with all that was happening with Moses and me, I needed a place to go to escape. When Moses went to the school and found me, he always embarrassed me, so eventually, I changed my routine."

"I started going to the library instead of the cafeteria or the student union. At first, Moses was mad and didn't believe me, but one day, he popped up in the library and saw me sitting there studying, alone. I guess he decided it was a safe zone and it was men free. After that, he stopped coming if I said I was in the library. Not only that, but I would pick up random books and read them. I fell in love with being between the pages of someone else's tragedy, instead of drowning in my own."

When she explained it that way, I understood because I found the same thing when I went to the library. She continued talking about how much peace she found in the library versus at home and went on to say she wished she could live there. She said that after she graduated, she immediately applied to grad school for library science, and while she attended, she worked as a library aide. Once she graduated, she was able to get a job at the local library through some of her networking, and that was her way of escaping her reality with Moses.

For some reason, I tensed up when she mentioned his name. I could still feel the anger swirling around in my head but talking to her calmed me. I almost forgot about everything that had transpired until Dante popped his head into the room to see if I was still on the phone.

Seeing the curious look on Dante's face made me ask Paola, "Where is that nigga Moses anyway, he straight? I meant to, I mean, I didn't mean to..."

She cut me off mid-sentence and said that she had called the ambulance and reported that he had been jumped. She said when the ambulance asked if she would be coming to the hospital, she told them to call when he was conscious. I chuckled slightly at the nonchalant tone in her voice, glad that my actions didn't scare her off and even more happy that she was able to call me without having to look over her shoulder.

"What are you gonna do?" I asked her while waving Dante off and requesting a few more minutes by myself.

She said that she was going to pack up her stuff and leave while he was in the hospital. A smile spread across my face, and I suggested that she stay with me for a while. At first, she declined, but once I told her that I would feel better if she had someone looking out for her when he got out the hospital, she agreed that having somewhere safe to stay was important.

"You remind me so much of my father, that's the reason I am going to come."

I maintained my composure over the phone while I hid my excitement. I offered to help her pack before we hung up. Although she denied my help, she told me she would call me when she was ready to leave. And just like that, my library girlfriend was now my girlfriend, and Dante and I had a new roommate.

~ ~ ~

In 2016, Ollie's appeal was looking good, and he was rumored to be scheduled for release in late summer. I had it in my mind to start school as soon as Ollie made it back to the city. I knew Dante didn't support me leaving to go to school, but he knew how much it meant.

Dante and I still hustled the weight we would get from our Cleveland guy, and Paola had quit working in the library to avoid contact with Moses. It was no secret that there was an ongoing beef between Moses and me. I never spoke much about it because when I thought about it, I was still the same timid Rilei who was unsure of himself, even if others had a different idea of who I was.

Paola always reminded me how similar I was to her father because of how protective I was of her, and Dante summed me up as spasmatic. I always tried to lay low and keep my head on straight, but with the help of Dante, the streets developed a nickname for me—Spaz.

I am not sure where all the status came from, but it seemed as if everyone knew Dante and me. I wasn't the type to go out, but when I did, people would speak and yell out "Spaz!" People whose faces I could not recall approached me as if we were old-time friends. Dante loved the attention; I shied away from it. Dante seemed to enjoy being known as a dope boy, but I enjoyed not being known at all, let alone known as a dope boy.

I could picture my mother's disappointment at that type of label, so I always rejected it. I wasn't a dope boy; I just wanted to survive. I was a survivor.

Despite what people thought of me on the outside, Paola thought much more of me. She tried to convince me that I was both a scholar and her hero.

Even though she quit working at the library, we continued going to libraries. After Paola moved in, she made it a point for us to go to the legal library at least once a week to read different law books. She always talked about how her father said that if she was going to do something, she needed to know the ins and outs of what she was doing. She told me that if Dante and I were going to be involved with illegal activities, then we should at least know everything about the laws that we were breaking. So, we studied all the laws that Dante and I had broken and continued to break.

Through those law library visits, I put together rules on how Dante and I would proceed if we were going to continue selling. I wanted to make every risk we took a calculated risk. I planned it so that we would always be shy of a prison sentence. The first order of business was to rent out a stash house where we would keep most of our product. We would never have over 9 grams of cocaine on our person or at our house.

Instead of cooking at the house, I would cook at the stash house. When it was time to pick up from our Cleveland plug, we would rent three cars, hire a 3rd driver, and bring back a total of 27 grams on each trip. Instead of taking more grams, we would take more trips. At most, if caught, it would be a 3rd-degree felony without mandatory prison time. I knew that my plan needed improvement, but it was better than continuing to freestyle our penitentiary chances.

At first, Dante complained about the changes, but when he heard that a guy he knew had been put away for 11 years on a mandatory drug trafficking sentence, he quickly got into the swing of things.

Paola never complained, but I wanted to make sure that if anything ever happened, her name was free and clear. I talked to her several times about moving out and keeping another place somewhere else, but she always declined. Part of me admired her loyalty while the other part grew annoyed with her determination to be around all the risks we were taking. I knew I couldn't handle it if she were ever to get caught up because of me. As much as I worried about her, I couldn't help but feel that Paola was built for this life and seemed to, at times, know more about it than me.

Chapter 10

Penitentiary Chances

"Victim or Victor?" —Jairo

Paola and I became closer than what I could ever have hoped for. She kept me grounded and close to earth while the rest of the world kept me up in arms. Everyone had adopted the name "Spaz" for me. Paola continued to call me Rilei. Even something as simple as calling me by my name, which Teigen felt I was worthy of, ensured me that she was my peace in this world. She always said that the streets don't get to choose who I am. There was something about the way she said that let me know it was true.

The closer Paola and I became, the further away Dante drifted. He tried to convince me that we needed to focus on getting shit right for when Ollie got home and to quit spinning our wheels by making so many trips back and forth to pick up less weight. I never considered Dante to have any logic, so I ignored him as usual. I was tired of going back and forth about the way we were conducting our business when Dante refused even to step foot in a library or pick up a book to learn anything about the consequences of the shit we were doing.

Eventually, Dante grew tired of trying to convince me that my ways were counter-productive, and we stopped speaking about it. I found that when we weren't arguing over the way we should conduct our business, we didn't have much to say to each other. I figured that Dante was agitated by my demands, but I hoped that, in the end, he would realize that it was to keep us at a minimum risk level.

Dante started spending more time away from home, which left Paola and me at home alone most of the time. Time with her always seemed to fly by. We could discuss any topic or any issue. Most things we agreed on, but even the things that we didn't agree on we discussed or debated in logical ways.

Aside from being beautiful, her vibe was addictive. She had a smile that reminded me of a rainbow after the storm. Her scent carried my mother's essence, and her eyes had a way of making me feel naked. It was more than a physical attraction with Paola. Everything about me was attracted to everything about her.

In many ways, she was my first. She was my first crush. I had encountered many women before, but never any whose name was worth remembering. My childhood was so disarrayed that I didn't have time or space to think of anyone else. I always tried to keep focused and survive. My priorities always centered around surviving. Paola was the first person who made me want to rearrange my priorities. Putting a smile on her face was as important as surviving.

The way I carried myself with Paola was different. It wasn't something I had to make myself do. It was more like something that I just found myself doing. When we left to go anywhere, I opened doors and held them. If we were out somewhere and she had to go to the bathroom, I walked her to the bathroom unless she specifically asked me not to. When it rained, I sacrificed what I was wearing to cover her. At times, I would catch her crying, and before I could figure out what caused her tears, my insides started to cry too. I always wore a strong face in her weak moments, but I hurt when she hurt.

The day she left Moses to come to stay with me was the start of a new life for me. I had never loved anyone as much as I loved my mother until I met Paola. I knew that I had to keep her close and protect her in ways that I couldn't protect my mother. I couldn't fail her the way I had failed my mom. That meant I had to be her shadow. I had to be her medicine when she was sick, extra oxygen when she was short of breath, and extra comfort when she was finding things hard. Everything she asked for, I supported.

She had mentioned out of the blue one day that she wanted to go to law school. I, as always, was game for whatever she decided. She explained that with everything going on around us, there was always a need for legal advice. With that in mind, she spoke to her father and requested the money to take LSAT courses.

Part of my pride sunk when she asked her father. Paola was aware that Dante and I had lost a lot of money with my new system of transporting. I even recognized that we were losing money, but I figured that the loss was worth a get out of jail free card. It didn't take me long to realize that the new system wasn't working just as Dante had suggested many times before. Part of my ego wouldn't allow me to change it, and the part that didn't involve my ego was the fact that I didn't know how to minimize our risk and increase our revenue.

Hearing Paola ask her dad for money, bothered me more than hearing Dante complain about the way we did business. I scratched my head for days trying to work out a better avenue for our transport, and I never came up with any ideas that could make a difference. The more I thought about it, the more agitated I grew. I felt incapable of providing for Paola the way I needed to, so I began to distance myself. I knew she could feel the difference in my attitude, but I couldn't shake it.

Dante sometimes came home, and when he did, I noticed that he and Paola would go outside to talk. I knew it was about the changes and the differences in me. I wanted to revert, but not being able to do for her what I wanted to do was my fault. It was my decision to cut into our profits. That agitated my soul to a whole new extent. I thought she would eventually leave. I wondered what would keep her with me when she still had to ask her father when she wanted something.

On one of the days that Dante and I had planned a pick-up, Paola pulled me to the bedroom and sat me down. She said she needed to speak with me. I knew what was coming. I noticed that she had just gotten off the phone. I was sure that the pending conversation was something to do with whatever conversation she had had on the phone.

"Rilei, you know I think you're smart. I know you want to look out for everyone and that you feel you are doing what's best to keep us safe, but a risk is a risk babe."

I sat still while she spoke, taking it all in for what it was worth. Dante had been speaking with Paola. It sounded like something he would say when he was arguing to change the way we transport. Not only was Dante speaking with her about me, but he was complaining. "A risk is a risk." What the hell else could that mean? There were such things as good and bad risks, and I wasn't fucking with any bad risks.

My demeanor must have changed without my knowledge because I could hear the cautionary tone in Paola's voice when she said: "I don't want you to get so caught up in trying to avoid risks, that you put yourself at more risks. I was talking to..."

"What did Dante tell you?"

While softening my face, I stared at Paola. I couldn't help but feel a fire in my stomach. Dante knew how much I wanted to keep Paola out of our business. He knew I didn't want Paola involved in anything that had to do with this life. What kind of man whines to a female because he can't get his way?

"Why do you feel like Dante told me something?"

"Come on Paola, I'm not in the mood for the extra right now, what's up? What he tell you?"

Paola looked at me and studied my face. I knew she was reading every emotion and every thought going through my head. She could see through me. I crumbled with her. I was Teigen's Rilei with her. She placed her hand on mine and spoke calmly.

"It doesn't really matter what he told me; it is more so what I want to tell you. I think it's time that you speak to my father."

I was shocked. Not much had been said about ever talking to anyone in Paola's family. She spoke about her father often, and she called him what seemed to be ten times a day. I wasn't sure why she wanted me to talk to him. I wasn't sure what I would say to him or what he would ask me. I was sure that no matter what it concerned, it was a big deal to Paola. Not wanting to disappoint her, I agreed.

"Alright. Call him."

She had a better idea, "Naw, that's not what I had in mind. I want you to speak to him in person."

I felt airy s thinking about explaining my fuckups to her father. I had no idea how I would explain my inability to provide for her. I knew he would think if I couldn't provide, then I could not protect her. She must have seen the thoughts swirling in my head, or maybe she noticed my nervous disposition. She placed her hands on my cheeks and said everything would be fine. She eased all my tensions with her eyes. I felt like "mush" sitting on the bed.

She continued to ease my anxieties with her voice. She massaged my ears as she leaned in to whisper, "Lend me all your insecurities, and I will transform them into confidence."

As she spoke, she moved my hand and pressed it against her cheek. Tingling sensations zinged through my body at her touch. The melodic tone of her voice sent vibrations through my spine. Her gaze never left mine. Her eyes commanded that I move closer. I wanted to see everything that she could see, especially all the things she could see in me. As I leaned in, we met forehead to forehead, and she allowed me to stare into her eyes to get a glimpse of the world as she perceived it.

We were paused at that moment for what seemed like an eternity, but it was only seconds before her lips found mine. She gripped my lips lightly while grazing them with her teeth. I froze with anticipation. She navigated my hand to her covered breast. Her nipples stood erect underneath her shirt. I could feel them in the palm of my hand as she continued to guide the massage.

Her hands departed from mine as she used them to hoist herself over my lap. All my insecurities drained into a focal point ready to meet at her rallying point.

As she rotated her hips at the head of my insecurities, I grasped her waist to let her know she had piqued my interest. I took time to admire the sexy curves of her figure while I slid my hands from her waist to her breasts, and back down to her waist again. Her nipples sat still taunting me from beneath her white t-shirt. I could feel the warmth of her center settling through my basketball shorts.

Removing all barriers became my goal. I slid my hands under her t-shirt and moved them against her bare back until I reached her shoulders. Her legs wrapped behind my back, and she rested her arms across my shoulder, interlocking her hands behind my head. I stood up with her legs wrapped as she pressed into me.

Once I turned and positioned her to lay back on the bed, she slid her legs down to the brim of my shorts. As she pulled herself up, she pulled me closer. Her eyes found mine, and without releasing her stare, she removed my boxers and shorts. All my insecurities rushed to the head as my endowment stretched to cover all my years of turmoil. I felt anxious to release.

With my emotions weighing on me, I grabbed her hands and allowed my weight to push her on her back flat against the bed. I took my time entering her. I wanted her to feel the weight of my world, but I wanted to please her. Her nails scraped my back while she gritted her teeth at me. Her aggressiveness made me feel that I could pound out my burdens, and she could handle the fight. With each stroke, I felt safer. Inside her was warm and snug. I wanted to pack my bags and move in. The more I dove in and out of her sea of confidence, the more I felt my own spirit transforming.

Before I knew it, my hips were meeting her hips in the center with a rhythm that would have put any dancer to shame. We ground in and out of consciousness. Her moans and quick pants kept me in rhythm, but they also drove me insane. When I would almost lose control, her muscles would grip me back into our sacred space.

"Es tuyooo Papi," she moaned.

I only recognized Papi. Hearing her speak in her native tongue was like having someone jam a battery in my back, and I exploded with energy. Her walls collapsed against me, causing me to slow down and steady my stroke. We continued our dance for what felt like hours. It was not just a dance of passion, but one of forgiveness, understanding, and solitude.

I felt everything in her. I felt the potential she believed I had with each long stroke, and the love she had for me with each short stroke. The faster I went, the more I felt her squeezing every drop of my insecurities from inside of me. I sped up and sped up until I collapsed on top of her and deposited everything I had ever known into her sea made for transformation.

It was nothing like what I thought I witnessed in pornos. It wasn't a bunch of flipping her around or hitting her from the back. It was a complete revival. It was like going to church after the world had just fallen on you, and hearing the pastor preach a sermon that was made just for you; she had cleansed my soul. It was like she said, and I did, lend her all my insecurities as I watch them magically transform into confidence. And with the last stroke, I dug deep and planted insecurities inside of her while I came out a new man.

When I could go no more, Paola let her fingers tickle my ears while my head laid planted on her stomach. We inhaled and exhaled in unison. She grabbed both sides of my face and lifted my head until I was looking her in the eyes.

"Soy tuya," she said, "puedes dejarlo todo conmigo, para siempre. You hear me, Rilei. I am yours. You can leave everything with me, always."

As she spoke, I knew at that moment, I would meet the pope if she asked me to.

And that is exactly who the fuck I was scheduled to meet. Everything was set into rolling motion. Not a full two weeks had gone by before Paola made the announcement that her father was coming to town. Her excitement did not outweigh my nervousness. I had never met anyone's family before. I was not sure how the visit with her father would go, so I carried more anxiety than I have ever had in my life.

Paola bragged about her father a lot, and she was crazy about him. I knew I had to present my best self to him, but I had no clue who my best self was. I was Teigen's Rilei, Paola's shapeshifter, and the street's Spaz. I was whoever I needed to be when I needed to be him. I figured that there was probably a version of myself that I would have to be for Paola's father as well.

He landed on a Tuesday and wore a Monday face and attitude. His face left me with no doubt that he didn't want to get to know me. It was Friday when he finally spoke to me. Dante and I had been sitting on the couch, and Paola was out at one of her LSAT study sessions. I was reviewing the itinerary to pick up our shipment when he chimed in.

I was so focused on what I was doing that I didn't notice that he had spoken until Dante slapped the back of my neck and yelled, "about fucking time."

Irritated, I looked up at him, trying to figure out what the hell he had touched me for. Dante was pointing at Paola's father, saying, "you need to listen to that man. He knows good shit."

His name was Jairo, which I knew only because Paola told me. He was tall and slender with smooth ebony skin. He wasn't what I had expected. He didn't fit the description of a man in this lifestyle, especially one who had been at the head of it.

He started in on me like he had been in the conversation the whole time. "Selling drugs is the risk," he started. "A risk is a risk, and there is no safe risk in this business; there are only smart risks." I focused on him while he spoke. It was almost like listening to Paola speak.

"Young man," he said as he continued his effort to brief Dante and me on his experiences, "this is not a business for the faint of heart."

Jairo told us his story, emphasizing that he grew up poor in Colombia. His mother and father were farmhands. Jairo had no formal education and blamed it on Colombia being a poor country. He and his brother used to roam around while their parents worked the farm since they were not required to help. There was a poppy field right next to the land on which his parents worked. Jairo said the poppy fields were supposed to be off-limits, but they hung out there anyway.

"Awww man, my brother and I would rip through those fields wrestling and playing. The most excitement came from knowing we were not supposed to be in them."

Jairo said he witnessed his first murder in the poppy field when he was eleven years old. He'd been with his brother as usual when he saw a few guys arguing in the area. The men were pulling the buds by the bundle while he and his older brother played far away enough that they were out of sight. When they noticed the men in the field, they made a game of dashing throughout the area to get close without being seen. The closer they got to the men, the more audible the men's voices became.

When they were only feet away from the men, hiding behind the tallest of the poppies, he and Dominic laid their bellies against the earth. Jairo and Dominic laid still enough not to be detected while the strange men's discussion turned to a heated debate about farming the poppy.

Jairo recalled that they were shouting about when and how to pick the buds. While they were yelling, Dominic lifted his head just in time to see a man with a suit on and a ponytail pull the trigger. The sound scared them, so they took off running. Jairo said he ran so fast that the wind was loud against his eardrums and he couldn't hear anything in his surroundings.

By the time he reached the farm, he had looked around for Dominic, but he was nowhere to be found. Jairo scared and alarmed, returned to the poppy fields to search for Dominic.

Not more than a few feet shy of where they laid on their bellies practicing being spies, laid Dominic. He was flat on his belly again, but he wasn't playing a game. Blood covered the ground around him, and he was lifeless.

Jairo's voice cracked as he described dragging his lifeless brother across the field back to the farm. When he got to the farm, his parents cried out all the tears they could muster before law officials arrived and pronounced Dominic dead.

"Poppies changed my life twice, once for the worst, and the other for the better," Jairo said adjusting himself in his seat.

"You see Rilei, you can be a victim, or you can be a victor. I was obsessed with what I observed on the field that day. I lost my brother to what I saw in that field. I had no idea why what happened had to happen. But I sat in that field until I figured it out. Heroin. Heroin is why it had to happen.

Poppy is the cash crop in my country. I watched my mother and father sweat years off their life farming when there were shitloads of cash in the field that my brother and I just thought of as pretty flowers. That's what they should have been farming.

I waited, day in and day out, on the people who killed my brother to return to the poppy field. Soon after that, I waited for anyone at all to return to the poppy field.

I struck gold on a day when the Colombian sun barely peeked over the mountains. I saw three guys come into the field and I watched. I watched and studied everything they did. I visited the field so much I could have lived there. Day and night, I lingered around the poppy field; I wanted to see when they were interested in the field and when and how they farmed it. My parents were so distraught over Dominic's death that they spent most of their days farming trying to work the pain away.

They never noticed me or cared where I went, so I left just as often as I came.

Hanging in those fields taught me two critical things: how to be quiet and listen, and how to read my situation. When the last of the petals would fall from the poppy flower, men would come and show interest in the field. After studying their habits, I finally grew balls and approached the men in the field one day. They were mild men; I knew that from watching them. I don't know what I expected from the encounter, but I started pulling poppy pods for them and adding them to their collection. In return, I learned about opium. I met them on the field several times afterward and helped them collect pods. Sometimes, they would let me sit with them while they cut the pods and harvested the opium.

The more I learned from watching them, the more I practiced on my own. When I was content with what I learned, I waited to make my next move. Their last visit to the poppy field was late at night. I had hung in the field all day waiting on them. When they finally showed, I helped them pick pods as usual. And as usual, they cut a few pods to ready the opium so that they could smoke before they were done in the field.

I continued to pick while they smoked. Once they were high and nodding, I grabbed the razor blade that they used to cut the pod and quickly slid it across each of their necks. When the third man woke, I was already standing over him with my blade at the ready. I wasn't sure who it was, but I felt in my spirit that Dominic had been avenged. Now, I was the victor, and it was time to let poppy change my life for the better."

My attention was entirely on Jairo as he regurgitated his younger life. I had so many questions, but I wasn't sure what was appropriate to ask; after all, he had just shared information that I would have taken to my grave with two strangers. He recounted every detail of the story that made me either shudder or empathize with a blank face and a "matter-of-fact" tone.

Paola had led me to believe that her father was out of that lifestyle, but I could tell that he wasn't. He was so open with his tale that I figured he wasn't a beat-around-the bush type of guy. I also assumed no question was off-limits, and I jumped in boldly to ask mine for the sake of progress.

"Can we do business?"

Chapter 11

Putting 'Rights' Back in the World

"I do a lot of wrongs, Rilei, it is important to a man's soul to put something right back into the community."—Jairo

Jairo stayed in town for the better part of a month during his visit. After the ice was broken, we became closer. Dante was even more attached to Jairo. He was fascinated by Jairo's way of operating, and I could tell that Dante clung to Jairo like the father he wished he had.

Paola was usually somewhere studying for her LSATs, but when we were all around each other, we would go out to dinner or watch movies while we joked. It felt like a real family. We enjoyed each other's company. It was like what I saw on Family Matters when Mama used to watch it. Paola was Laura, I was Urkel and Stephon, and Dante, well, he was still Dante, but it worked.

Dante and I were watching T.V. on a Friday afternoon while I was waiting on Paola to come home from her study session. Jairo had come from my room and motioned me over to talk to him. I thought nothing of it and hopped up immediately to see what he needed.

Upon entering the room, he looked at me with intense eyes and told me to sit. Instantly, my ass hit the bed like an obedient dog. I was irritated by the command and by my immediate instinct to follow it, but I brushed it off. Jairo hid his hands behind his back as he stared at me. He paced the floor.

"Do you love my Daughter?"

"Yes, Sir. "

"And my daughter clearly loves you. She's just like her mother, that one—-resilient, loyal, determined… and she's smart."

"Paola's mother died when she was young, and I had to figure out how to take care of her and teach her everything I knew. It was shameful because, well, all I knew was poppy. Her mother was my balance. Her mother knew how to live life and be happy. She was supposed to teach Paola those things, but because of me, she was never able."

I sensed the conversation getting deep and began to wonder where all of it was coming from, or why it was coming at all.

Jairo continued, and his face grew solemn. The look on his face caught me off guard. Not too long ago, he had recounted the story of his brother's death to me without emotion, but emotions flooded his face when speaking about Paola's mother.

"I did everything I could to keep her alive. I was going to give it all up. The drugs, the money, anything she wanted me to give up, I was going to give. She didn't let me. When they kidnapped her, those sons of bitches …"

Tears swelled in Jairo's eyes, and his voice was groggy.

"She said to me on the phone, she told me, 'Jairo, te amo. Cuida nuestra hija, sé fuerte por ella. Se feliz y juguetón, no tan serios. Muéstrale el Jairo con que me enamoré. I love you, and you take care of our baby girl. Be strong for her. She wanted me to be happy and playful for Paola. She told me to be the person she fell in love with instead of being so serious. She wanted me to do her job, and before I could say anything, before I could even tell her all the reasons that I couldn't do her job, she hung up. Can you believe that? She hung up. Those fuckers could have had my whole world. I would have given it all for her, but she hung up.

Her body was found in an abandoned house a few days later. I was sick to my stomach. I wanted to die. But not before those bastards were dead. The anger in me was so thick that I couldn't see or think clearly. I did all I could do by going home and lying next to Paola. I swore on my life that I'd protect her as her mother wished."

I sat still. I could hear his voice breaking. I knew something like the pain he felt, but I couldn't find any words to remedy his pain. I looked down at the floor while Jairo continued to pace. When the thudding sound from his constant pacing stopped, I looked up, and Jairo was standing right over my head with a pregnancy test.

"I found this in your bathroom—in the trash. "

I blinked a few times and then rubbed my eyes to remove any debris that may have been altering my vision. Unable to gather my thoughts, I asked stupidly, "what's that?"

His eyes hardened, and then he diverted them toward the bathroom. "If Paola is pregnant," he started, "what are you going to do?"

Still stunned by the test, I ignored his question for a moment. My head raced with several thoughts, several ideas, several emotions; and of all that went through my mind, the only thing that made it out my mouth was "I don't know."

I could tell he was not pleased with my response. I was also not pleased with my answer. I knew exactly what I would do. I would do whatever she wanted me to do.

As the initial shock started to wear off, I started feeling excited. Jairo face softened at the smile he saw form across my face.

"That's the same way I smiled when Isabella told me she was pregnant with Paola."

I looked at him with my most genuine smile and said, "She's in good hands, sir, I don't have everything figured out, but I will figure it out. She is in good hands. Trust me."

Jairo returned the pregnancy test to the trash and put his finger to lips, "Let's keep this to ourselves until she says something, shall we?"

"Indeed."

"Indeed, we shall. Rilei, I like you. You're a calculating kid; you think. From what Paola says, you overthink. I can work with that. See, you can teach a man how to rationalize his thoughts, but you cannot teach any man who doesn't think at all. So, I have a proposition for you, my son."

My son. The words danced in my head as he continued to speak. My son. I haven't been anyone's son since Teigen. He kept talking, but I was fixated on "my son."

"Rilei, you listening?"

"Repeat that please."

"Don't get clumsy on me now," Jairo said pausing mid-pace. "I need your focus kid, this opportunity is not one that I grant to everyone, so if you want it, you need to act like it. If Paola is pregnant, then you are family. You need to be able to take care of her and take care of the family."

Jairo continued speaking and segued into an introduction to his philosophies on heroin, the proper way to market and distribute it, and the rules on its use. Jairo had only one rule regarding its use: DON'T.

Jairo was firm about his product. I always thought of this hustle as a crutch until I could move on to better things. It was clear that Jairo thought of this as his business. He talked passionately about his trade, and I could tell that he was serious about everything he said. I could feel the vibe, and what I picked up most, was that anything was disposable when it came to protecting his business.

I listened as Jairo spoke endlessly about his glory days and how he discovered the best time to farm his poppy, pick the pods, and harvest opium. Opium was Jairo's natural sell. Jairo said that he could pluck the pods and cut them, and the opium was ready.

Jairo was a genius. Even though he was small in stature, he was intimidating. I could tell that he was unbothered, well-respected, and very influential. I was sure that he had killed many people based on the ease with which he spoke about death. Jairo was a dangerous man.

He continued his lecture by telling me how he went on to making morphine from his opium, and finally heroin.

"I found a little spot where I could make a refinery. Big production, none of that small-time shit."

Jairo couldn't do it all by himself, so he had several workers under him. Jairo mentioned that he had a few less trustworthy workers, but he said that fear conquers all.

Jairo made people fear him, and I could understand how.

He continued to brag about his knowledge and the building of his empire. He had such a wealth of knowledge and experience that it was hard not to lose myself in his wisdom. He said you must love what you do to be successful.

Jairo claimed that his fascination made his brother's death mean something. He said his brother died to give him a new life, and the poppy field was a sign. "My brother died February 21st, on the brink of spring, where everything dies, yet everything blooms. He died at that time to show me that we were supposed to bloom into greatness."

According to Jairo, he honored the anniversary of his brother's death every year by visiting the poppy field where his brother died and sacrificing someone to allow a new life for someone else. Jairo said that he also paid tuition for the poor city kids who showed promise in a different lifestyle.

"I do a lot of wrong Rilei. It is important to a man's soul to put something right back into the community." Jairo fell somber at his own statement.

"No one ever tried to put anything 'right' back into my world after they destroyed it. They took my brother and my parents away from me on the same day. They might as well have taken me."

At his last remarks, I understood him. I thought about my mom and watching her on the cold floor. I thought about the hospital room. Seeing my mother mummied up, never sat well with me. Finding out I had a father who never wondered about me after he violated my mother always sat at the back of my mind. I was like Jairo; no one ever tried to put anything 'right' back into my world either.

Chapter 12

Sunflowers and Dandelions

"The jealous are troublesome to others, but a torment to themselves." —William Penn

Jairo returned to Florida not long after Paola had wrapped up her LSAT courses. He and I continued to develop our relationship during his visit. When Paola confessed to her pregnancy, Jairo and I got even closer.

I told Jairo about my fear of not being able to provide because of the dip in my profits. I explained to him that I didn't want to take any risk that would take me away from being there for Paola, but I also couldn't afford to do business the way I was doing it. Before Jairo left, he purchased me a round-trip flight to Florida and told me that I would be expanding my horizons.

At Jairo's departure, Dante was grim. It was as if he had lost his best friend. Dante had taken to Jairo. He clung to Jairo's every word as if it were gold. Jairo seemed to like Dante to an extent, but I felt that he was mostly tolerating him. In fact, Jairo told me to watch out for Dante because he was just as dangerous to my cause as he was useful.

In the days before my flight, Dante and I started preparing for Ollie to get out. I assumed that he would be out later in the year, but Dante swore that he would be out within the next two months. I stuck with my thought because we had constantly been awaiting Ollies release only to keep getting disappointed each time we speculated.

With Paola being pregnant, I wanted to move. I felt that we needed to be in a different type of environment, and I wasn't feeling the idea of her being alone in the house with two of my friends. I trusted Ollie and Dante, but I thought that, as a man, it was not the right situation to put a woman in.

It was time for me to figure out how to take care of my family, and I wanted a place of my own to do that. I did what I thought would be best and signed a new lease for Paola and me.

The day before I left for Florida, I told Dante that I would be moving out in the next month so that he and Ollie could keep the apartment. Dante was a man of few words generally, and I didn't think much of his silence in response to the news. I knew we were both excited to see what the trip to Florida would yield, and I figured he was quiet because he was reflecting.

Dante wanted to go on the trip. He tried to buy a ticket. Jairo liked Dante on the surface, but I could tell by the way he watched Dante that he did not trust him. On several occasions during Jairo's visit, he alluded to Dante being envious of me. He said, "Dandelions are flowers too, but they are pulled and treated like weeds, while sunflowers are nurtured. They are a part of the same family, but one seems a beauty while the other seems a nuisance."

It was the same thing Mr. Donald told me years ago except that it was metaphorical coming from Jairo. I gave Jairo the same respect I gave Mr. Donald, but no one understood Dante like I did.

After hearing some of Jairo's stories, I was sure that it was best for Dante to hold down the fort while I went to Florida. Since Paola had been stressed about studying for the LSAT, I figured that I could put her up in a hotel while I went to meet her father.

I wanted her to go, but she insisted on staying and studying. I gave in and made sure to book her the best room that I could find to allow her time to relax and study.

After I had all my affairs in order, I was ready to depart. I arrived in Florida before the sun fully had a chance to rise and was on a private jet with Jairo before noon.

I had no idea that we would be taking another trip. Knots filled my stomach, and I started to think of all the reasons Jairo had to kill me. I did impregnate his daughter. I wasn't his prime choice for a mate for Paola. He had made it clear that he wanted Paola to be different and not associated with slums. I was a slum by his definition. I didn't have the stability that he wanted Paola to have. I wanted her to have it too. I made the trip for the sole purpose of giving it to her.

"Relax," Jairo interrupted my thoughts, "you have to love what you do to be successful. You cannot love what you do if you do not know what you do."

I eased off my anxiety enough to satisfy Jairo's command for me to relax. Jairo's philosophical explanations always triggered my interest, but the thought of being killed gripped my insides so much so that I felt a tiny droplet of urine escape me. I kept thinking of seeing Paola again and then never seeing her again.

My body became heavy, and his voice began to go in and out like a bad cell phone connection. I started breathing faster and faster as thoughts of an impending death filled my mind. I felt my fists clench, and my fear began to morph into anger. Just as I was about to lunge to save myself, the jet landed, and the doors flew open.

"Bienvenidos a Colombia," Jairo stood with his arms outstretched. I opened my eyes to the most beautiful house I ever seen. The yard was filled with flowers, and the sky was bluer than I had ever seen it before.

I instantly felt calm standing on Jairo's estate. All thoughts of me being a pig for slaughter vanished, and all I could imagine was Paola and our kids laying in the flower beds laughing and smiling at all the nothings in the world.

I wanted this for myself. I never placed much emphasis on anything material, but this was more than material. This looked like freedom. It looked like what my mother had been working for, and I had finally found a way to get it.

After touring Jairo's estate, we went off to the fields. Jairo showed me how to plant poppies, nurture them, and distinguish which pods were ready for opium harvesting. After gathering for the better half of the day, we returned to what Jairo called a refinery.

Inside the refinery, Jairo showed me specific ways to cut the pod for opium harvesting. We went on to dry out the opium and boil it with lime. I had been curious about the process, but I had never thought to ask. I had wondered if heroin came readymade or if it had to go through a process. I got my answer in Jairo's refinery.

A film had settled in one of the barrels and Jairo shouted out, "Now we have morphine, my son. This is one hell of a drug on its own mijo. I have some stories about this one." Laughing, Jairo went and grabbed a bottle.

"Ammonia, that's next. You have to know what you're doing."

I watched Jairo as he reheated the morphine with the ammonia. He then filtered and boiled it again, and I watched as it turned into a brown paste.

"We are almost there," Jairo said.

He worked around his refinery like a mad scientist. At times, we sat around like bumps on a log, talking shit, and shooting the breeze while waiting on the next step. When it was time to complete the next step, Jairo got excited and start moving anxiously around the refinery again.

"Keep up Rilei, this is what you Northern Americans call on the job training, huh mijo?"

When it was all said and done, Jairo disappeared into an office-like room and reappeared with a bottle labeled "ether." He began to add the ether to his work surface.

"This, this is how we purify it. Rilei, I have the best product because I put time into it. I take my time, and I use shit that other people are too cheap to use. I have the best shit because I use the best shit. I have people who do this, but I never get lazy, I always come back and get my hands dirty."

I looked at Jairo in disbelief. There was not much powder on his work surface, but what was there was pure and white. Jairo marveled at his work. I could tell that he was proud.

"I assure quality," he said, looking over at me waiting on my approval.

By the time we left the refinery, it was a new day. We rode back out to Jairo's estate, leaving the evidence of our night in the lab behind. Once at Jairo's, he immediately began going over business arrangements. He mapped out and gave direction on everything, including price.

He ordered that every six months, I come back to Colombia with him to keep sharp and remain humble.

"The first load is on me. The second load is on you, and the responsibility of it all will weigh on you. It is no secret that you are not what I had in mind for Paola. It is also no secret that you love her, and she loves you. I trust you with my daughter, which says a lot. Now I need to trust you with my legacy. I will hold you accountable. I expect you to hold those around you accountable."

Jairo stared into my eyes with both his hand against my cheeks. "For now, a soldier, later a general. Don't fuck this up muchacho."

After the process and operational order were explained, we were back on Jairo's private jet to Florida. Jairo set up rentals and loaded me down with as much product as he thought I could handle. He told me to think of it as a welcome gift and that once I proved myself, we would start building my own industry. I was honored that he had taken me on. The better part of me did not want to be a drug lord, however; the truest part of me knew that I had found my silver lining.

"I want to give an anonymous tip. There's a truck coming through traveling northbound. I believe that they are smuggling people from the border, and I think they have cocaine." He paused.

"How do I know, ayyy Mija, I saw enough with my own eyes. Take this license plate won't you."

Jairo gave out a license plate number, hung the phone up, and winked. He could sense the nervousness in me. I had always made conscious decisions not to travel with anything that put me in a mandatory prison predicament.

"A risk is a risk," Jairo said as he handed me the keys. I had enough weight to put me in prison until Jesus returned to earth. He explained that I was to drive two cars behind the decoy truck. He had loaded the decoy truck with pounds of marijuana and a few bricks of what he called "knock off" cocaine; meanwhile, my car was weighed down with nothing but "Colombia's finest," pure heroin.

As Jairo expected, when we went through the border patrol checkpoint in Miami, the white decoy SUV was pulled and searched. I was shitting bricks while driving through, but I maintained a poker face when the border patrol agent got to my window. He performed a quick glance over and waved me through. I rode all the way back to Ohio on high alert. I did not breathe until I was parked at home.

As soon as I shut the engine off, I texted Paola to come home and went up to meet Dante. When I got up the steps, Dante was sitting with a female I had never seen before perched between his legs. Dante's head was rolled back, and they were in a moment that did not allow for them to notice that I had entered the room.

I contemplated interrupting but decided that the conversation that I needed to have with Dante would have to wait until his company left anyway. I returned to the rental car and sat there until Paola arrived back from the hotel.

Paola pulled up fifteen minutes later. I hopped out of the car to meet her at the door. As I was opening her door, Dante strutted down the steps with his friend. He shot me a quick look. I didn't know what to make of the gesture. He stared me down and hopped into a car that I had never seen with the female that I had never seen. I brushed it off and continued to help Paola out of the car and into the apartment.

Paola fell asleep almost immediately after getting into the apartment. I wanted to spend the day with her, but pregnancy seemed to keep her in a slumber most of the time. If she was not out studying for her test, she was eating. If she was not eating, she was asleep. I missed our conversations, but I knew that once this pregnancy was over, there would be more than enough to talk about.

I couldn't get the look that Dante had given me off my mind. The more I thought about how he looked at me, the more Jairo's words played back in my mind. I felt ridiculous for letting the thought cross my mind. After all, I had been there for Dante through everything. When Dante lacked a mother, I lent him mine. I shared everything I had with Dante. He was my brother at the end of it all.

Still, I could not help but hear ringing through my head, "Sunflowers and Dandelions."

Dante had to know that my life was nothing better than his and nothing to be desired. Our lives had been nothing short of intermingled pain. Mine was no greater than his, and his was no greater than mine. Everywhere we went, we went together. Nothing separated us, not Helena, not Unc, and not the system. Dante was my brother, and with that thought in mind, I sent him a text to meet at the house to discuss business.

I broke down the game plan to Dante on a need to know basis. I felt like I could trust Dante no matter what our differences were now, or whatever the oddness between us was. Even with trust, I still acknowledged what Jairo said about accountability. I couldn't afford to let my trust put me in a precarious position that would cause me to have to take responsibility for Dante. I knew Dante's attitude, and he was stubborn at times. Jairo wanted everything done a specific way, and I wanted to deliver and stay alive.

After everything was set straight, I told Dante in the same way Jairo told me, "there is one rule as far as the use of his shit Dante, DON'T."

Dante nodded in passive agreement, and we started putting work forward to become suppliers of everything moving north of Virginia.

Dante had a few friends he claimed to have met through Unc a few years ago that resided on the east coast. He convinced me to supply some guys out in Philly and wanted me to talk to his friends in New York.

I knew that the amount we sold and the time it took us to sell it would make all the difference in how Jairo wanted to proceed, but I still wanted controlled movement and numbers since I was just stepping into this relationship with Jairo.

I chose to stick with the guys from Philly and to develop our own business at home before we pushed out further.

"Dante, we got a lot of time to expand. We only got one time to fuck this up. Let's figure out what we are doing and our numbers, and then let's move this shit up. I ain't fucking with New York right now bro."

Dante twisted his face up, but I was done with that discussion. Jairo trusted me, and it was my ass on the line. I wasn't willing to let the product spread until I knew I could grip where it was spreading.

I knew that Dante was starting to feel a different dynamic in our relationship. I tried to assure him that we were partners, but I could see in his eyes the type of resentment that a worker has for his boss. I figured it could be the relationship I was developing with Jairo. Dante admired Jairo, and although Jairo liked Dante, he thought of Dante as impulsive and jealous. Jairo was convinced that those were two qualities that didn't make for a suitable partner or a trusted friend.

"He's useful but dangerous," was the way Jairo described Dante to me.

"Yeah ok, Unc." Dante gave me a shoulder as he walked past me with his head slightly hung.

Unc. I thought about all he could mean by calling me Unc. Unc, the one who took us in and looked out for us, even if it was harsh? Unc who abused Dante because he was white? Unc, who killed his father and kicked his ass? Unc who he shot? Unc the oppressor or Unc the philosopher? Hell, did it matter when it came to speaking about Unc? What the fuck did he mean by calling me Unc?

It weighed on me. I was nothing like Unc. I looked out for Dante, and I was trying to keep us both safe. He must have forgotten who played the part by his side since kindergarten. I could have reminded him, but for what? He would remember on his own once he got out of his feelings.

I thought of calling Jairo for advice on Dante. After thinking about it for a while, I decided that I didn't want to cause concern for Jairo since he had already made it known that all issues on my end would have to be handled by me.

I went to Paola instead. Despite how much I hated involving her in my situations, she thought a lot like her father. Paola knew Dante better as well. She didn't know him as well as I did, but she knew him enough. Plus, she had a heart like my mother's, which made her advice more valuable to me.

I didn't expect any of what I got when I asked Paola. Paola, like her father, suggested that Dante might have some jealousy about me. I refuted her suggestion with the same counter ideas that I'd used to resist her father's words. In the end, Paola said that she saw a friendship that was on thin ice and that I should move carefully with Dante.

It was a pill that was hard to swallow. I could not fathom that Dante would ever turn his back on me. The thought made me sick to my stomach, but I could not say that I haven't felt sick to my stomach at some of the looks Dante had given me these last few months.

I knew when I was honest with myself that things had started changing when Paola came into the picture. Even with the changes, I felt that it was just an adjustment and something that we would have to get used to. Dante wasn't used to me being attached to anyone like I was to Paola. Thinking more on it, I could imagine the way it might have made him feel, but I never tried to exclude him, and I kept him close as well. I defended Dante more than I defended myself.

Mama would have warned me if she had seen anything different coming of Dante, but Mama was gone. I didn't have her foresight on situations to prepare me for when I saw Dante with Hitler's *Mein Kampf* tucked under his arm. I ignored it because, for all I knew, Dante couldn't even read. The image of the book lingered in my mind, and I would be lying if I said that I didn't feel a rush of irritation at the sight.

A month went by with tensions rising between Dante and me. I had expected Paola and me to have moved out by this time, but with the loads going faster than I imagined, the moving into our own place process slowed.

At first, Dante seemed excited at his assumption that we would be staying because we did not leave when I had said we would. When I confirmed that we would be moving after the next shipment from Jairo, the tension grew again.

Jairo informed me that the next shipment would be delivered to us. I was pleased that I would not have to make a pickup but curious about why I had to drive the first shipment down if he had delivery service.

One of Jairo's many teaching points was revealed when I asked about delivering all future shipments. Jairo quickly let it be known that there would be very few times that he would deliver to me. He didn't entertain my question at all. He quickly snapped back, "why should I take all the risk? Before I can take a risk on you, I have to see that you can take a risk on yourself."

In many ways, Jairo was the father I never had. I learned a lot from him, and he never missed an opportunity to drop one of his philosophies on me. Although he didn't approve of Dante, he respected my stance on the relationship. He challenged me and kept me aware. At times, he would drop a line for me to get a count of all my product and my team. He was teaching me to stay sharp. He was molding me for greatness, and I could tell. He was teaching me the business from a distance and working to ensure my success.

"Always watch the News and always read the papers," he told me.

He would ask me what's going on in Philly. He would ask me to name at least two people involved with my business at each level.

"Treat the foot soldiers with as much regard as you treat your upper ranks. Your soldiers will keep you straight," he advised.

"Ears to the streets as they say. Know what your competition is doing and what they are selling. Know what they are selling their product for. Know when they are out and know when they are reloaded. Know their quality, and the bonus is knowing what they do it for. Know what they have to lose, why they are in this business, what their goals are. That Hijo is what gives you your advantage."

Through Jairo, I became more observant. Instead of leaving the Philly line to Dante, I knew I had to get involved. I started speaking to at least one or two people on each level. I thought at first that there was supposed to be anonymity between the distributor and the soldiers, but Jairo made me understand that that was an idea put in place so that the distributor could avoid the rift raft. Jairo believed that soldiers always wanted a way up and would usually be willing to work harder and look out if they felt they had somewhere to grow to.

Jairo inherited his first poppy field because he expressed loyalty to the man in charge. Jairo said he farmed the pods and noticed that there was talk of stealing and eventually overthrowing. Jairo had grown fond of the man who ran the field because whenever he visited, he gave Jairo shoes, clothes, food, or money to take care of himself.

When Jairo heard of the plan to take over, Jairo alerted him. Jairo was summoned to give all the information he had and was told that if he eliminated anyone who spoke ill or with ill intention, he would be rewarded.

"Soldiers are important, and the worst thing you can do is take them for granted, Rilei."

Jairo was right. After moving out, I made frequent trips to Philly to follow Jairo's advice. I had heard from the street that Ollie had been released from prison around the time I got back from my first trip with Jairo. I never paid it much mind because I knew that I would be one of the first stops if Ollie were released. Dante and I would know before anyone else would. We sent letters to Ollie at least once every week or two. Dante would mail them off, and we were sure to put money on his books. I hadn't gotten a letter back from Ollie in months, but I knew he was stressed and waiting on his release. I had not been able to visit because Jairo had me running like a chicken with my head cut off since I left Columbia.

Teigen's Rilei is hardheaded. A couple trips to Philly and I found out all I needed to know. It turned out Ollie had been in Philly for at least 2 months and was running the Philly trade. Not just any Philly trade. He was running Jairo's shit, my shit.

My head ached with confusion because I couldn't understand what was going on. I had never been short on cash or product, and no one ever mentioned being hit. I would have put Ollie on anyway, but how he got on without me, even knowing he was home was beyond me. Dante was the only one outside of me that could have supplied Ollie. It was the only thing that made sense.

Even with everything in my gut telling me that Dante knew, I still convinced myself that Ollie being released would be news to Dante. I called Paola to talk to her and get her take on everything so I could avoid a lecture from her father. Paola encouraged me to remain silent and watchful.

Even though I had a lot of questions, I returned home without a word. Paola held my head and watched the tears fall from my eyes. That's what I loved about Paola. It was okay to cry. Some would call it sensitive, but Paola understood what it meant to part ways with Dante. It meant separating from memories that got me through the rough patch with my mother. A lot of memories with Mama and me had Dante in them. If Dante would betray me, it wasn't just me he was betrayed; it was Mama too. Paola understood that. Instead of judging my weak moments, she joined in on them with tears of her own.

I couldn't deny questioning if Dante were still the friend I had in kindergarten. I couldn't help wondering if I were paranoid by questioning Dante's loyalty. We had seen each other through so much, and I couldn't help but feel that he would never do anything shady to me.

Feelings being what they were, I knew I had to lead the organization with my head from that moment forward. I texted Dante the day after I arrived back from Philly and told him to open up the lines to New York. I figured that it would keep Dante busy while I investigated everything happening in Philly.

I wasn't sure if I was over-analyzing the situation, but every reason that I didn't know was every reason I needed to find out. I needed to have a talk with Dante and find out what was going on. I didn't want to approach him with accusations. I needed all the facts. To have facts, I needed to see and speak to Ollie.

There were many things I needed to address with Dante. I needed to ask him about the "Unc" comment, *Mein Kampf*, and his overall attitude. I kept Paola's advice at the forefront of my mind: silent and watchful.

I had two months left until I had to go back to Colombia for what Jairo liked to refer to as "Humble Remembrance." With Paola getting further along in her pregnancy, I wanted everything to be a well-oiled machine by the time she delivered. To do that, Dante and I had to be on the same page, and if Ollie were involved, we all needed to be spearheading our campaign. I had to make things right.

I made several trips to Philly over the month. Sometimes I would drive out there to see who the major players were coming in and out, and other times, I was hoping to catch Ollie. I felt like Ace from *Paid in Full,* sitting in the streets observing. I was in a position of power. I was becoming a big figure. I was a somebody, even if it wasn't the somebody Mama would have wanted me to be.

I was learning to understand the business. I understood how Jairo found love in it. Yes, it was drugs. Yes, it was possibly destroying homes, and yes, it may seem like a selfish business venture, but it was a business. Jairo said, and he made it clear, that people were going to use drugs regardless of where they got them from.

"If they have the will to use, they are going to use. Why are we so different from Big Pharma? Opiates. Doctors handing out prescriptions like stickers. All you got to do is grease their palms a little. Legal drugs or illegal, what's the difference, is it tax dollars? Is it control? Medical benefits? Yeah, that's what they say, but most drugs started through a medical basis, eh?"

I didn't know enough to agree or disagree. I was interested, though. Jairo was into that type of thing. Arguing political interest, conspiracy, drugs, war on drugs, or anything of the sort, made his blood pump faster.

A month before it was time to take our trip to Colombia, Jairo made a surprise visit to town. He flew in and met me right before it was time for me to meet his delivery driver. Dante wasn't around, but I knew he'd pop up that day because the shipment was coming in.

Jairo rode with me to pick up the shipment and drop the product off at the storage house. When Jairo saw the storage house, his face dropped with disgust.

"Is this where you keep my legacy?" Jairo showed obvious disapproval.

I attempted to explain my logic before Jairo cut me off and asked, "who has access to this house?"

After answering his question with just Dante and me, Jairo dropped his head low and said, "I'm not gonna go into this with you mijo. Change the locks tomorrow, but for today we clean this shit up."

Jairo was serious about cleaning the storage house. We spent the day and into the night cleaning. Once it met his approval, he decided not to wait, but to change the locks that night.

After the work was done, Jairo smiled and said, "now this looks like something worthy of housing my legacy. Poppy out." He saluted the packages as we walked out and blew them a kiss. He was passionate or crazy.

On the way back from the storage house, I got a text from Dante that he had gone to pick up some of the product in the morning. I was so tired and ready to get to Paola that I didn't think about the fact that Jairo and I had changed the lock. I sent Dante an "OK" text reply and continued home to Paola.

In the morning, when I woke up, I saw a text from Dante that he was going to go by in the afternoon to pick up the product. He said he couldn't get in.

Every thought that crossed my mind caused me to panic. I knew that he would flip out about my changing the locks, and I didn't want to argue with Dante. I wanted us all to get on the same page. I started to shoot him a text to let him know that Jairo had wanted the locks changed. Before I could hit send, Dante followed up his message with another text that said he couldn't find his key.

I was thankful that the fault was on Dante and that he had not yet discovered that the locks had been changed. I figured it would save time and suspicion if I just went to the house and offered to meet Dante. It was the best idea I had to buy myself time to explain the new arrangements to Dante.

I jumped out of bed and threw on some clothes. I kissed Paola on the forehead on the way out of the bedroom. I closed the door as quietly as I could and turned to walk out the door. Not more than two feet in front of me stood Jairo.

"Where you headed so early?"

I didn't want Jairo to think that I couldn't handle Dante. I wasn't ready to explain the locks, trust, distrust, and address all the tension between Dante and me, so I told him I was heading out to get Paola something to eat.

"I'm hungry too mijo, I'll ride with you."

I didn't debate, I didn't want to draw unnecessary attention to myself, but my heart pounded loudly enough for Jairo to hear my nervousness. If there were ever a time to clear things up, I knew that the time was now. I had to let Jairo know how close Dante's dealings were with his product and about the tension. If anything were to occur, I didn't want to be on Jairo's bad side. I hoped that he would be able to give me advice on how to handle the tension. I could explain to him Dante's and my relationship, and then he would understand.

I started off slowly by small talking Jairo. He picked up instantly and gave me that intense stare that I had encountered so many times before. I explained the situation with Dante to him and even went into Ollie. What started out as a quick rundown turned into a serious conversation that caused me to have to pull over.

I knew what Jairo was going to say, and I had been trying to keep accountability while holding others accountable. Dante was a soft issue for me because even with all the evidence in the world, I still only saw the kid with too little clothes fighting for a place in the world. Several sleepovers at my house built a brotherhood between us. No one was there the night Helena chose the pipe over her son. At times, my mother held him more than she held me. He rescued me when I was at my most vulnerable moments, and I couldn't see all of that going down the drain.

I listened to Jairo as he lectured me about my dealings with Dante. When he finished drilling me with all his philosophies, he leaned his chair back and told me to make my next move my best move.

I thought that stopping by the storage house would be the best move, but before I did that, I wanted to show Jairo that I had heard him. I pulled up to a gas station and bought a newspaper. When I got back in the car, I passed the newspaper to Jairo and offered a quick smile. Jairo picked up the paper and started to thumb through the pages. He exchanged a quick look with me, and I could tell he was pleased.

Although the timing was not perfect, the vibe had settled so much that I wanted to ask about marrying Paola. It had been on my mind for what felt like centuries, but the opportunities were always few and inconvenient. I was not into the traditional way of doing things, but Paola was so close to her father that I knew it would mean the most to her if I asked him.

Jairo was so intrigued by the paper that he didn't notice that we had pulled up to the storage house. I sent Dante a text to let him know to meet me at the storage house to grab his product. After the text was sent, I focused my energy and attention on Jairo.

I had been thinking for some time, and I knew I wanted to marry Paola. I had plans, and I didn't wish to see any of them coming to fruition without Paola by my side. I had thoughts of living in Florida and keeping Paola closer to her father when the baby was born. I even thought about Colombia; it was beautiful. I wanted Paola to have everything she needed: family, friends, her father, everything. I was tired of dealing with unnecessary tension and drama. I wanted to find Ollie so that he and Dante could make all the big decisions, and I could just distribute and focus on being better for Paola.

Outside of Jairo's charity, I didn't have anything to offer Paola and the baby. My mother was dead. She would have loved Paola, and I could only imagine her face knowing that she had a grandchild on the way. My baby would have no grandmothers. I couldn't even offer Paola a mother in the way that I had offered Dante one.

I wanted to do right by Paola because Mike had never done right by my mother. I wanted my child to see what I didn't see growing up, a father. I wanted Paola to feel the love my grandparents shared throughout their years of marriage, and I wanted her to get it all from me.

Sweat poured from my pores like rain while I anticipated asking Jairo about Paola's hand. I didn't know if this was the right time or if Jairo had really come to terms with the idea of me being Paola's suitor. I knew he had seen something in me, and I hoped it was enough.

"Jairo, you know I was thinking…"

Fixed on the newspaper, he let out a chuckle without turning his head. "It's some sick people in this world," he said without acknowledging me. I almost lost my nerves and retreated from the pending conversation, but between the anxiety and excitement, my adrenaline went full steam ahead, and I snatched the paper from Jairo.

"I want to marry Paola, shit ain't perfect yet but…"

I tried to explain while every word I spoke after snatching the paper seemed to have the effect of poking a bear. Jairo stared at me until I started to feel small in my seat. When he finally let up his stare, he snatched the paper back and made an exaggerated "thwap" sound while opening it back to his previous article.

I felt defeated, but more than defeated, I felt annoyed. I had a mind to snatch the paper again, but I wasn't sure if I had the mind for all the potential consequences that plagued my brain.

"Old ass man touching on little girls. That's sick, este cabron."

Jairo was so intrigued by the paper that I immediately ruled out snatching the paper again. I figured I would approach him with finesse and show interest in his article. I stared for a minute as I thought of ways to initiate my move. After seconds of anticipation, I blurted out, "What it say?"

At first, Jairo scoffed. I felt my opportunity had probably passed when I snatched the paper and started to hang my head in defeat. Before I entirely dropped my head, I caught Jairo inching the paper towards me.

I looked up and peeked over at the article, and in a bold headline, it read: "City's Council Member Michael Morehall Charged with Rape."

My chest clenched tight, and my lungs collapsed. I started gasping for air, but the air would not come. I felt a hand clench my shoulder and, in a panic, I jerked my shoulder and stared at the passenger seat. I felt a look so cold come across my face that I tensed up. My brain felt like it was splitting several different ways, and an instant headache came on.

I convulsed with confusion.

I needed air.

I reached for the handle and swung the door open. Unable to get out of the car fast enough, I threw myself onto the cement catching myself with my hands. With half of my body still in the car, I crawled out, and before I could get entirely out of the car, my insides loosened, and I began to throw up everywhere.

Chapter 13

If It Ain't One Thing...
"Not my circus. Not my monkeys." —Polish Proverbs

I was going to fucking kill him. I became obsessed with keeping up with the Mikes case ever since I read the article. It was said that Mike had been accused and charged with statutory rape of a minor. The story had it that Mike had impregnated a 16-year-old 2 or 3 years ago and Morgan had tried to pay the family off. The girl went public with the rape when Morgan couldn't settle on a figure. Her family pressed charges, and it had just started making its way through the media mainstream.

I hadn't read the papers like Jairo told me to, but I always kept my ear open for what was going on around me. I never knew the whereabouts of Mike. I never even heard his name until the year my mother died. I boiled with anger at the thought of him.

Charged. Charged with rape. I had mixed emotions. He should have already been charged with rape. If he had been charged and convicted before, maybe he wouldn't have been able to do it again. He wasn't charged, so he was free to pass out his HIV like candy. I couldn't help but wonder what was different about this rape that got so much attention. Meanwhile, my mother died with no regard from anyone, especially the justice system or the DA's office and their charges.

I knew I had to make it right for my mom, and I knew exactly what to do. I just had to figure out how to get it done.

Paola was glowing in her eighth month of pregnancy. She had taken and passed her LSATs and was waiting to hear back from her chosen law schools. Her GPA alone had schools waiting on her, but she needed her LSATS for admission.

We had discussed moving to Florida once the baby was born but had not set anything into motion. Jairo was visiting frequently and keeping a close eye on his shipments. I had missed a few shipments since I had found out about Mike's case, and I had let Dante take over for a while. Jairo disapproved.

Paola had explained to Jairo the significance of Mike, and at first, Jairo was repulsed and wanted her to stop seeing me. After coming and talking to me with one of his long drawn out lectures, his disgust turned to empathy. He gave his blessing for marrying Paola; after that, Jairo started trying to bring me in on more of his projects. I noticed that he would call me more and talk about random shit like baseball games and basketball games. Jairo was usually all about business and Paola, but now he expanded his interests to include me. I could sense the change. Jairo was trying to be the father I never had.

I told Jairo about my plans to make sure Mike disappeared. He didn't argue. He even agreed. "It's a necessary thing," he said every time I spoke of new ways to torture Mike. Jairo had even offered up some of his own ideas and offered to participate if by some chance Mike ever came to Colombia.

With Dante running the shipments and Jairo micro-managing Dante, it left me all the time in the world to focus on Mike. I took my time creating the perfect plan because his death was necessary, but I couldn't afford to get myself caught up with a murder case.

I thought about enlisting help, but I knew that fewer people knowing would be for the better. The only person I had told at that point was Jairo. Paola sensed it, but I never confirmed. I wanted to tell Dante, I figured he would be most apt to help me, but when I mentioned telling Dante to Jairo, he said it would be my worst mistake to date.

I understood where Jairo was coming from, but I also knew Dante loved my mom like she was his own. I knew he would want to see Mike fall just like I did. It was true that things were different with Dante and me now. It was also true that Dante still had not told me Ollie was out and it was still being kept secret months later. The truth I held onto most was that Teigen was Dante's mother when he needed one most.

Like all the other things I noticed going wrong with Dante's and my relationship, I also noticed that money was coming up short. It was never enough for me to spark attention, and Jairo was collecting his money upfront, so I never brought up the issue. I had learned from Paola to make mental notes, to watch the board closely, and to never speak about my next move, so, I kept quiet. When

Jairo started micro-managing things with Dante, he noticed shortcomings too. Jairo didn't keep quiet.

"He's smoking my shit, Rilei."

Jairo came in one day after leaving the storage house ranting and raving about how someone had been getting high in the storage house. He swore it was Dante, but I knew better. Dante saw what heroin did to Helena and never forgave her or the heroin.

"Nah, Dante wouldn't smoke that…"

I could not finish my sentence before Jairo was in my face.

"I know what I fucking know. He's out. That motherfucker is out. And you're going to fucking tell him. Today. To-fucking-day. And if he lays his thieving paws on any more of my shit, that's it. Just like his fucking ancestors, entitled thieves."

I knew Jairo was serious, but I had no idea how I was going to approach Dante with the news. I had a lot going on trying to figure out my situation with Mike, and this did nothing but complicate matters more for me. I had hoped to take care of Mike, propose to Paola, and be moved to Florida by the beginning of the year. Taking Dante out of the business operations would mean more work for me and less time to take care of what I needed to do. Letting Dante handle the product meant steady profit without getting my hands dirty. I liked the dynamic we had set up, but I knew Jairo, and I was in no position to test his orders.

I eased my way into the conversation, hoping to soften the blow. The news was going to piss Dante off, and I had no way of preventing that, so I told Dante about Mike. He hit a state of confusion like me, and I told him that someone else would run shipments while he and I took care of Mike. I hoped he would say something about Ollie, but he didn't. He swore that he was good to run shipment and handle Mike, but I insisted that he be off.

"Bro, you ain't using this shit, is you?" I asked Dante laughing, hoping it would ease some of the weight off the question.

Dante denied that he was using, but his face flushed red, and I could see in his face that he was. I hated that Jairo was right and I hated even more that I was wrong. I was satisfied that I had gotten him off the shipment for now and I decided to let good enough be good enough. I added a verbal note to Dante before I completely let off the topic, "remember Jairo's rules, man."

"Fuck Jairo," Dante let out with irritation in his voice.

"Yea, fuck Jairo," I said looking at Dante with a look of disbelief on my face, "until Jairo finds out you're fucking him."

"Who back you got anyways, Rilei?"

"I ain't in that shit. I don't know what the hell going on with you, but we ain't doing no unnecessary shit. Let's focus on this Mike character, alright."

The vibe I felt from Dante was different. I could see in his face that shit was different with him and all I could think about was how long had this been going on. I grew irritated with myself at how stupid I was for bringing heroin to his face like that. We were fine when we were selling cocaine, but now, things had changed. The more irritated I grew, the more I regretted telling Dante about Mike.

Chapter 14

"Alright Unc"

"Love all, trust a few, do wrong to none." —William Shakespeare

I had to order my priorities. I wanted to get out of Akron so bad that I could taste it. Things had gotten even more sour between Dante and me since I was forced to remove him from our operation. I knew Dante felt played, but Jairo had made the call. The only thing Dante showed interest in was Mike. He would only call me to talk about Mike and only come by if he needed to discuss some shit about Mike that we couldn't speak about over the phone. It was hard not speaking to Dante like I wanted to, but I was thankful that he showed passion about Mike.

After planning for weeks, I managed to track down the girl who was the victim in Mikes case. That was the thing about Akron, if you left your ears close enough to the streets, you could find out whatever you wanted to learn.

I caught her at a neighborhood park after I had been following her for days. She was a slender girl with blond hair and blue eyes, and she carried her son with her on her hips while she walked the park. I approached her first by trying to pretend I was interested, but she showed no interest.

Not wanting the opportunity to pass, I broke down and confessed that the baby she was holding was possibly my brother. She looked at me with disdain then suddenly busted out in tears. I thought the tears were out of sympathy, embarrassment, and hurt; until she began to cry even louder. I attempted to quiet her, but she started to yell.

"Why do they keep doing this? I am so tired of these games. Mike knows what I want." She breathed heavily and started again. "Did Morgan put you up to this? Who sent you, Melissa? I know it was Melissa. You tell her I don't care what she says. Mike is either going to leave Morgan, or I am going to testify. She could have at least sent someone half believable. You're clearly a Nigger. Mike would never touch a..."

The sentence went incomplete, and my hands collapsed around her neck, daring her to continue to speak. Her son busted out in tears while his mother tried to remove my hands from around her neck with one hand and hold him with the other.

His cries pierced my ears. I wanted to let off her throat, but I couldn't. I noticed her son clinging to hang onto her while I squeezed. I fell limp at seeing him watching me take life from his mother, and I released my grip. She coughed for a while, sucking in all the air she possibly could.

I wondered if he would remember the image of me holding his mother by the neck. Would he remember me like I remembered Mike? I wasn't there, but I remembered Mike violating my mother. I could see it when she spoke to me. I wondered if he would remember me if he would see me like I saw Mike.

I sat on the park bench and stared at her as tears formed in her eyes. I wanted to apologize but for what? I knew that I had come only to talk to her. She was the hostile one.

I continued to stare at her while she cried. Her screaming child still had the look of fear blanketed over his face. I watched her hold him and kiss him while telling him everything was ok. She loved her son. I could see it in her face. She wore the look that my mom wore so many times.

I got up from the bench and turned to leave. Thoughts swam through my mind until I felt weak in the knees. I never ached so bad from being called a nigger. I had heard it before, but I had never heard it the way it left her mouth. I thought about my mom. She was beautiful. I was always told that I resembled her. I never thought about having a father, let alone a white father.

I knew what she said was an attempt to invalidate my claim, but I also knew that it devalued everything my mom told me, everything she suffered, and what she died with. She said he would never, but he did, and I was proof that he did. My mother's claims were thrown out because the city swore "he would never," but he did. I grew up not knowing I had a father because everyone said, "he would never," and he did.

Developing a plan for Mike had become wearing. Paola was starting to complain about the lack of attention I was giving her while Jairo was complaining about my lack of focus. I made up my mind to pause on Mike until after the baby was born and focus on the product.

I wanted to get enough money together that Paola and I could leave right after the baby was born and we could start fresh. Jairo was for us moving to Florida because of Paola, but he wanted to find someone that could keep the lines to Philly and Ohio open.

Despite him never coming to see me when he got out, I figured it was time for me to talk to Ollie. I expected some things to be different, since he never called me. I also knew that Ollie and I had something in common, and the night at the hospital had started a bond between two black kids with no mother. I knew that I had not done anything that would shake that bond, so I planned to find out what was going on.

I talked to Jairo about finding someone to run the line up north, and he was cool with my choice if he met them. I planned to get Ollie and bring him in since Dante was a definite no for Jairo. Since I needed to make a trip to Philly, I figure that I could use the opportunity to make it a road trip with Paola. It would work if I recruited someone to run the product to Philly. I wasn't willing to risk much of anything, especially with Paola riding with me.

I had hit up Dante about finding some people to run the Philly delivery, and I told him that I was going to be taking Paola out of town for a little bit. I didn't tell him that I would be making a pit-stop to meet up with Ollie.

I started getting knots in my stomach when I talked business with Dante, so I stopped discussing everything that he didn't need to know. Since I moved Dante out of his power position, things had seemed off. I knew Dante wouldn't mess up a shipment though, because regardless of what Jairo had said, I made sure that Dante still had a way to make money.

Dante had found a middle-aged white couple to do the delivery. I brought the couple to meet with Jairo so that he could approve them, and we could start planning the route. Paola had wanted to go to Baltimore to see the Harbor and some of the historic sites. She had also made it known several times before when I was traveling to Philly, that she had a craving for an authentic cheesesteak. Pregnancy.

I wanted to take extra precautions because I had made the trip back and forth so many times already in my own car. I had never been pulled over, but in my mind, police knew my car from riding that route so many times.

I rented a car to change things up. I had a few things I needed to close with Jairo and the delivery drivers, so Dante picked the rental car up for me, and we all met up at the storage house.

Once the plan was made, I did a once over of the rental to made sure everything was in order, and I loaded Paola and my bags into the trunk. Dante loaded the product into the delivery driver's car and tossed in a few blankets and two suitcases to cover it.

"Not convincing at all," I thought to myself. Jairo was fine with it.

"Two middle-aged white people, best chance of any," was Jairo's take on the situation.

I tossed the keys to my car to Jairo and gave Dante a nod. I looked over the car once again to make sure it was completely clean.

Dante looked at me and said, "Alright Unc," as he winked and waved goodbye.

"You silly dude; lay off that shit for real."

I jumped in the car and looked back just in time to see Jairo give Dante an intense eye. Happy to be getting away from the tension for a while, Paola and I headed out letting the product lead the way.

Chapter 15

Protect and Serve

"If something can corrupt you, you're corrupted already." —Bob Marley

I called the delivery drivers to pull over at the nearest gas station so that I could make sure everything was a green light. I had texted the young guy that I met the first time I made the delivery; he knew about Ollie and gave me the number to contact him. I decided it would be best to make the call on my way to Philly. If he answered, I could get a vibe for what was going on instead of getting there and risking it being tense while Paola was with me.

Paola went into the gas station to grab snacks and use the bathroom before we got on the road. The delivery drivers were filling up the tank. I got irritated for a moment because I could not understand why the tank was not filled before we loaded the car.

After seething for a bit, I calmed down, realizing we were at the gas station and getting gas was some normal shit to do at the gas station. I kept feeling anxious waiting on Paola to get back to the car, and I couldn't figure out why.

It seemed like the best time to go ahead and call Ollie's line. Hearing from him could at least ease some of the pressure on my mind, so I sat back into the seat and dialed his number. It rang. I grew nervous. It rang again. Thoughts started to fill my head. What if shit really wasn't copacetic.

Ring.

"Hello."

On the third ring, Ollie answered the phone. Normal timing, most people answer on the third ring. I was surprised. I was so stunned to hear his voice that I got lost in the moment and didn't respond the first three times he said hello. Hopefully, it was just as normal to await a "three hello response," like it was a "three-ring answer."

"Yeah. Uh, hey. This Rilei Man. What's been up? Long-time, no speak?"

Everything was silent for a moment. If I were a betting man, I would have gambled everything I had that the earth stood still when he heard my voice.

"Yo, is that really you kid. Damn, I can't believe it's you. I thought…. Yo, hold up, this Dante on my line."

I yelled into the phone before he clicked over to delay him.

"Hey, don't tell him you talked to me. Hit me back, I'm trying to talk business with. And yo, Ollie, I missed you, bro."

"Fo sho. Don't tell Dante? Aww man, I'm going to hit you right back though. We on bro."

Just like that, we were off the phone. I had no idea what to make of the situation. He sounded like he was shocked to hear from me and that he didn't just neglect me when he got out. My stomach started to knot up as Paola was walking out of the gas station.

When she got to the car, she mentioned that she was feeling dizzy riding in the passenger seat, so she preferred to drive. I preferred that she rested, but she insisted that she be the one to drive. I gave in and moved to the passenger seat.

As Paola started the car, I looked over and nodded at the delivery drivers so they would know to take off. Once they pulled out of the parking lot, Paola and I pulled off. We didn't make it five seconds down the road when I saw red and blue lights pull up on the delivery car.

My heart started beating 10,000 beats a minute while I tried to convince myself that everything was straight. Paola got into the far lane so that we could pass where the drivers had been pulled over. As soon as we passed, I took a deep breath and sent up a quick prayer that everything would go smoothly.

I had never encountered problems making this drive before, especially when I hadn't even made it out of Akron. I didn't know what to make of it. I glanced in the side mirror to see how far back the load was and saw another set of red and blue lights coming up from behind. Quickly, I sat back in my seat and fastened my seatbelt while checking to make sure Paola had hers on.

There was an SUV between them and us, and there was an exit for a gas station coming up. I pointed it out to Paola and told her to speed up and pull up at the gas station. I looked behind us, and the police were still behind the SUV. I relaxed a little thinking that maybe they were pulling them over. I felt almost silly for panicking when I knew I had nothing on me but seeing the delivery drivers get pulled over had me spooked.

When we reached the gas station, Paola went inside to relieve herself again, swearing that her bladder was at its weakest. I hopped back into the driver seat to avoid any more scares with Paola at the wheel.

A few minutes had passed, and I saw Paola heading to the counter once again to pay out for some random snacks she had picked up, heading out of the bathroom.

I looked out the window and noticed Helena sitting on an Ice Box. Her skin looked pale and oily. I could see crater holes in her face from my car. I thought to myself, "Helena graduated from heroin to meth."

I thought to get out of the car and say something. It had been years since I last saw her, and I knew Dante would want to know I checked up on her. As I started to get out of the car, a white man in uniform threw his hand on my door. I hadn't even noticed someone coming up from behind. I hadn't noticed the lights flashing through my rearview.

"Stay in the car, please, sir. License, Insurance, Registration, please."

I looked in the store trying to catch Paola's attention. She was staring off the opposite way waiting in line to pay.

"License, Insurance and Registration please, sir," the officer spoke again. This time more loudly, which caught Helena's attention. I reached for my license and went to grab the rental information from the glove box.

"Keep your hands where I can see them, sir." By this time, Helena was inching closer to see what was going on. She looked kite high and sickly.

"Sir, hand me your registration. Do you have registration?"

I felt myself growing irritated, and without answering him, I reached for the rental information in the glove box again.

"I am not going to ask you again sir, keep your God-damned hands where I can see them."

I looked at him in time to see him placing his hand atop his gun.

My shit is in the glove box, you want it or not.

"This is a rental sir. The paperwork is in the glove box."

Mama had always taught me to be respectful, but I couldn't help feeling irritated at the entire ordeal. I knew I was clean, so I didn't care about spouting a little attitude back. I exaggeratedly and slowly moved my hands to the glove box again while I stared him in his face.

He seemed irritated, and I got a rise out of it. After he got the registration, he looked at it for a moment as if he were a lawyer reading a contract. I left him to it and scanned back into the gas station to see where Paola was. She was staring out at the car with a worried expression on her face. I waved her on hoping she would stay in the gas station until the officer left.

"What you waving at, boy?"

I could tell he was starting to taunt me. I didn't have a comeback, and I wasn't going to tell him Paola was with me because I could sense that he was petty. I looked over to see if Helena was still watching and, of course, she was.

"I'm waiving at your sister. Say hi."

The officer looked back and noticed Helena staring into the car. While he looked away, I mouthed at Paola to stay inside. The officer turned back around with an angry look on his face.

"You a funny nigga ain't you, boy?"

Before I could reply, the officer backed up and went to his car with the rental agreement and my ID. I grabbed my phone and texted Paola to stay inside until she saw them leave. After I sent the text, I sent a text to Dante, letting him know I had seen his mom at the gas station in Cuyahoga.

I peeked out my side-view mirror and saw the officer walking back to my car. I made a mental note to myself to get his name to file a complaint later. I had never been bothered much with what people called me, but with everything happening lately, I was getting fed up with what I felt were attempts to downsize me because I was black.

Cops were killing unarmed black man left and right and getting away with it, so I knew I needed to mind my manners, but I couldn't watch my tongue.

I saw another police car pull up. The first officer who pulled up on me walked back to my window. I looked out the window to peek around the officer to see what was going on, and I saw two more officers get out of the car. The original officer placed his hand back on his gun and motioned for me to step out of the car.

My spirit was telling me to sit still and not move, but I saw Paola looking at me with tears in her eyes, so I decided to comply. Without making any snide remarks, I pulled on the handle to open my door and tried to open it. I felt a slight push, and the door closed again.

"Get out of the car, sir," He said it loud enough to draw everyone's attention.

"You gotta move ya arm first, right? I mean how else I'm gone get out?"

"Get out of the car, sir."

I quickly understood what game he was trying to play.

"You trying to make this seem some type of way so you can shoot me like you did that boy Philando huh? Nah, buddy, we ain't bout to play them games."

"Last time sir, get out of your car now."

"Please move off of my door, so I can get out of my car, sir," I yelled out.

He smirked at me, but he did not move. He wanted to make me react. He wanted me to show any sign of aggression so he could shoot me. I wasn't going to give him the pleasure.

I cracked the car door a little to the point where I could feel resistance, then I thrust it open. I caught a glimpse of his name tag, and it read D. Brown. I stuck both my hands out of the car so that anyone watching could see I was unarmed and to double up on caution, I yelled out loudly,

"I'm unarmed."

As soon as I was completely out of the car, I felt something hit my foot. I looked down to see what it was, but Officer Brown had already put his foot on it and slid it over to him.

"What do we have here?"

He bent down to pick up whatever he had covered with his foot. The other two officers stood watching and waiting for instruction. Officer Brown flashed a baggie with a crystal-like substance in it.

I laughed as the two officers started to search my car. I knew they wouldn't find anything because I had made sure I was riding clean. I couldn't believe that of all drugs to get me hemmed up, it would be meth. What type of officer just walked around carrying baggies of meth?

I had never touched or sold meth a day in my life. I knew it had to be something orchestrated by Officer Brown. There couldn't have been more than two grams in the baggie, and I was sure that Paola and I had gone over the punishment for that weight.

"We got something."

Officer Brown guided me over to the trunk where the two officers held the flap that covered the compartment that holds the spare. There it was, lying where a spare should have been, two clumsily wrapped kilos of cocaine.

I glanced back at the gas station window with tears in my eyes. I saw Paola drop to her knees. I mouthed the words I love you, and I waited for the inevitable.

"You have the right to remain silent. Anything you say can and will be used against you in a court of law. You have the right to an attorney. If you cannot afford an attorney, one will be provided for you. Do you understand the rights I have just read to you?"

PART 2

Chapter 16

A Plantation Called Prison

All that dope was planted.

"All that dope was planted."

Who the fuck does Meth? Aside from Helena, apparently. She graduated quick. No fuck that, focus Rilei.

"Who does meth aside from Helena?" I asked out loud.

"Ay youngblood, I don't know who you talking to, but this ain't the cell for the mentally disturbed."

Salt and Pepper rolled over to the end of his bed and looked up at me. He sat up and began rubbing his eyes. Throwing his hands down to his side and gripping the bed, he hurled over and let out a violent cough.

"You alright, ol' school?" I asked him, halfway curious.

"Yeah man, I'm good. I might be dying. I would have died in my sleep if you weren't over there with all that bullshit. Now I gotta be woke for this shit."

"My bad, ol' school. I'm just trying to think."

"Think about what, you in a cell. You here, kid. Don't think about shit. Just take yo ass to sleep."

I paused. I wanted to reply. How do you not think about shit? All I could do was think.

"I hear you, old man," I replied.

"Hey young nigga, you got one more time. You want something to call me by then ask me for something to call me by."

"What can I call you by my guy?" I asked with a hint of sarcasm.

He coughed again, this time more violently than the last.

"Your guy, huh? You gone be somebody sissy. Keep yo soft ass where I can always see you. I'm going back to sleep."

He started to lay back down.

"What can I call you?"

He rolled over and pulled the covers up to his neck. He stretched out long and curled his legs back in. Nothing but gray and black hair remained visible.

"Young man..., shut up and go to sleep," he responded, showing his irritation.

"Call me, G."

Salt and Pepper's name was G. He was tall, about six feet two with brown skin and big eyes. Gray and black hair grew all over his head in a thick and bushy sort of way. He had a seemingly calm demeanor but gave off a vibe that left no doubt that he was not to be taken lightly.

I wasn't scared of him.

I was a little tired. It was an eventful day after all.

I could use a little sleep.

I hoped that they arrested Spaz too when they arrested Rilei; he might be needed.

I, Rilei, was not sure how to be. My closest experience to prison had always been through movies and TV shows. Spaz, on the other hand, was impulsive and able to fend for himself. I wasn't sure how I was so unattached to my alter ego, but I was aware that I needed to synchronize myself with him soon.

Being Teigen's Rilei is what kept me grounded, but it didn't protect me. The more I tried to hold on to all the facets of my life that I felt would make her proud, the more shit I got into. Teigen's Rilei trusted too easily, made foolish mistakes, and couldn't make executive decisions. I needed to reinvent myself.

I didn't want to be Spaz either. I knew that Spaz could handle himself, but I couldn't control him. I wanted something new where I was in control. I wanted to be like Jairo – smart and philosophical. I wanted to be like G, mysterious, and blunt. I wanted to be like Rilei, kind, and understanding. Like Spaz, I wanted to be able to do what needed to be done.

"My name is Rilei, just call me Lei."

Lei. Lei would be the new me. Enough of the name remained to keep me attached to Mama, but enough of it was gone to set me free. I was going to redesign what everyone thought they knew about me.

"Nigga, I wouldn't care if your name was Jesus, shut the hell up and go to sleep," G said holding in what seemed to be another cough.

I laid down on my bunk and stared at the ceiling. My back ached from the night I was arrested. Officer Brown had managed to fracture three of my ribs and did some minor damage to my back as well. I was in no position to start being Lei now. I would start being Lei first thing in the morning.

~ ~ ~

A month came and went in prison. It was the most adjusting I ever had to do for something so routine. G became my go-to in prison. He kept a book or three open at any given time. He was always reading, studying, and learning something new. He had an opinion on everything from dope to politics. Everything was a design to G. Prisons, welfare, poverty, drugs, if you could name it, it was designed to hinder Black folks' progress.

G's conversations intrigued me, although I didn't always agree. He was smart that I couldn't argue. Alongside G, there was Marvy. Marvy was another old school, just like G. Marvy had a more patient approach than G but shared his same interests when it came to the plight of Black people. Many conversations transpired within my first month of being in prison. It was enough to make me pick up a book.

"All the secrets is in books. That's where all the good shit is. The truths. It's a lot of truths out there. They all in books. You know why that is?" Marvy raised his eyebrows up at me.

"Because Niggas don't read. Too goddamned lazy," G answered before I could open my mouth to speak. "You want to hide something from a nigga, the best place to put it is in a book."

Marvy patted my back. His eyes looked somber and disappointed. His eyes remind me of Ollie's eyes the night my mother died in the hospital. There was a story there.

"Yep, we don't read until we get into places like this," Marvy said, looking suddenly misplaced.

Marvy got up from the table and dismissed himself from the conversation. I looked over at G. G shrugged. He looked back down at the table at his books and slid one over to me.

"I been reading. It ain't take prison to make me pick up a book," G said. "Here, I just read this for the 3rd time, you go 'head."

I picked the book up from the table.

Miseducation of the Negro.

That was the first book I read in prison. It was disappointing. I wanted to go to FAMU. I wanted to be a scholar. I wanted power words like Halie's dad. I wanted success. The book G gave me challenged what I thought of as success. It made me angry. I went back to G and told him just how I felt about the book.

"Good, now read it again. This time take notes."

I did. I read it again. I took notes. I asked for another book. I read before prison, but I read different material. I read differently. I read to escape reality and feel close to Mama. Paola and I read law books to keep a step ahead. In prison, I read to learn, to be informed, to be inspired, and to be angry. I started developing opinions just like G and Marvy. I started to dislike the American dream and those who invented it. I started becoming interested.

Marvy and G weighed me down with intellect. They took me under their wings. I was not to be messed with because they said so, and they were respected. G didn't let me get into the riffraff with the other prisoners. G said he had plans for me because I reminded him of somebody. We didn't talk much about who I reminded him of, but I could easily assume it was someone he was close to.

Between G and Marvy, it was hard to figure out which one was the most dangerous. They both passed as men of intellect and sophistication, even though they used improper grammar. Neither would discuss why they were locked up. If I asked G, he would say that I'd be best to mind my business. If I asked Marvy, he would tell me that it is rude to ask about a man's affairs. Either way, it was a conversation neither of them would have, and both advised me not to have it with anyone as well.

"Folks is nosy. They don't care about what you did. Shit, you say in here can come back to bite you. I suppose you would do best to keep your business your business," Marvy explained with patience.

"Man," G would say twisting his nose up, "what you gone tell them niggas anything for? So, they can run back and tell them peckawoods. How 'bout you just shut up?"

It was G's way of communicating that made me feel that he was more capable, more dangerous than Marvy. They were opposites, yet so much alike. G reacted quick, Marvy masterminded his plans. If you said the wrong thing to G, consequences were immediate and brutal. If you said the wrong thing to Marvy, you had to wait in suspicion, and you never knew who was going to deliver the blow. It was more of the anticipation that people feared with Marvy.

Marvy said that there was more than one way to affect someone, and he was always after the way that gave the most damage. Marvy bragged about having a white man's philosophy. He was content with affecting someone's situation long-term.

Marvy would say: "See you can beat them, but they heal. You can kill 'em, but then what's left? No. Affect they're living. That's what I learned from the white man. Make them live in fear. Make them live with struggle. Only if that fails, do I resort to violence."

G disagreed. He wasn't as patient. "Beat they ass. If you got to, kill em. I don't have time to be looking over my shoulder because someone got a vendetta."

G had the attitude of "get 'em done." G's philosophy was if you needed an ass-whooping, then he had one waiting, and if you needed more, he could make immediate adjustments.

If I had to best explain it, I would name G – Malcolm X, and Marvy – Martin Luther King. The only problem was, Marvy wasn't non-violent, and neither Marvy nor G cared to co-exist equally with whites.

When I first told Marvy and G that my best friend was a white kid from the projects, they scratched their heads in confusion. For G, it was the fact that I was still calling Dante, my best friend, after I had explained to G, in detail, the night of my arrest. For Marvy, it was a white kid being from the projects that confused him.

It wasn't hard to explain Dante's background, but Marvy couldn't register that being the lifestyle of any white person. As much as they intrigued me, I hated that their views of the world were so narrow. It gave me room to question whether what they believed had any validity to it. I knew Dante and his life better than anyone else. I knew that white people could have just as hard a time as blacks. I did my best to get G and Marvy to see the same.

They didn't see it my way. They set me up for an immediate intervention, which involved me listening to Malcolm X's *House Nigga vs. Field Nigga* speech.

"You don't have to hate white folks," G told me, "but you have to know who you are. I mean you really got to know who you are."

I didn't understand. G knew I didn't understand. Marvy stepped in to explain patiently and lead the way.

"You win when you understand. You can't understand until you rewire your mind. You will never rewire your mind long as you thinking that you in the same playing field. Where you from? And don't tell me no bullshit ass American state. Tell me something about your bloodline. About your history. Do you know anything about your history? What you know about Africa besides for Feed the Children? What do you know about the true

Jews? What is a white man doing on a picture claimed to be Jesus? I mean really, tell me something about the great library that was burned down, about them pyramids in Egypt and the stories told through the pictures. What do you know besides what you were indoctrinated with? You keep leaving everything for a white man to teach you, and soon they gone have you thinking that slavery was just a nice paying servant gig with benefits. Your president already confusing dead black historical figures with people working for him. I ain't spitting in your ear. Go pick up a damn book and quit being a nigga."

G laughed. It was all the words G wanted to say in a way that G couldn't say them. G wasn't patient enough to say them.

"That cat cold-blooded ain't he?" G asked me.

G opened up for the first time with a genuine thought. "Let me tell you something. My grandmother was a slave. Here you are, right now, talking to me, and I am telling you my grandmother was a slave. I knew my grandmother very well. Sweetest old lady you could ever meet. Pretty woman with long hair. Light complexion and a hard worker. A white man's baby probably, and she was a slave. So how long ago was slavery really? Them crackers walk around here telling folks what they need to get over and move on from, but they want me to remember 9/11, nah fuck that, I remember my grandmother."

I remembered my grandmother too. I didn't remember her as a slave. I remembered her as my morning reminder to eat all my breakfast before I could drink my orange juice. But, what about her mother? It was hard to imagine that my grandmother's mother could have been a slave or even the mother before her.

I wondered if Mike's great-grandfather owned or fathered any slaves.

It was these conversations that helped me to define who I needed to be and what I needed to know. All my life, I had been fed direction, but Marvy and G challenged me to give direction. To give direction, I had to read.

My first month in prison was like a caterpillar in his cocoon. I transformed. I hadn't spoken much to Jairo or Paola, and I had not spoken to Dante at all. I communicated with Ollie the most. I felt like a failure to Paola and a disappointment to Jairo. Paola was a new mother, a single mother, like Mama, because of me. I couldn't forgive myself for putting her in a situation like that.

Jairo had been working to find a suitable lawyer for me to file an appeal. I had put Jairo in contact with Ollie since Ollie had been through the process before. After I put Ollie in contact with Jairo, I distanced myself. I couldn't stand the idea of letting down the only father figure I ever had aside from Mr. Donaldson.

Damn.

Mr. Donaldson.

Chapter 17

Price of Life

Freddie Gray. Damn. Alton Sterling. Philando Castille. Michael Brown. Damn.

Sirens blared through the TV screen. I would have sworn I was at the scene. The sirens were deafening as if the room had surround sound.

My mind continued to race. Eric Garner. Akai Gurley. Amber Monroe. Sandra Bland. No matter woman or man; the threat was all the same.

G sat next to me glued to the television. He didn't even blink. Marvy sat near enough for me to hear his mocking sound of shame.

"Umph umm unh."

"Shhh," I put my fingers to my lips, ignoring the stares that would follow such a bold act. I couldn't hear myself think. The lady on the television murmured on in the background.

Tamir Rice.

"Matthew Donaldson shot dead this evening by Akron police. Police said that Donaldson appeared to be holding what looked to be a gun." The news lady carried on her conversation without me.

Matthew Donaldson shot dead.

Akron Police.

"Ayyy, rewind that back," I shouted out loud. The group of orange jumpsuits near the front laughed. G looked over at me and shook his head.

Marvy whispered over, "this here is cable. Won't be no rewinding. But what part did you miss? Same shit. Another nigga dead."

The News reporter looped her report, "Matthew Donaldson shot dead by Akron Police."

His picture flashed across the screen, and I lost it. I flashed back to the night I was arrested. Officer Brown beat me bad. He was allowed to do it. Everyone saw it, but nobody stopped him. I didn't have a gun, but I had a smart mouth. Mr. Donaldson didn't even have a smart mouth.

Mr. Donaldson didn't own guns. He hated guns. He told so many stories about his Army days and his time at war; he never wanted to own another gun. He was obedient, disciplined; he was a soldier. He was all about respecting authority figures. He even had a punk ass "back the blue" sign in his manicured lawn in the bougie part of Akron.

"Several burglaries in Merriman Valley."

Her voice rang back in disrupting my thoughts. I could hear her every word loud and clear.

"Donaldson, a possible suspect was confronted by officers while he was believed to be breaking and entering into a car." She continued to hammer on.

A picture of Mr. Donaldson's house flashed across the screen. I felt an itch in my nose as warm tears started to flee from the corners of my eyes. I could feel a hammering in my chest, and my head started to pound.

Possible suspect.

"Discharged from the Military in 1992, Military record show Donaldson received disciplinary action resulting in his dismissal from the..."

"Turn that shit off," I screamed across the room.

Disciplinary action. Mr. Donaldson was a war veteran. He fought in the Gulf War. He was infantry, he suffered PTSD, he dealt with survivor's remorse. He came home and lost his mother the same year. He was homeless. He slept on the streets for months before he was able to land a job. He worked hard, met a woman, fell in love, and found out he would never have a child to carry his name because he married a woman who could not bear children.

Suspect.

He had medals on top of medals from his service to the Army.

Disciplinary action?

Of what fucking sort?

"Criminal record showing possession of marijuana in 19..." Her voice was still humming.

"I said turn that shit OFF."

I got up from my seat. I could feel G and Marvy's eyes burning into my back. I marched to the front of the room near where the orange jumpsuits had camped out.

My head was pounding. I couldn't think clearly enough to care that I had walked through a gang of Aryans. I reached my hand up to the TV with tears stinging my face. I felt around for the off button.

Front of the TV.

Back of the TV.

Sides of the TV.

Not one damn button in sight. A firm hand tapped my shoulder, and a remote magically dangled in my face. I stood still for a moment to try to control my next movement. I didn't want to be Spaz anymore. I wanted to be more like Jairo, more like G, less like Rilei and Spaz. The remote continued to float in my face.

I spun around to a face taunting me. He was red as if he had just got done blushing, or crying, or both. His head was completely bald, and his neck carried around a swastika on its side.

"A dead nigga, in the good ol' days that was something to celebrate. You tryna turn off our celebration boy?" He jigged at me.

I pleaded with myself for control. G and Marvy's eyes still burned into my back. Mr. Donaldson's name still bounced around the prison walls. Adjectives that were the furthest from who Mr. Donaldson was continued to be tossed out.

"Don't worry, boy, you in here where you're needed most. Them fine fellas is making America great again, don't you worry."

He laughed. All the orange jumpsuits laughed. I turned to look back at G and Marvy. They were no longer in the same seats that they once sat in. I spun back around to the court's jester.

"Fuck out my face, and turn that shit off," I said calmer than I intended.

"You heard him, Robbie, he said turn that shit off huh," Another skinhead with a swastika on his face said looking over at me.

"I do believe that is what he said gentlemen," Marvy's voice interrupted.

Marvy appeared from the side of me. I looked back at the chairs where he and G once sat trying to figure out where he came from.

"I know one thing; I don't plan on asking any of you crackers for shit."

That was G. I could hear his subtle inpatient command coming from behind me. He moved quickly and snatched the remote from Robbie who had once dangled the same remote in my face. G tapped the power button, and the TV flickered off. An older man appeared from the back of the orange jumpsuits. His face was calm like his blue eyes. His hair was gray, and he looked friendly, or like a
pedophile. He wasn't bald like the others, but he wore the same hate swastika on his neck that the others wore.

"How bout we leave the happenings to the young folks G."

The older man walked over to G and placed his hand on his shoulder. They liked to put their hands on people's shoulders, it seemed. G wasn't having it. G shrugged his shoulder away and twisted up his nose.

"Man, Lou, what the fuck is you talking about 'happenings. Get the fuck out my face with that shit. You cats is something you know that" G said to Lou as he handed the remote to me. "Don't you put your motherfucking hands on me. I'll cut you to the white meat if you touch me again."

"What he means is..."

"Shut up Marvy, I know what the fuck I mean. You hear me, Lou. I'll cut you wide the fuck open. Don't forget about Guy." G's face was stuck in a confused frown with his nose bunched up into his eyes. He spoke with his teeth gritted and his finger-pointing. Lou did not appear intimidated, but he turned to his gang, and they dispersed.

"What you go and do that for? You know that shit ain't never-ending." Marvy's patience seemed to be wearing thin while he addressed G's actions.

"You know why I did it," G said to Marvy while looking at me.

I didn't know why he did it, but I was happy he did. I couldn't stand to hear any more about Mr. Donaldson. I needed to call Mrs. Donaldson and find out what was going on. I needed to talk to someone. I couldn't think while the lady on TV was delivering all her inaccuracies about Mr. Donaldson.

Thwap.

I felt a cold ringing in my ear. I turned to see what had just happened.

Thwap.

I caught a glimpse of his fist as it connected with my chin.

Spaz freed himself. In true Spaz fashion, the deed was done before I realized what happened. I looked down at my orange jumpsuit. It was decorated in blood. I looked to my left and my right. G stood shoulder to shoulder with me and handed me a homemade shank.

"Cut that shit off his neck."

Marvy chimed in. "Leave it be. Let's move around."

I was Rilei again. Not Lei, not Spaz, Jairo, or G. I was Teigen's Rilei. I saw Mama again, in my head, bathroom floor, lying still in all that blood. She was mummy wrapped in the hospital, dead at 4:04. I glanced up at the clock near the TV. It wasn't 4:04, no one would die today.

G snatched the shank from me and bent over to operate on Robbie's neck. I thought he was cutting the swastika off like he had ordered me to do. When G came up from surgery, I peered down at Robbie. He laid still, unconscious. Right next to his swastika, G had carved the words "Black Power." Marvy laughed and patted G on the back.

"I suppose he will have a change of heart if he wakes up, huh?"

G laughed, "yea, I suppose Lou will be to see us in the morning. Head on a swivel."

I laughed to keep from crying. Robbie didn't look like he would be waking up. I couldn't say I cared much if he woke up, but I feared what would happen next whether he woke or didn't wake. I let my fear settle to the back of my mind as thoughts of Mr. Donaldson crept back up. I had to call Mrs. Donaldson first thing in the morning when we received phone time.

~ ~ ~

Or write her a letter. I spent the next couple of weeks in solitary. Robbie didn't survive G's surgery. G carved too deep when he went in with his shank, or better, rumor had it that G had coated the blade with something that took Robbie out. I didn't get a chance to ask G before the guards came busting into our cell. G had been having serious coughing spells throughout the night and was in no position to be handled by the guards. When they came in asking about Robbie, I made sure their fingers pointed to me.

I was carried off to solitary without any questions. Solitary was different. It was quiet. It was a prison inside of a prison. Quieter than my mind could handle, I started humming tunes and having conversations with myself to fill the silence. Every so often, I would hear the guard's footsteps pacing through the corridor. I made a game out of counting the footsteps or trying to guess how many keys were jingling when he walked through. Every game I created while in solitary only held my interest for a few moments. So, I spent most of the time conversing with myself. Once my conversations with myself got boring, I broke down and asked for a book.

The guards refused me. I asked for a pencil and paper. The guards refused me. I asked for medical attention for my nose that felt broken after Robbie's fist had met it. I was refused. I was refused on all my requests until one day, or night, I heard footsteps pacing down the corridor that were unlike any footsteps I heard before. They were heavier and faster than the footsteps I had become accustomed to.

"Hey, can I get a book in here or something?" I shouted through the slot in the door. He answered with: "Let me see what I can do for you, man."

"A brother," I thought to myself.

Next thing I know, not too many days later, I had a book, a pen, and some paper. I knew from that point on to listen to the footsteps for my request. I timed my days based on the sounds of the footsteps and made my request when the times were right.

I wasn't sure how long I had been in solitary. It felt like forever, but there was no way to be sure. I had read three books and written eight letters – two to Mrs. Donaldson, two to Paola, two to Jairo, and two to Ollie. I hadn't received any letters back, but I hadn't considered asking if I even had mail because the right footsteps hadn't been pacing the corridors.

I heard the doors open and clank shut to the left of me. It had been quiet for the longest time with the only signs of human life being me and the guard's footsteps. Now there was another sign of life. There was humming from the other side, a voice that spoke to itself – I recognized the signs.

An odd feeling rushed over me. I anticipated conversations to help the day go by and helping ears to detect which guard was on duty. The idea of having someone to talk to after only speaking to myself for what felt like forever overwhelmed me. I stuck my ear back to the door to listen for footsteps before I introduced myself to my neighbor.

The corridors were quiet. It had to have been the cool guard shift. He took more frequent breaks. I took my chance to speak to my neighbor.

"Hey, what's up?"

I waited for a reply.

Silence.

I thought I heard a mouse piss on cotton. I stared at the cement walls. I knew he could hear me. Whoever was over there could hear me. The sound barrier was not great in solitary confinement. Sometimes I could hear the guards up the hall whispering. So, whoever was in that cell could hear me.

"The hole, huh? How you manage to get in here?"

Silence.

And, I had broken one of G's and Marvy's rules. I wasn't quite sure if the rule only applied to what someone did to get in prison, or what people did while they were in prison as well.

"I'm not trying to be rude or nothing. It's just, well, when you been in here for a long time, conversation is a hot commodity. You feel me?"

Silence.

I backed up off the wall and walked over to my bed. I sat down and put my hand in my head. I was going to go crazy. I could feel my mind slipping through my fingers. I started to hum a tune to myself. One of Mama's favorite songs when I was growing up, was *Poison* by Bell Biv DeVoe.

I hummed aloud.

"Never trust a big butt and a smile. Dun duh dun duh dun du dun DUUN. Poison..."

I started beatboxing. I had forgotten how much I loved that song. I had forgotten how much Mama loved that song. I stood up and start sliding across my cell. Singing. Dancing. I could feel Mama dancing with me. I could hear her singing along. I sang even louder.

"It's driving me out of my mind..."

"That's why it's hard for me to find," He sang out loud and clear from the other side of the concrete wall.

I stopped humming, dancing, singing, and sliding all at once. He wasn't invited to this song, and when I tried to talk to him, he ignored me. Now, here he was, singing on my song, and off-key. I was in no position to argue. I needed conversation.

"Ay, what you know about that," I asked to start a conversation.

Silence.

I heard the guard's footsteps creeping back toward my cell. I moved back over to my bed and laid down.

"You gone want to talk sooner or later. Going to go crazy if you don't," I warned.

I felt desperate. I had talked to myself enough times to know that it wasn't the same as talking to someone else. The silence was so loud that my head started to ache. I heard the footsteps creeping back up the corridor. They were heavy. They were tired. They dragged down the corridor. I reached under my pillow and grabbed one of the books I had hidden underneath. I flipped open the front cover and stared at the title page.

Mein Kampf.

I had seen Dante with this book. It had taken a lot for me to get my hands on it because of the material content. I stared at the title page for several minutes. I wondered what G would think if he saw this book in my hands. I could picture him telling me, "no book left unread." G would tell me to understand and know what I am talking about. G would remind me of Mama if he knew what to say, he would say, "Solve the mystery."

Marvy. Marvy would claim poison and tell me to watch what I read. He would say something about a skewed truth. He would look at the authors' name and condemn the book before he even looked at the first sentence.

I, on the other hand, held the book firmly in my hand and flipped the page. I was determined to find out why this book was the holy grail for so many, and more so, what Dante got out it.

Chapter 18

Is This Thing Broken: Criminal JustUS System

"Manslaughter."

His voice was heavy and carried a thick southern accent. He dragged his words and sounded like he had a mouthful of tobacco.

"I got three years in this shit hole."

Three years.

His southern draw continued to loop in my head.

Three years.

"Manslaughter, three-year bid. Not bad," I whispered quietly while my head churned with thoughts.

My chest tightened. Three years for killing somebody. That's it? I was surprised at how cheap the price was for taking someone's life. All these years, I worried about being put away for Unc, but Unc was cheaper than drugs.

"Yea, they tried to get me with murder second degree. I took the plea."

The plea.

I didn't know you could plea these days. The way I was looked at when I waited on my plea deal was comical. There were hints of laughter behind every face that was in the room. They told me there was no plea deal for me. They didn't need a plea. I sat there battered and bloody, charged with possession of a controlled substance – meth, and trafficking. Neither of which belonged to me. No one cared about my story.

It didn't matter that Officer Brown had assaulted me and beat me half to death. All that meant was I got charged with resisting arrest. The only deal that came my way involved omitting my story about Officer Brown in exchange for the resisting arrest charge not being added to my other charges.

I started off with a bomb lawyer. He walked in the interrogation room in a suit made for a king. He was clean-shaven, with intense eyes. He looked around and spoke once, everyone cleared the room. He had power. He instantly reminded me of Halie's dad. He listened to my story and felt the emotion behind it. He talked a good game. We were going to trial, and Officer Brown was losing his job.

"You won't do a day. This is ridiculous. We got the fruit of a poisonous tree, we got illegal search and seizure. You said someone recorded this. Do you know who? How to get in touch with them?"

I did. I felt confident. Plenty of people in the gas station witnessed and recorded the night of my arrest. Including Helena. I was sure that the case was just as open and shut as the lawyer suggested.

"It doesn't matter about the cocaine in the back of your car, they never had permission to search your car."

My attorney was sure. His confidence had me ready to talk shit to everyone in the courtroom. However, even with the confidence, I still asked about a plea. I wanted to know all my options. The attorney told me there was no plea deal offered, but we didn't need one anyway. When I told Paola, she said it sounded strange, but the confidence of the attorney won Paola over as well. Jairo said It was a sure thing. And it probably was a sure thing, until my attorney traded places with a public defender.

"Don't worry, I can't represent you, I got some real bad family stuff going on. Emergencies. I just can't do this legal stuff, but I know this guy. I mentored him through law school. Clever guy. He is me at his age."

But he wasn't him when I needed him. There was no attempt to reset the court date and no real sympathy in his voice. His confidence lingered on, however, and at the last moment, the public defender and I sat in the courtroom both listening to the judge echo out "FIFTEEN YEARS."

I closed my eyes to channel what G or Marvy would say. I could imagine Marvy shaking his head with solemn eyes. He would be disappointed but not surprised. I couldn't channel G. G was unpredictable. His patience was thin as well. I could imagine G giving a lecture just as much as I could imagine him flipping out. I didn't know what to do. I pried.

"How they drop murder to manslaughter?" I asked him not fully expecting an answer. I was digging through someone's business despite G's advice. I wanted an answer. I needed an answer. I contemplated saying 'never mind' as soon as the words slipped from my lips. My voice wouldn't allow me to retract my question. I leaned against the wall and slid down after several seconds of awkward silence.

"They don't just drop 'em," his thick southern accent rung in.

My ears perked up. He was going to talk or continue talking. He was going to explain away my fifteen years with a logical explanation. He was going to explain why inflation on drug sentences was up, and murder was down.

"It's all about who you know and what you can afford," He said it matter-of-factly. He was right.

"I'm a first-time offender. I ain't never been caught before. Shit is crazy. My cousin, he is serving 10 years of probation in Texas. He ain't never been sentenced to no time. I'll tell you what it is, tainting stock." Again, he presented his story as if it were nothing new.

"Huh?" I didn't understand. Perhaps he didn't know that he wasn't telling his story in a way that only a person truly listening could follow.

"Ten years, three years. For what. I'm sitting on fifteen for something that ain't me."

"Ain't you. Aww man, it ain't none of us." He laughed, "Ain't no one ever did nothing. You wouldn't be in here for doing nothing."

"They use your story to bite you in the ass." G's words rang through my head. I wanted to speak on what I felt was my injustice, but I bit my tongue instead.

"Well," he continued, "they getting lighter on the sentencing. We getting off with a lot more shit these days."

I was confused. Who was getting off with a lot more shit? Surely, he couldn't be talking about me, *my kind.* I stayed quiet and let him continue.

"My cousin, he was hauling them drugs from across that border in El Paso, made a couple stops along the way and made it all the way to Dallas. He was home free. He had even gotten pulled over for speeding in Abilene near the prison. No one searched him. He was free and in the clear. We call him Lucky. Should have named that kid Retarded. He gets home from Dallas and goes to the bar. I tell you, he got shit faced. Got in the car, left it running at a gas station. Well he got a drug charge. Man Del, something. I forget what they call it. He had the whole kit and caboodle. Lucky had a few pounds of weed, a shitload of methamphetamines, and some personals. I don't remember how much he had, but I know what was left after his drop-offs. I'm willing to assume he had a good amount.

But see. It's who you know. The lawyer swept in the courtroom, and all the sudden, it wasn't my cousin's meth. The weed, nothing. Well, the personals were found on his person. Pretty much, they settled. Deferred adjudication for the drug charges. I don't know what happened with the DWI."

I sat on the other side of the concrete wall in a cold sweat. My head throbbed. Meth. I had seen people who used meth. I wasn't a judgmental person, but I judged people who used meth. I noticed the signs on

Helena when I saw her the night I was arrested. She had the holes in her face with the sunken eyes—tell-tale signs. I couldn't see how people used that shit.

"I can't see how people use that shit." Damnit. Slipped.

"No really, I can't either," He said agreeing with me. "I was using that shit. It will fuck your mind up, man. That's how I got here. My cousin, he violated probation twice because he was high on meth doing crazy shit."

I was surprised that the conversation continued. He was quiet at first. I was practically begging him to speak, and now he was speaking more than what I required. He had my attention. Every word he spoke left me more irritated. Yet, every word he spoke, I clung to, compared, and craved an explanation.

"What happened to you?" I asked him more curious than I was before.

"Well, man. I don't really like talking 'bout that shit. Things just went awry. I didn't mean for them to go the way they did. It was a young gal. She said the wrong thing. I shot her. The lawyer said the gun went off. The DA had a plea. I had three years and manslaughter."

His story ended, and I was left unsatisfied. I wanted to probe deeper, but the sound of footsteps started down the corridor again. My eyes were starting to weigh heavy, and my headache was in full swing. I ended the conversation requesting his name.

"Derek."

Derek was his name. No last name is given. Just Derek. Many things were left floating after the conversation. I felt no peace from having talked to him, and I felt no more enlightened or understanding of my sentence than I did before he gave me his and his cousin's undetailed stories. There were too many gaps. He didn't tell stories the way I needed them told. He told them as if I was supposed

to understand the particulars; I didn't.

"Read." G's voice rang in my ears. G would tell me to read. He explained many times that there was no way to get to the truth without picking up a book. I laid on the bed with my curiosity eating away at my mind. The quietness in the corridors allowed me to think to the point of a headache. My obsession with understanding my sentencing drove me insane. Solitary confinement helped me none. G and Marvy made my time feel doable, but they were not available in the quiet confines of solitary.

Fifteen years were not doable in solitary. I had too much time to think. I could envision myself reading and becoming focused while in prison. I would come out of prison a scholar like so many others. I would possibly quit eating pork and proclaim myself to be Muslim. I would be enlightened. Woke. I would change my name to Shareef or some shit like that.

I could picture many nights and days passing by. Getting older. Being fifteen years older than I was now. My child would be 15 years old. So much for the theory of only doing two days like Marvy said. He swore you only did the day you came in and the day you got out. The joke was on me, I had already done 116 days in prison. Not including what I had spent in solitary confinement.

I didn't mean to count the days; the days counted themselves. I couldn't help but keep a running record of the mornings I opened my eyes to the same thing. I felt a strange gloomy feeling start to come over me. I never felt one quite like it before. My mind started to shut down, and tears started to build in the corners of my eyes. The feeling was nameless, but I could tell it wasn't going to be a passing feeling.

I closed my eyes several times, trying to sleep. They wouldn't stay closed long enough to count. Eventually, I quit fighting and allowed my eyes to peel open and stare at the ceiling. My mind fluttered about. Faces wove in and out of my head. *Paola. Jairo. Paola. G. Marvy. Paola. Dante. Paola. Paola. Mama. Paola. Mr. Donaldson.*

Damn. Mr. Donaldson.

It had fallen from my mind. He had fallen from my mind. Now it swarmed around with the other thoughts that I couldn't free myself from. It was true that one could become so preoccupied in one thing that they forget the others. I could not forget Mr. Donaldson. I could not forget *suspect.* Even more, I could not forget my sentence. The strange gloomy feeling hit me again. This time harder than before, and I cried. I cried like I wanted to when Mama passed. I didn't have enough time to cry then. I had to figure everything out. I had time now. And I used it to cry.

I cried until my eyes got heavy enough for me to fall asleep. Before they could fully close, images of Dante popped into my mind. I felt anger. I wasn't quite sure why. His face swam around in my head, laughing, and taunting me. I closed my eyes to get rid of his face. It didn't help. His face was engraved in my mind, laughing. Then, Mike's face made its debut. Fat, red, and teasing, his face filled my mind. It laughed as well. For a second, it seemed as if Dante and Mike laughed in unison.

I tossed and turned across the small twin bed. The laughter continued. I smacked my face to get rid of the sound. No result. I clasped my hands to my ears and pushed them in so tightly that my arms grew tired. The laughing only increased in volume. It was beyond deafening. It sounded like nails on a chalkboard. It was so loud I was sure the guards down the corridor could hear it. As the laughter continued, my tears dried up and started to stain my face. I laid still allowing the laughter to torture me. Once I stopped trying to get rid of the sound, the laughter died down. A smile cracked across my face, and a small chuckle rose from deep within me.

It was a chuckle at first. It was a small chuckle that turned into a big chuckle. From that big chuckle erupted laughter. It was laughter more sinister than Dante's and Mike's. It felt good. It felt like revenge. It felt like control. It felt like a laugh got stuck in my throat, and I began to choke on it. I coughed to get it out, and instead of the laugh that relieved me, I coughed out a cry that sent me back into a dizzying spell of tears.

Thump. Thump. Thump.

"You alright in there? You having a mental break or something?"

I didn't respond.

Thump. Thump. Thump.

"Answer me, boy."

It must have been the rude guard. I hadn't listened to pay attention to the footsteps, but I could tell by his tone. I sat still in silence. I quietly refused to obey his command. I readjusted my pillow for comfort. My book slid out and fell to the floor.

"Alright. You're obviously alive in there. Next time you answer me, or I'll have you hang yourself like that Bland bitch," he whispered the last half into my cell.

Bland. Sandra. She had a name. She didn't hang herself. She was killed. Murder, not suicide. I coughed again to recover my laugh. I leaned over to pick up the fallen book.

Mein Kampf.

I clutched the book and darted over to the cell door to catch the guard's attention before he made it too far down the corridor. I slid the book through my meal slot and waited to hear it hit the ground on the other side. I heard the footsteps scurry back to my cell door, and once I could tell they were in front of my door, I whispered through the doorway, "You remind me of Hitler's bitch."

I walked calmly back over to my bed and laid still as the keys jingled in the cell door, and I saw his face for the first time. He was every bit of what I pictured him to be. He was heavy with brown eyes and brown hair. His cheeks were rosy pink, and his uniform fit like a plumber's dream. *Sloppy,* was the first impression he gave me. The ass-whooping he gave me was everything but.

The other guard on duty never came to see what the commotion was about. It was just the plumber and me. The more he beat me, the number I felt. When he finished, he turned to exit my cell and snapped a "Hitler Salute" as he walked out.

I couldn't help but laugh as I finally closed my eyes to get the sleep I had been fighting for. Hitler, I thought to myself. I chuckled slightly feeling accomplished. I had to suffer an ass whooping to make it happen, but it happened. While the guard was connecting his boot with every surface area of my body he could find, I made sure that he connected with my ribs and I made sure that I would bruise. I knew a lot of things were overlooked in prison, so I made sure to catch a name as well.

I slept in pain peacefully that night thinking of the letter that I would be writing to Paola and Jairo regarding my new beating. Paola would have a fit and without a doubt, call a lawyer. I would make sure to get placed into the infirmary to document my injuries. In my mind, this ass whooping, along with the one from Officer Brown, would work to my benefit.

~ ~ ~

My request for medical attention would go unanswered until I was released from solitary.

Chapter 19

If it is by Design,
Fire the Designer

"His name is Derek," I told G, relieved to be back in my old cell talking to someone I could see. G finished putting on his orange flip flops and turned to make his bed.

"He said he in here for killing some girl he was dating." I continued to talk to G while his back faced me. G wasn't engaged in the conversation; he was too fixed on making sure the corners of his bed were tucked neatly. I contemplated whether I wanted to keep telling my story to G, and I decided against it. I figured it would be better to wait until we were around Marvy. Marvy would pay attention.

"I am tired of making up this bed," G spouted.

I glanced over at the bed. It wasn't really made. The neatest part of the whole spread were the corners that he spent too many minutes tucking. The top of the bed looked as if someone had been wrestling on it. I got up to help him smooth the top of the bedspread. G was heavyset, and his labored breathing was becoming more audible with every finger he lifted. G was undeniably lazy, but he was also ill, and I knew he needed help.

"What was you saying about this Derek, kid?" G asked me as I smoothed the top of his bed, making all the wrinkles invisible.

He was listening. I thought to myself. I still thought it might be better to wait till we were around Marvy, but being typical Rilei, my mouth started moving at one-hundred miles an hour as I tried to recount my whole solitary confinement experience.

"Awww shit man, that's that little white kid that be running around here talking all that shit. He a little liar. That's what he is," G sat on the bed, breathing hard after his quick rant. I helped him onto his bed while my eyes begged him to tell me more. Once he was seated and his breathing calmed, I asked, "why you say he a liar?"

"He a pervert man. That boy raped and killed a young girl. Burned the house down behind himself. What should have been arson, rape, and murder was manslaughter. You tell me how that shit work. It was a big story, man, how you miss that?"

I don't know. I was hustling trying to survive. I was trying to make a living and make things right for my family. On the outside of the prison, the real world was happening, and it wasn't stopping for anyone. Jairo always told me to stay informed, **READ,** but the hours in the day didn't add up to enough time to do it all. Now, here I was with G, listening to him start another lecture.

The guard came and opened the cell. It was time for breakfast. G paused his lecture while we were ushered out of our cell and patted down. Once we made our way to the chow hall, we were greeted by Marvy.

"Rilei, my man. You back," Marvy greeted me with excitement and a strong pat on the back.

G eyed Marvy, "let me tell you what this nigga done."

Marvy stared at me with an "uh oh" face. "Tell me what he done, G. He just got out here. He couldn't have done much."

"That kid Derek, the pervert, the one that raped that young black girl..."

My eyes lit up as G voice trailed off into the distance of my mind. *Young black girl.* I heard it repeatedly in my head. I don't know why it tripped me up so much, but I thought of mother. She was a young black girl.

"Wait a minute, if he did all that G, why was he only charged with manslaughter? He got a three-year sentence," I said as we sat down at our table with our trays.

"You think I gotta lie to you. First, I told you not to go around here sniffing out other people's business and not to be out here telling yours. Why you know so much about this kid in solitary? Solitary is a solo experience. Now you up there mingling and sharing bunk stories with..."

"A deplorable," Marvy said, cutting G off, "Look Rilei. I know you. I was you. You out here lost trying to make sense of something that ain't gone never make sense. It's bad blood with them kinds from Derek's side."

"What you mean 'Derek's side'?" I had to ask. I was confused about how this conversation turned from a simple conversation to such a serious one. I wanted to tell them how he had three years and find out what else they knew about the case. I wanted them to help me make sense of my fifteen-year sentence.

Marvy looked at my face closely, "I know you hate hearing this, but white is white in here, and black is black. It's like that out there too, beyond this fence. It's just like that; which is why for the life of me, I can't understand how you was running the streets with a lil' white kid at your heels."

"It's different times, man," I said to Marvy and G with a straight face. "If you knew Dante, you would understand. He didn't have it easy. His mom was strung out, his daddy dead, man he was living in the 'jects, sleeping outside, trying to survive just like me."

"No, not just like you." G eyed me carefully, making sure that I registered how serious he was. "Look, I know what they say about the race card. I know what you thinking but let me tell you what's real. Dante was unfortunate, maybe so, but he's a casualty of the design, a casualty of war."

"Yep, that's right, the war on black people," Marvy chimed in.

"Listen here, man," G leaned said seriously, "YOU are part of the design. You are the motivation for the design, the victim of the design. It is as it was intended. For that, you and Dante could never be the same. You don't know how to look past yourself, that's why you're worthless. You too caught up in your own shit, you're no good for your people. I don't say this shit to offend you, I say it cause it's true and if I tell you the truth you can do better."

I felt worthless. I had felt this way plenty of times in my life, but I never had someone bold enough to confirm it for me. I challenged G, "How do I do better man? How you figure I'm worthless."

G gave a reckless laugh that intimidated me a little. "Nigga, 'cause I said you is."

Marvy chimed in, "Rilei, in the months you been here, have you learned nothing? Your mother, you said she was raped, where is her rapist? Why isn't he in jail? You in here on a fifteen-year sentence, for some drugs. It's murderers in here for less time. Why you think that is? It's so much going on in the world today, what you know about any of it? Nothing. How can you change shit and you don't know shit? You don't care. You don't care that a white man got off scot-free raping someone; you only care that it was your mother. You selfish. A selfish man is worthless."

"I'm no Martin Luther..." I started as G cut me off.

"Fuck Martin Luther King my ass. He was a pawn. Yea, he had some good moments, he did some good things, but he was a pawn. A black man that can be controlled and led by a white man can't do nothing for me."

"Hold on now G," Marvy interrupted. "Don't say fuck, Martin; we may disagree, but he was an integral part of getting us to where we are. We gotta respect that. The man took a risk and ass whippings. He not worthless."

"Marvy shut up. Y'all listen here. He set us up to think equality was what we wanted. Who the hell wants to be equal? Malcolm X said in his *House Nigga vs. Field Nigga* speech that the white man gave us a little something to hold onto, and we started running around thinking life is great. Separate the 'have a little, from the don't have shit,' and the 'have a little' will be loyal to you. They sold us a dream, gave a few of us a path to get there, and shut the door to the rest of us. Then they blamed us for our own downfall. Now before you start in on your philosophical shit Marvy, listen to what I am saying. I'm telling you that all this shit is by design. You know that Marvy, but for this stupid motherfucka right here, it's a design. You got fifteen years because it was designed for you to get fifteen years. Psychological theories from way back in the day described the biological features of a classic black man and used the features as the forefront of their study. They called us degenerates. Our features were indicative of criminal behavior. Can you believe that shit? The first features of man, indicative of a fucking criminal. That's how I know criminality is defined by society and oppressors. Move further, start talking about control theory and all that other goofball shit. It always describes the climates that blacks are put in.

We were brought over here during the Trans-Atlantic slave trade and stripped of everything we knew. Our culture was ripped out of us, and we were forced to conform. Then we got some idiot talking about slavery was a choice. How when they mind-fucking us? Got rid of our language, separated us from our families, and beat us. They made you scared to live but gave you just enough to not want to die. Maybe you had a kid around or a wife. They left a will to comply is what they did."

"Man, what this got to do with my sentence G. What this got to do with anything," I asked. It was too much information for me to process. I believed G, but what he spoke of was from the olden days, and I could not find how it applied to me or my life.

"Marvy talk to him before I fuck him up." G ordered Marvy. "No better yet, I got this. What happened to you in solitary, Rilei. Tell Marvy about what the guard did."

"He beat my ass."

"Don't be modest. Tell him what the guard did."

"He bruised my ribs up really bad because I was talking shit. I was trying to get sent to the infirmary. Figured I could get a phone call because I was injured. At worst, I thought I would catch G up there for his shots. I was gone tell him to phone my peoples about the guard and the original police. I wanted to see if it would help with an appeal. They didn't send me."

Marvy cracked a smile. I could tell he was trying to contain his laughter. He couldn't. He busted out into hysterics.

"You thought they were gone send you to the infirmary after a guard whipped your ass. You thought that it would help with an appeal. Rilei, you too smart to be so damn dumb. An appeal deals with your court proceedings. If things didn't go right in court, not no shit you doing in here. Next, these guards don't give a damn 'bout you. Ain't no one risking they job by sending yo black ass to the infirmary, especially if they the one who whipped yo ass."

"Ok, I get it. But what does that have to do with the shit G was saying," I asked Marvy getting irritated by his and G's long-winded lecture? I couldn't see where it was headed, and I felt like it was an attempt to make me feel ignorant.

"All G is saying was it is by design," Marvy said calmly.

"No that's not all the fuck I'm saying. I'm ranting. A school in Georgia is teaching kids that Europeans did not go to Africa and kidnap slaves. They telling them that Africans were obsessed with 'fancy' European goods, weapons, and shit. They teaching them babies that they traded prisoners for these things. You talk about a half-ass truth. You from that era, huh Rilei? This the shit you learning in school, huh? Yea, Africa sold off its prisoners. Africa was a rich continent, not no dump like what they put on the TV. We were somebody we came from greatness. They sold us, traded us, true. The Africans swore they didn't know the treatment we would receive, but that's neither here nor there. The other half of that is that Europeans also kidnapped us.

See you gotta know ya history Rilei. You too selfish. Only concerned with what directly affects you. Let me tell you a secret, what affects your people, affects you. Now, look at you. In jail. Crying about fifteen years. Welcome to the new form of slavery, if ya eyes was open you would have seen it coming. How you get your hands on them great drugs from out the country. U.S know everything about everyone, air travel is communicated. Dope used to be shipped over here on military planes. Yes, that shit is coming over here from other countries and you telling me the government don't know. They let you get it in your hands. Sell it to your people. Rip apart the black family dynamic. Take the black man from home. Leave a single mother to raise a son and repeat the cycle. Then they arrest you and throw you in prison for it."

I agreed. I wondered if the higher powers knew about Jairo if they knew that he had flown drugs in and out of his country. If not, I wondered would they care if they did know. I thought about Dante being a casualty. He was the son of a single mother due to drugs. I wondered if the higher powers would be angered at the flaw in their design, or if it was just a risk, they had to take for the greater agenda.

Marvy saw me in deep thought while G continued to speak.

"They're indoctrinating you from a young age. They're teaching you what they want you to know and how they want you to think. They're teaching, through their textbooks, about you. Got you believing your own kind are savages, ignorant, and the only way to be normal is to fit into their standard. They got our women believing in European beauty and not their own. What that sound like Rilei? Do it sound like when I just told you they brought us here and stripped our culture?

They make you work for them. Blood, sweat, and tears to build they country. Make you think it's an honor to fight in their wars that benefit you none. They burn, tar, lynch, and drag you by the tail of their pickups. Then, they say that a peaceful protest is the best protest if it is out the way and does not bother them too much. If it bothers them, they blackball you, or they arrest you. What that sound like Rilei?

A white officer kills an unarmed black man; it's broadcasted on the news. His body is left to sit, it's a warning. It warns niggas pay attention and beware. Stay in your place.' What that sound like dammit?"

I hadn't counted the seconds that Mr. Donaldson body laid on the cold pavement in front of his house. I wasn't there to know how long he was out there. I could understand G's point, however. It was like parading the death of our people like a warning. It was like saying, this could be you if you step out of line.

G continued. I continued to listen.

"They argue the relevance of our death by police, an organization meant to protect and serve, with black on black crime. The design. They never mention white on white crime. White on everyone else crime. No, the fact that we kill our own kind makes it ok for anyone else to join in. 'Shut up nigga.' What that sound like, man? Come on, Rilei, I know you hear me talking.

That white cop in Dallas went in that apartment and murdered that black man. Man, his record was squeaky clean without a scratch on it. They had to bring up the weed in his apartment.

They just killed a black security guard who stopped a mass murderer. What that sound like, Rilei?

Mr. Donaldson was his name right, the guy you were up in arms about?

They just killed him. You knew him. Was he a burglar, a robber? You think he was breaking and entering. Is this too much for you Rilei?"

Tears swelled in my eyes. G continued to talk. I continued to listen as my ears accepted what G was saying.

"I ain't tryna make you cry, man. I'm trying to paint the picture. You see the little strokes, but you standing to close to see the painting for the picture it's showing. Look. If you have all the food in the world. If you have control of it and you tell a group of hungry people with families to feed, that you are going to place a single piece of pie out there and the first one to grab it is the one that will eat, what you think they gone do? You gone have a real, live hunger game out here. That's what we have. Few opportunities, given at random, and we gotta fight for 'em. Fuck that, how about like I said, white people kill white people. We don't talk about that, though.

Mass murderers, they always gotta have some shit going on with them that justifies their crime. I mean really what the fuck. That kid in Los Angeles involved with that gang, he got off without even a conspiracy to commit murder. He got off with absolutely nothing. Why? Because he was just obsessed with gang culture. He didn't understand. If it ain't in your face Rilei, it's because you walking around here blind. I'm going to tell you what it is. Nothing fucking new. We still slaves. Comply, nigga.

I know I danced around the point, but I'm going to drive it home. You just ain't ready yet."

~ ~ ~

That night, I laid still in my bed, mentally exhausted. We had gotten mail earlier from mail call, and I had a dozen letters from Paola, Jairo, Ollie, and Mrs. Donaldson. I stared at the letter from Mrs. Donaldson the longest. Her delicate writing stretched across the heading of the letter.

"My Dearest Rilei,"

I didn't have the mental strength to read her letter. I looked at the letters from Jairo and Paola, they came in together in the same opened envelope. I had at least eight letters between the two of them. Three of the letters came from Ollie and just the one letter from Mrs. Donaldson. I tucked all the letters in my pillowcase and laid still.

Not one letter from Dante, I thought to myself. As much as I didn't want what G had said to me to ring true with Dante, I was starting to question it. I had made a lot of bad moves and decisions, but Dante wasn't one of them. He had been my brother since the beginning, and despite any problems we had, they were not bigger than our commitment to each other.

Or were they?

I had noticed changes with Dante, but I noticed changes within myself as well. Other people noticed things in Dante that I couldn't see, or that I could understand from knowing him. People had always been quick to give me their warnings about Dante, but I figured it was them being overprotective of me. No one ever gave Dante a chance. This much I knew to be true. Only me and Mama.

With those thoughts lingering on my mind and after months of incarceration, I decided to write Dante a letter.

~ ~ ~

Dante,

I haven't heard from you in a great deal of time. How are things holding up?

I been doing a lot of thinking in this hell hole. You know losing Mama was a lot on both of us. I appreciate everything you did to look out for me after she passed. I called myself trying to take care of us and get us in a position to where Mama would be proud. Look at where that ended me.

It is so much I don't understand about that night. So much shit went wrong that night.

Oh yea, shit. That reminds me. I saw Helena that night at the gas station. She looked like she was on that upgrade. Had holes in her face and everything. She might have been with some dude that I seen recording the event. Even so, she saw the shit that went down that night, she was so close, I wouldn't be surprised if she could tell someone what happened play by play. With those being my hopes, try to find her bro. Her knowledge could help me in an appeal.

Look, I'm going to be straight with you. I read Mein Kampf. I can't understand what you would be doing with a book like that, but I don't judge you, man. I saw you with it before, and I made it my business to read that book because I felt like you were different at the time. I had heard of it before, so I made sure to read. I don't know what the fuck you would be doing with a book like that, but I won't judge you!!

It was dope in the rental Dante. That officer planted that meth, I know he did. I don't think he planted the dope though. You brought me the rental. They researched who it was rented under, the rental agreement was under some female name with me listed as a driver as well. I have to serve, Dante. I don't want to point fingers. You weren't at any of my hearings. I haven't had anything come my way from you. It feels different. I won't lie.

I defend you when folks point out what seems to be obvious. Mr. Donaldson is dead. I defended you with him. I hate to think that I would be missing 15 years of my kid's life, my family, man. You knew what this shit was to me. I just hate to think that I am missing out and that you could possibly be the reason. I know you don't gotta answer me, especially while I am in here. For the sake of our brotherhood though, clear up what is unclear for me. Solve this mystery.

You are on my visitor list. If I don't see or hear from you, I guess I know what it is.

—Rilei

Chapter 20

Heard It Through the Grapevine

Time passed quickly. Every day was easier than the last. It came to a point where I could predict the time of the day just by what was happening around me. A lot of tension died down, or at least it wasn't apparent.

G continued with his rambles and lectures, as did Marvy. I was learning a lot. I was reading more books than I ever had before. That was something I knew Mama would be proud of. Jairo and Paola were working with Ollie, and the lawyer on my appeal; Marvy and G were impressed with my growing knowledge of my history.

I had read Mrs. Donaldson's letter but never wrote her back. So much pain was revealed in the letter that I could never put the right words together to console her. So, I didn't try. She had made me aware that she intended to sell the house and move. She promised she would send me a new address as soon as she had one. More than anything, she revealed what happened the night Mr. Donaldson was shot. He was attempting to get into her car because she had locked her keys inside. She was parked on the street in front of their house, and Mr. Donaldson felt that he could free her keys himself.

Mrs. Donaldson made it clear that Mr. Donaldson would never do the things he was accused of doing and that law enforcement had no intention of clearing his name, even in death. She was more upset that they tried to make a criminal out of him once they killed him, rather than simply apologizing for their mistake.

Her letter was so intense. You could feel the pain while reading it. I hated knowing that a woman who cared so much about other people was being disregarded in the death of her husband; yet, I didn't know what I could say to make her pain go away.

Mr. Donaldson was unarmed when he was shot. He wouldn't be the first unarmed man killed this year by the police. All I could think of was what G and Marvy had said so many times before: "They only make you think you can have a piece of the American Pie."

Many times, I wanted what G and Marvy said to be anything but the truth. Time and time again, things kept happening to make their words seem fact. Including Dante.

Dante never got back to me. He never responded, never wrote, and never visited. When the lawyer for my appeal requested character letters, he told me that he personally asked Dante, and Dante didn't hesitate to refuse.

It was long before I had heard from Ollie that Dante had been caught up in a drug raid. I was sure that Dante would meet the same fate I did, and we would have plenty of time to discuss our differences while he was locked up alongside me. Like everything else that I was sure of, I was wrong.

Dante didn't meet my same fate. Ollie informed me that Dante had received probation. Five years of probation to be exact. In all fairness, he wasn't caught with as much dope as I had been, and it wasn't in a car. All being the same, Dante had priors as an adult. I didn't. Ollie also said Dante had a bomb lawyer. I didn't.

I didn't know how to make these things fit into the scope of what Marvy and G would preach to me, yet, I also didn't know how to make them not fit. Dante's and my situation were different but equally punishable. Marvy and G would have me to believe that this was strictly because he was white, but they would have bypassed the fact that he had a good attorney by his side.

I had started to notice the difference in treatment in the prison that convinced me that maybe G and Marvy weren't far from the truth after all. Gang relations in prison were high. It seemed that the black gangs were reprimanded and given official misconducts more than anyone else. Of course, this would be me on the outside looking in, but it became clear when a fight broke out in the chow hall one day.

Several guards and witnesses were around to verify the start of the fight. It was the result of the racial conversations struck up by none other than Marvy himself. The conversation was the focus of almost every black in the chow hall. So much was going on with police shootings, and black murders that it had crept its way into prison conversations.

It was then, at the peak of the conversation, that some uninvited bystanders chimed in. At first, they had my attention. Although uninvited, the guy who spoke up – spoke with logic.

"It's the way you all carry yourselves. Pants down your ass, no couth. Lazy bunches of people, entitled. You all think the world owe you something, but the world owes no one nothing. I'm not saying that no wrong has ever been done to your people, but you guys want to live on that and build off that, and the rest of the world is over it."

He made sense to me. I didn't let it show because it would be the end of me, and G would never stop complaining.

And just like I knew he would, G jumped in. "Oh yeah, tell me more about my people."

The young white guy bit the bait.

"Well, look I don't want to come off at you all wrong," the young white guy spoke timidly, "I just think that sometimes people add to their own problems. The *Black Lives Matter* movement, for example. You guys will rally for police shooting your kind, but you all shoot your kind every day. I'm just saying, police shoot white people too. We don't parade around saying white lives matter.

We don't all come from wealth and the best neighborhood, some of us work hard to get where we are. Some of us lose a spot that we earn fair and square due to affirmative action. They say we are racist, but the truth is some of you are more racist than we could ever be. My parents taught me not to see color, but to see a man's heart and judge his character. My dad hired mostly blacks to run his shop, and he never took so many losses until he did, from his employees stealing from him."

Marvy interrupted him this time, "Say, young fella, gone find you something else to do. You don't even know the meaning of racism, let alone what the hell you talking 'bout."

The white guy stood his ground, timid, yet determined to make his point.

He started to speak again, "I mean no disrespect. I just thought you could use another side of the story. You know that there is three. Life could be so much simpler if we all learned to live together. We have to let go of the past to build a better future. It's easy to demonize whites, but that's because y'all need someone to blame. I get it, but how do we move forward?"

He was in the wrong area of the mess hall. I looked around the tables, gathering the looks on everyone faces. Half of them were in a stupor, the other half were enraged. G spoke first.

"Racism, young man, racism is about power. It's a privilege to be able to be racist. My kind, as you put it, don't have that privilege. I'm prejudiced as a mothafucka though and let me tell you why Emmett Till. That white woman admitted to lying. What's that, conspiracy to murder? What's the statute of limitations on that Marvy?"

The white guy interrupted again, "OJ Simpson. He killed that woman. Never did a day in prison for it."

A guy sitting at the end of our table, not much younger looking than myself, cut his eyes at G. It was obvious by his face that he did not understand how we were allowing someone to talk to us in such a manner. G held his finger up, silencing anyone who thought it would ok to speak up or rise up. G had that kind of power. Many of the youngsters knew better than to disobey G, and the old heads respected him.

"Listen, I got an invisible leash around the cats at this table, all of them are ready to eat you alive, but I'm curious. My curiosity is saving you right now. OJ is an idiot, went to prison for stealing his own shit. But we both know what the problem is, and until everyone acknowledges, there will be no moving on. Now, let me let you in on a secret." G spoke seriously through gritted teeth.

"What's that?" The white guy asked less timid than before.

A crowd of white onlookers started to form around the white guy. I could tell that a touch of confidence surged through him that had not there before. The guards stood still in their designated areas, watching.

Tension filled the air. There was so much obvious hostility that my adrenaline kicked into full swing. My heart was beating uncontrollably fast, and I could feel a more physical confrontation coming our way. G remained calm.

Marvy removed his reading glasses from his face and placed them on the table. He looked up at G with irritation, as if to say, "you always starting shit."

G didn't bother to acknowledge Marvy's stare. Instead, G kept his eyes on the white representative and allowed a full smile to cover his face. G was excited, this kind of tension seemed to entertain G.

I looked around to get a better picture of what was going on. Around the white guy who had spoken boldly and out of turn, now stood several other white guys. I didn't have the patience to count them, but I could estimate that there were more of them than us.

In prison, the lines were clear. You belonged to your race. Stronger than any gang wars were race wars. No lines were more clearly defined than the lines of race. I hated that. Not everyone was an enemy. I had spoken to several cool white boys while I had been locked up. One of them I even worked with on laundry detail. He was a cool guy from Michigan. I could relate to him on many different levels. But at this moment, he stood where he had to stand, and that wasn't with me at my table. At this moment, he had also become an enemy.

G looked at the gathering crowd and said in a playful tone as he watched them continue to gather: "Don't you threaten me with a good time," G looked back over at the white guy who had spoken his truths, and with a sinister and eerie tone said: "Run."

No one moved. The white representative's faithful entourage stood still. I blinked once and opened my eyes to a tray flying across the table that we sat at. G dropped his finger that once held everyone at bay. All at once, it was as if the invisible leash was dropped. The guy who sat at the end of the table leaped into the air onto the table and took a running start into the gathered crowd of white people. He leaped off the table directly into the middle of the crowd. Not even a second later, his body dropped with a loud thud. Through the crowd, I could see one of the men pulling what looked like a toothbrush out the side of his neck while those closest to him kicked and punched him.

With that, G stood up, and everyone else at the table followed. Everyone moved so quickly that the table flipped over, and we trampled over each other to get to our assumed enemy.

There was no organization. I stood back for a minute and watched as everyone collided with anger and emotion. It looked like a civil war on a World War III scale. I could see G and Marvy moving through the crowd of white men swinging. G still wore a smile on his face. I could tell he was enjoying every moment of it. Marvy wore a more serious look. He didn't seem to get much pleasure out of it. Instead, he seemed to be annoyed.

I continued to observe. I felt guilty for watching, but I was more interested in seeing the action than being a part of it. I noticed Marvy using his eyeglass handle to quickly stick and move through the crowd. I admired Marvy's tactics. He was resourceful, wise, and understanding. He was also reliable and always ready to do what he needed to do.

In my moments of admiration, Marvy made eye contact with me. He noticed me standing in the corner, uninvolved. A look of disappointment started across his face as the guard came up from behind him and clocked him in the head with a baton. I looked around and noticed all the people who had been sitting with me being clocked in the head one by one by the guards. The white guys either continued to fight or were pulled off and held down.

I started to move toward the commotion to warn G, but before I could take a step in that direction, I felt something move swiftly across my head, and the room went dark.

I woke up to find tear gas clouding the room and everyone being evacuated out of the chow hall. The fight resulted in telephone, commissary, and visiting privileges being stripped. Some individuals were thrown into the hole, but none that I knew personally.

With all the punishments being thrown around, it was painfully obvious that everyone wasn't punished the same. Namely, the white guys who were involved. I found it funny because a prisoner died during the brawl. The young guy who sat at the end of my table and was the first of us to take a stand was fatally stabbed. It was obvious at that point that all G had felt, was relevant, as I watched the man who was responsible for killing him, make his commissary run.

Marvy had taken a different stance with me. He had noticed that I was not involved with the brawl in a way that he felt I should have been and had limited his communication with me. Marvy made G aware, but G didn't show obvious signs of sharing Marvy's disappointment. Instead, G cautioned me that if I ever stood still in a brawl again, I would not have to worry about serving my fifteen-year prison stint.

I heeded G's warning, but I felt compelled to explain my side of the story. I explained to G that I didn't intentionally avoid the confrontation, but instead, I froze at the bigger picture of the confrontation. I told G that seeing the brawl was like watching everything he said come to life. I had noticed how the guards separated the brawl and noticed the methods they used to do so. I was so entranced by it that I couldn't interfere.

"I thought about that guy, Dylan Roof, G. I thought about how he shot up that church and made it out alive, armed, and dangerous. I thought about his public claim of hatred. I thought about the guy who killed those people outside of Kroger. You know, the white man who killed that black woman and that black man for no other reason than they were black. I don't know G, watching that brawl, I thought about all that. I realized something that you and Marvy been trying to tell me, and I shut down."

G was interested. He could tell that his and Marvy's lectures had finally settled.

"Oh yeah," G said, "and what did you finally realize."

"I realized that all this shit is by design. I realized that we are an inferior people because we allow ourselves to be inferior people. We don't unite strategically, we unite out of emotion and anger, but not out of sheer necessity. G, they outnumbered y'all, but I still seen y'all fighting as if life depended on it. It took the guards to intervene to save their asses.

I realized that we come from greatness, and we gotta tap into it before we let them convince us any further that we don't possess it. We gotta unite because we simply must unite, we can't wait until shit happen. We can't only stand by each other in prison, or in time of emotional distress. We gotta stand by each other period, G. I'll be there in any brawl from now on, standing by my brothers. Not because we are angry at what someone said or at some bullshit that went down, but because that's the bigger picture. I fucked up G. I am sorry. "

G stared at me with a smile spreading across his face. It no longer mattered that I did not fight alongside him and Marvy. G knew that I understood at that moment, and that was the only fight he cared for me to win.

~ ~ ~

After the brawl, things changed. Once privileges were reinstated, I received all my mail and was able to call out to Paola and Jairo to check on the appeal. After receiving the news that all was going well with the appeal, I was able to gather the courage to call Mrs. Donaldson

Gathering the words to say to her was still a challenge, but hearing her voice eased all my anxiety. Through the phone, she sounded as if she had aged a bit. Her voice was weary and tired. Hearing me on the other end of the phone seemed to put a small amount of excitement in her tone.

We talked until my time was up, never once mentioning Mr. Donaldson. I had decided that if she did not bring him up, then neither would I, even if during the whole conversation, my mind continuously wandered to him.

Mrs. Donaldson rambled on about her new apartment and her new living conditions. She was excited to hear about Paola and find out that I was a father. She said she always wanted to be a grandmother, and that I was still a son to her. She apologized for letting CPS take me away all those years ago and blamed herself for my being in jail. She felt that if she had fought harder to keep me, then my life would have been different. And maybe it would have, but I explained to her that my path had to go as such because I had my own path to follow.

She noticed the new man I was becoming. She recognized that I had always been smart, but she noticed something different about my intelligence. Mrs. Donaldson said she noticed that I had become more enlightened. And with that, she asked me about Dante.

In all the years that Mrs. Donaldson dedicated to me, she told me that she put effort into Dante because she could tell that it meant something to me. Mrs. Donaldson assured me that my heart and kindred spirit were nothing to be ashamed of, but instead, something to cherish. "You will be blessed," is what she said to me.

Mrs. Donaldson said that she noticed that things were different in Dante's spirit than they were in mine. She hoped that love would change it, but she knew that it was a slim shot. She was relieved to hear that I had severed ties with Dante, and she believed that it was for the best.

It made me feel better to hear these things coming from Mrs. Donaldson. It was different than hearing it from everyone else because I knew that Mrs. Donaldson cared. After ending the conversation with Mrs. Donaldson, I returned to my cell and started another letter to Ollie.

While locked up, Ollie had been a reliable source for me. He kept in contact and, along with Paola and Jairo, he made sure to keep as much money as I could need on my books. He visited just as much as Paola and Jairo and showed just as much interest in my case.

Jairo grew to like Ollie and told me in one of his letters that he was going to extend an olive branch to Ollie for all the loyalty he showed to me. Jairo was nothing like the man I thought he was. He was ruthless, but underneath it all, he was a man about his family. If he considered you family or found you to be loyal to someone then he considered his family, he would go to extremes for you.

Ollie had shown great loyalty, and he showed a great work ethic. Jairo loved that. In Ollie's letters, he described everything going on in the streets in so much detail that I felt like I was out there with him. He kept in communication with Dante, but he reported back to Jairo or me all that was going on.

Ollie had grown to distrust Dante after finding out that Dante was possibly the one who planted the cocaine in my car. Ollie, the one who I once thought of as the "Gentle Giant," was anything but. He wanted to plot revenge on Dante, and the only thing keeping Dante safe was my unwillingness to approve anything happening to Dante.

Ollie had informed me that Dante had been in contact with Helena and was possibly getting the relationship he craved from her since they were using together. It was unrealistic to me that Dante would take a turn in the direction of a junkie, but I didn't let the thought consume me. Far as I was concerned, Dante could be whatever he wanted to be, if it wasn't having an impact on my life.

Ollie understood how I felt. He was like the big brother I never had, and he looked out for me. He once questioned where I was when he got out of jail and why I had stopped communicating with him. He told me that for a period, only Dante wrote to him, and he questioned my loyalty. Dante had told him that I had run off to Florida to go to school and do my own thing while abandoning him and showing no regard for Ollie. Dante had also told Ollie that I had killed Unc.

Ollie held hard feeling about Unc's death. I never put much thought into figuring out Ollie's and Unc's relationship, but I later found out that Unc was really Ollie's Uncle. I thought that it was just a nickname Unc had gained from being an OG, but it was what Ollie called him because it was short for Uncle.

Unc was Ollie's mother's baby brother. Ollie said that Unc was all he had left of his mother, and when Dante told him I killed him for no good reason, he had washed his hands of me. He connected what Dante told him about my leaving for Florida with me killing Unc. He thought I was on the run. He didn't want to believe Dante because he felt I wasn't that type of person, but Dante told him to ask the streets about 'Spaz,' and the streets painted him a different image of who I had become.

It wasn't until I called him that night while sitting at the gas station, sounding like the same Rilei, that he felt like he heard a ghost. He said he could feel it in his spirit that I couldn't have done what Dante accused of me of doing. He said he didn't hear it in my voice. Ollie swore he had always been a good judge of character, and hearing from me assured him that he still was.

Then, he asked me about Unc. I admitted to having jumped on Unc, and I admitted that I had beaten him up pretty bad. I also told him why. Ollie couldn't deny understanding what caused me to 'spaz' on Unc. But during one of our visits, I informed him that it wasn't me who killed Unc.

I told him about how Dante froze at Unc's story, and once I had jumped on Unc, Dante followed up by unloading a clip on Unc. At this news, Ollie got up from the visiting table and left the prison without saying another word to me.

Chapter 21

No More Bad News

Things had slowed down in prison. No fights, no revenge for the young guy who was killed, no problems. Things were more relaxed than I had ever seen them before.

I had grown used to the thought of serving out my time, but I didn't allow myself to grow used to the sentence. For that reason, I stayed on Ollie, Jairo, and Paola about my appeal. It was always good news as far as filing and starting the process for my appeal, but there were never any promises of court dates or actual progress. Waiting on someone to verify that the appeal was in motion sent me into depression.

It was like experiencing let down after let down. G had warned me not to get my hopes up, but the team I had behind me was fierce, and it was hard not to place my faith in them. I knew that it would be a long process because I had watched Ollie go through it, but nothing felt longer than going through it for myself.

Paola kept my spirits going with constant pictures of our baby boy and letters. She was on top of holidays and birthdays, and I was proud to see her handling my responsibilities like a champ. I was also angered at the fact that she had to handle my responsibilities. Watching Ramon grow through pictures angered me. It wasn't the type of father I wanted to be. I could see my features in him, but I wasn't there to put my personality into him. I wasn't there to mold him. I was, in a sense, like my own father. I wanted to be anything but my father.

I wrote letters to Ramon, apologizing. Although I knew it would be a long time before he could read them, I knew that if I had to serve fifteen years, that I would at least make sure he knew that I thought of him every step of the way. It was hard to write out everything that I felt I was wrong for, but I wished that Mike would have done that for me. So, I did it for Ramon.

Jairo showed me more loyalty than I deserved. It was odd to see so much love coming from another man that had no biological ties to me when a man that was the reason for my existence didn't even acknowledge my existence. I wrote Jairo letters and made sure that at the end of every letter, I thanked him for being the father that I didn't have. Maybe even the father that I didn't deserve. Jairo admired the way I held my head up. At least he admired the way that he *thought* I held my head up. The truth was, I was drowning in misery.

Jairo was proud of the fact that I inserted Ollie into my position. He was honored that I made sure that my family was ok with whatever I could while I was incarcerated. I had Ollie checking on them daily, and I was constantly building new connections in prison to pass on to Ollie. I was putting my hands on anything I could to make sure that Paola would be straight on the outside.

Jairo knew this. He said that my heart and my efforts could be felt from miles away and that even with me in prison, he trusted Paola in my hands. I was honored, but I knew better. Everything I did was out of guilt for putting her in a position that I would have never wanted to see her in. It was the same position that my mother was forced into.

Every morning during showers, when I looked in the mirror, I could see Mike more and more. I was turning into Mike. I wasn't a pervert like Mike, but I was his son. I was a man who abandoned my child. I was a man who neglected his family, who neglected his son. I became so obsessed with a lifestyle that I put all Teigen's lessons on a shelf. I should have taken my black ass to school.

I would never tell Jairo this. It would sound ungrateful. I appreciated Jairo taking me under his wing and teaching me the ins and outs of his legacy, but I didn't want that to be my legacy. I wanted something that Mama and Ramon could be proud of. I wanted the type of money that didn't cost me *fifteen* years. I wanted legal money. I knew that when my appeal finally did come through, I would re-enter the streets a new man. I would be an enlightened man, doing it for my culture. A father, doing it for his son. And for Paola, I would be a husband, doing it for his wife. I would be a changed man, no more Spaz; but Rilei, the family man. For that reason, I mailed out every letter I sent to Jairo, Ramon, and Paola – *Rilei, the family man.*

~ ~ ~

With so much time on my side, I started looking into and reading inspirational books. I still dabbled in books meant to educate me about my culture, but I had G and Marvy for that, so I spent less time with those books.

My mood stabilized for the most part. I felt better about life and all the possibilities it had to offer, and the best part was that I was confident in who I was becoming. I knew how to defend myself when I needed to, and I knew how to stand silent when my voice was worth more than the topic of discussion. I was really coming into my own, and I had G and Marvy to thank.

The two of them taught me how to really see the person in the mirror. I was pro-black but rational. I was able to hold my own in a conversation with Marvy and G without them looking at me like I was the ignorant young kid. I was satisfied, and my past was behind me. I was no longer insecure Rilei who waited on everything to go bad. It didn't matter who I was, though, because everything eventually goes bad.

Paola came to visit me on a Saturday in the winter before Christmas. She didn't bring Ramon, which I was fine with because I didn't like for him to be in a prison. Many lessons from G and Marvy taught me that we introduce our kids to society's expectation for them when we bring them into the prison. I always asked Paola to leave Ramon home.

It was my second Christmas behind bars and the prison allowed for visits where I could touch Paola. It was different than before when there was no touching allowed, and every visit seemed too long. It was always a risk, and I was always just seconds from pouncing across the table just so that I could feel Paola's touch, or smell her vanilla scent.

This time it was different.

I sat at the table in my tan jumpsuit. I was a trustee in prison, and the tan jumpsuit signified such. I watched Paola as she entered the room in a pair of yellow pants that hugged her hips and cuffed her ass with enough respect for me not to get jealous. She wore a red, yellow, and blue blouse, and red heels. She knew I loved her in red heels.

It was our thing. She always got dressed up nice when she was coming to see me near a holiday. Her hair was pulled to the top of her head and twisted into a bun with only her baby hairs outlining her face. She was fine, with minimum effort; she was the most beautiful woman I had ever seen. My heart skipped two beats as she strutted over to the table where I sat and took a seat.

I was puzzled. I imagined her running into my arms with a huge smile on her face, but that wasn't what happened. I stared at her for a moment, confused, wondering if she remembered that we could hug now. She didn't look at me. She held her head down, and the vibe that shot across the table put a sour taste in my mouth.

"What's up Paola?" I asked her with a voice staler than the toast the prison served us for breakfast. I could tell that something wasn't right, but I was a different Rilei, and I knew how to transform wrong into right. She refused to answer me, and even worse, I saw a tear fall from the corner of her eye.

"Dante's dead, Rilei," She managed to stutter out her comment between deep breaths and quiet sobs.

I froze.

"Dante's dead?" I repeated for clarification. Before she could answer, I spoke again.

"Dante's dead."

I said it quietly to myself a few times, but I couldn't find any emotion. The words felt empty. I looked at Paola sobbing and touched my own face to see if any tears had slid down unnoticed. There were none. I had no reaction to the news, and the only thing that bothered me was seeing Paola cry.

"It's going to be ok," I told Paola getting up to console her. I wanted to feel something, but nothing came. I wanted to ask her what happened, but I didn't really feel like hearing the answer.

Hugging her, I could smell the vanilla rise from her skin. It tickled the hair in my nose as it reminded me of Mama. I remembered Mama hugging me at random times of the day and always smelling like fresh vanilla. I could hear her voice, *"what mystery did you solve today?"* I could see her standing outside on the porch looking down the street, looking toward the corner, looking, and staying up late waiting on Dante to come in. She would wait on him to come in just so she could tell him that he couldn't sleep there if he didn't respect curfew and if he insisted on staying in the streets.

"It's hard for Dante. He is going through things that we may not ever understand, but that doesn't mean we stop loving him. He needs to know he is loved. I hate seeing him without a mother. It's eating him alive. Shame, Helena doesn't see what we see." Her voice rang through my mind, and I could hear it as if she were right in front of me.

I backed off Paola. The vanilla scent quickly became overwhelming. The sudden movement caused Paola to look up at me. When she made eye contact with me, she quickly wiped away her tears and stood up in front of me.

"Aww baby, don't," she took her hands and placed them on my cheeks. I was confused. Don't what? I stayed quiet; at least she was touching me.

She took her thumbs and moved them to the corners of my eyes, and she wiped her thumbs down my cheeks. I wanted to tell her to quit being weird, but I was too busy appreciating her touch.

"Don't cry, baby."

Cry, I thought to myself. Who's crying? She took her thumbs and rubbed them from my eyes to my check again. I moved her hands and put my own to my face. There they were, tears.

Feeling the warm drips of tears flow down, my face bothered me. I wiped them away, and they kept coming. Paola stared at me while she bit her bottom lip to keep her cries in. Watching me rub my face seemed to make her tear up more. I wanted to stop and soothe her, but I couldn't because the tears were coming faster and faster. Agitation began to take over, and I could no longer take it.

I heard my voice crack as I tried to fix myself to ask Paola about Dante's death. I wasn't even sure how she could really know. Dante had been off the grid for months now. No one could track him. Ollie had kept in contact with him before, but his communication started to die down once he found out the truth about what happened to Unc.

Jairo had even been looking for Dante. Jairo thought that he could convince Dante to be a character witness for me after the lawyer made his failed attempt. It wasn't a huge deal for Dante to be a character witness. I had enough people to speak to my character. But Jairo was convinced that Dante needed to write a letter for my character whether we used it or not. He was even willing to physically force Dante to write it.

During a previous visit, he told me, "That little fucker is going to write a letter. It just goes to show you that everything I said bout that boy is true. He is a fucking weed. A damned dandelion. He needs to be plucked. He is going to write that letter, or I'm going to pluck his ass."

I believed Jairo, but Jairo couldn't find Dante. In fact, I was happy that Jairo had never found Dante. Although I sometimes had homicidal thoughts concerning Dante, deep down, I never wished him any harm. I always figured there had to be deeper reasons why Dante did what he did to me. The truth of the situation was hard enough to accept, but the thought that he did it just to mess up my life was completely unacceptable.

The fact of the matter was, I still saw Dante as the kid in class who got bullied and picked on. Dante would have been the prime candidate for a school shooter. The things he went through in school were everything that a school shooter was made of. I couldn't help but feel that Dante's life had been a constant nightmare.

I thought back to the days where he used to beg Helena to stay home. I even remembered the day we picked the table up from near the dumpster and cleaned it to the best of our ability so he could surprise Helena. Helena was Dante's undoing. She constantly plucked away at him until he was just a shell of a person with no soul.

Mama and I gave Dante soul. If not both Mama and me, then certainly Mama. She took him in and loved him as hard or as soft as he needed to be loved. She wouldn't give up on him. Even when Dante ran from her discipline, I saw Mama sitting up late at night worrying about him. It was strange how she could love a child more than the child's own mother. Just like Jairo, he loved me as if he were my own father.

I was from a disadvantaged world, like what Marvy and G spoke of so often. But so was Dante. Dante was from my world. We had both experienced the real world. If anyone could relate to my pain when it came to Mama, or when it came to simply being beaten by the world, it was Dante. With all the misunderstandings between us, I would gladly forgive Dante just for Paola to take back the news of his death.

"Wh... Wha... What happened?" I managed to stutter with my voice cracking at every word.

She looked at me and dropped her eyes as if looking at me brought pain to her.

"Paola," I called her name to grab her attention again.

She refused to look up and acknowledge me. My mind started racing, and I felt my temperature rising. A small feeling of irritation started to creep into my chest, and I could feel myself becoming angry. I slapped my hand on the table and raised my voice loud enough that she would know I was serious, but not loud enough to alert the guards. I didn't want to draw the guard's attention because I knew any act that seemed aggressive to them would end the meeting between Paola and me.

"Paola!" I called her name through gritted teeth and carefully monitored volume.

She looked up. Her eyes were red, and her soft brown cheeks were turning to match her eyes.

"Rilei, I'm so sorry. Lo siento mucho mi amor."

"Sorry for what. Paola, what's going on?" I was growing more and more irritated by the second. It was as if she was speaking in code, and I had no way to translate. I wanted her to get to the point. I wanted her to tell me what was going on, not to apologize.

"Ol...Rilei. Ol..."

"Damn Paola, spit it out."

She paused and looked at me with tears streaming down her face.

"Ollie baby. Ol..."

I paused. Ollie too. Not Ollie. I looked at Paola with my face balled up. I scrunched my nose tight hoping that it would help me keep my composure. My head began to pound, and the room started to become blurry. I closed my eyes so that I could hide from the world.

Paola was in full hysterics. Hearing her cries confirmed what she wasn't saying, or what she couldn't say. Ollie was dead. It felt as if my heart had stopped, and the air in the room was cut off. I couldn't breathe. I stared around the room to see if anyone else was having trouble breathing, but everyone else appeared to be fine.

It was always strange to me that everyone could be so happy when my world was crumbling around me. Everyone in the room breathed easy while I suffered. The world was exactly as G and Marvy said, even if they said it in different contexts.

My struggles and my fears were invisible and non-existent to others because they couldn't relate. I picked my head up and stared at the only person who might be able to understand.

"Ollie gone too, man."

"Oh, heavens no. Baby no. No, Ollie is not gone. Ollie is fine. No, wait, no. Ollie isn't fine baby," She leaned across the table and whispered in my ear, "Ollie is the suspect in Dante murder."

She sat back in her chair and looked at me. Her eyes searched my face trying to detect any emotion. The tears in my eyes instantly dried up, and everything around me seemed to stand still. I searched Paola's face for any sign of misunderstanding, hoping that maybe she had gotten her wires crossed.

Looking into her eyes was all I needed to see that she was delivering me real news. Staring at her for so long caused her face to appear distorted. I scooted my chair back from the table. She eyed me suspiciously. I didn't know what to do, the longer she sat there looking at me, the more she looked like something far from what I could describe. She looked like the bearer of bad news.

As she became almost unrecognizable, I began to feel sick to my stomach. I needed air. I looked at Paola once more, staring into her face hoping to be able to make out the beautiful woman who had walked in before she opened her mouth. I knew it wasn't Paola fault for what happened but hearing the news from her was too much for me. I scooted my chair even further back.

"Ollie." His name managed to get out even though I was making a conscious effort to purse my lips so tight that nothing could escape.

Paola continued to stare at me with curious eyes. I stared back, allowing the uneasiness in my stomach to grow. I could see Dante in her face. His smile, his bowl haircut, and his red cheeks that would usually surface when he was either angry or embarrassed.

I stood up from my seat. Paola mimicked my movement. She started to make her way toward me, but I held up my hand, signaling for her to stop. I took a step back, and she eyed me. This time, a single tear danced on her cheek as her eyes searched me.

"Ollie," I said again, but this time it was because Ollie had taken over Paola's face. His thick eyebrows were raised, and his eyes were lowered and beady. He looked angry or desperate, or both. He looked the same way he did the last time he came to visit me after I told him the truth about Unc.

Damn. I told him the truth about Unc.

I looked at Paola and continued to step back further and further toward the door that led back to the cells. With every step I took backward, she cried harder and harder. Tears filled my eyes as I tried to think back to how I felt before Paola came in. I tried to think back to my inspiration books or back to my self-help books. I couldn't. I couldn't think back any further than the moment when I realized that I had killed Dante.

I motioned toward the guard. I felt guilty. I needed to be handcuffed. My fifteen years were unjust until now. Now, my fifteen years made sense.

"I killed Dante," I said to Paola as the guard walked toward me to let me out of the visitors' area.

"No, Rilei. No. Please, don't do this," Paola cried out as the guard guided me through the doors.

Paola's cries fell on deaf ears. As much as I hated to end our visit, I couldn't stand to stay any longer. The guard turned me toward the window that looked into the visitor's room as he patted me down. Paola sunk to her knees, just like the night at the gas station. I was putting her through the same shit again.

I couldn't do right to save my life. I was reading and doing everything that I knew to do to be a better man, but here I was, still a fuck-up, still a small, scared little boy. Paola deserved better. She deserved a real family man. I was a felon. I was a dope boy, and not even a good one. I was a murderer. But most of all, for the first time ever, I realized, I was a coward.

Chapter 22

Break to Rebuild

I removed everyone from my visitor list. I stopped writing letters. I stopped reading letters. The letters poured in, but I tucked them away. I didn't bother conversing with G or Marvy. I didn't bother reading. I treated myself as if I were in solitary and drove myself insane with forced silence. I wouldn't speak to anyone. I completely isolated myself.

G was worried. I had carried on this way for weeks without explaining why. My silence worried G the most. G always said that I talked too much, and I didn't know how to hold my lips together, but I was proving him wrong. I wasn't talking at all, and he was getting fed up with my silence.

"You gone have to say something 'cause I'm not going to keep dealing with this shit," G had reached his limit with me, but I hadn't reached my limit.

I remained quiet. I respected G like every black man in the prison did. Those who didn't respect him, white, black, or other, feared him. His commands were usually met with obedience. He was a different type of man. He was true to his word, honest, and he looked out for people. He was also dangerous and quick to act.

Even knowing that, I kept quiet. I wasn't ready to deal with everything going on in my head, and if I told G about it, he would tell Marvy. Together, they would force me to deal with everything while picking me apart.

Nope, I would rather keep quiet.

Once G noticed that I was serious and I refused to discuss what was going on, he sat back down on his bed. He stared at me so long I began to feel uncomfortable.

"I get it. I know how to respect boundaries," he said as he continued to stare me down.

"You want to sit here in pity, that's fine. This world gone move on without you. Believe that. You remind me of my granddaughter. That's why I handle you the way I do. You smart, you stronger than you think, but you rely on self-pity because it's easier than dealing with the real you."

His granddaughter. I knew from the moment I met G that he saw someone else in me. I never knew it was a female. He had my attention, but I didn't want to let him know it, so I sat quietly, not uttering a sound.

"I don't understand people like y'all. All this knowledge, all this potential, but instead of going out and fulfilling your purpose, y'all would rather tell yourselves all the reasons why you can't. You two are just alike. So self-absorbed but in the wrong ways. Can't see the world outside of yourself, so instead of shit just happening because it's life, y'all think everything is happening to you, or because of you. Everything ain't about you. The forest for the trees. Damnit, Dia."

At that moment, G looked directly into my eyes. His face was moist from the tears that fled from his eyes. For the first time, I saw G cry. He looked at me as if he had just told on himself. I never seen G so vulnerable.

I spoke.

"Who is Dia?" I asked G not thinking about whether it would cause him pain, but it did. Tears filled his eyes and cycled down his cheeks again. I could see the pain in G's face.

"Dia killed herself. No, that's not who she is, that's not who she was at all, but that's all people seem to remember. You know what helped her kill herself, that shit you doing right there. That same shit. You ain't gotta talk to me. You ain't gotta tell me a goddamn thing. Sit there and sulk, you will be dead before me. I'll be done outlived you and my grand-daughter."

I felt a tear escape my eye. I quickly wiped it away as I noticed G turn over in his bunk. G mumbled, "I got a life sentence; I gotta die in this place. You choosing to die in this place."

I wondered if he were right. G had spoken nothing but truth since I met him, but he didn't understand what I was going through. I wanted to tell him, but I couldn't, so instead, I laid down on my side and shut my eyes until I drifted off to sleep.

~ ~ ~

A few mornings later, while sitting in the TV room watching News, G and Marvy surrounded me. They sat down next to me and didn't say a word, not even to each other. They just sat there. It felt good to have their presence surrounding me, and even better because it was a silent presence.

We all stared at the TV and watched the news lady go over her segments. Marvy had a secret crush on her, so anytime Fox News played, he was sure to watch. Other than that, he couldn't stand Fox News for political reasons.

Normally, Marvy would comment on the News anchors tight-fitting clothes or her young brown skin, but not this time. He just sat there quietly. I knew they wanted to talk to me or to check on me. Marvy hated being silent. He would much rather share his new philosophical ideas or his newest discoveries about black culture. I was thankful that he was able to contain himself for me.

As I stared at the news, I saw Dante's picture flash. The lady went on and on about a troubled man who was killed outside of a suspected drug house on a bad side of town.

My heart dropped as she spoke. She called it a wrong time, wrong place scenario. I chuckled to myself. Anyone who knew Dante knew that anywhere near drugs was a place that Dante liked to frequent.

The lady continued to speak her inaccuracies as Ollie's picture flashed on the screen next. Immediately, she dove into Ollie's criminal background. She pointed out his kidnapping charge and drug charges. She then dared to state that Ollie may have been obsessed with Dante being that Dante was the victim in his kidnapping charge. She labeled Ollie a violent offender and used every word to describe a thug, except for the word "thug."

She talked about Ollie being a high school dropout and brought up his Juvenile record. She had mangled his reputation so badly that by the end of the segment, I questioned if I even knew Ollie. I was so disappointed in the way she represented Ollie that I couldn't wait until we were able to use the phones. I needed to check on him.

As I continued watching the news, Helena appeared on screen. She was made up without a flaw. Her face was so heavily powdered that she was almost unrecognizable. She cried and pleaded that someone would bring Ollie to justice for her son. She bragged about how her son was a pillar in the community and that he always looked out for anyone he met. She really laid it on thick. The field reporter ate it up as did the large group of people behind them.

"Animals took my husband from me years ago, and now, one has taken my son. We have to stand up and do something. We have to say no more. We have to get justice." Helena spewed on sounding more intelligent then I'd ever known her to be.

Her teeth were rotted and nearly hanging out of her mouth. She was clearly still up to her old tricks, and the news had the nerve to let her speak on behalf of Dante. They had the nerve to let her slander Ollie even further. I was appalled.

I looked over at Marvy and G who watched intently. No expressions or emotions crossed their faces.

They were stale faced. I should have expected as much. Nothing surprised Marvy or G. They expected the worst of everything. If I had told them this was going to happen, they would have said that they could see it no other way.

I couldn't help but compare. I knew without a doubt that Dante had a record a mile long, even as a juvenile. I couldn't ignore the fact that he had never been in prison. I also knew that Dante killed Unc. Even though Unc's case went unsolved, I knew the truth. It was me that gave a few of the local crackheads on the block a couple rocks to go inside the house after Unc was killed. I never told Dante because he thought he knew everything and would never approve of giving away free drugs. I, however, knew that if they went in there, they would contaminate the scene enough for it to complicate any investigation.

I saved Dante. I spent most of my life saving Dante. Part of me knew what telling Ollie about Unc would do. I wasn't completely sure what would happen, but I knew that Ollie would be upset. I knew that Ollie would react. When I was completely honest with myself, I knew that I had set Dante's murder into motion. I was the monster and the mastermind, even though I didn't necessarily mean to be.

My emotions were mixed. I felt like I had lost two people at once. I had allowed anger and resentment to build up in me so long regarding Dante. I was passive, I let things go, I turned blind eyes, but things people said to me were registering. Because I could not be real with myself, Dante was dead. It was my fault. I didn't do what needed to be done. I didn't cut him off when I should have.

Jairo said I would be accountable, and I took it too literally. I thought that meant if Dante messed up with the drugs or money, then I would have to take responsibility for it. Jairo had said so much more. He meant that I would be accountable for not handling those around me period. Even if I let things go like Dante giving me the cold shoulder, Dante lying or bringing suspicious characters around, then I would ultimately be held accountable.

The more I thought about things, the more I realized that my sentence made sense. I was serving time for being stupid and not for drugs. Dante had given me many warning signs that he was not capable of being loyal or trustworthy. He had changed, but I denied the signs. I was too caught up in wanting to make things right. I was so busy trying to catch back up to a time when I had my mother, and everything was simple. Dante was just trying to protect himself.

My mind slipped back into when I saw him reading the Mein Kampf book. It puzzled me, especially after I read it and understood the content. For Dante to be able to read a book that sophisticated was amazing to me, but for him to have the book in his possession was a disappointment. The book preached superiority of the white race and I had always thought of Dante as no different than myself. Dante was black as far as I was concerned. His struggles were just like mine.

Suddenly it hit me. When Dante stopped spending so much time at the house, and when I left the house,

Dante changed. I knew he always resented the way Unc treated him, and I knew finding out about his father was a hard blow. Dante had started spending time with his cousins from when he was younger and trying to find himself. Since Helena was no longer around, and Dante was grown, his father's side of the family accepted him with open arms. I remembered.

I remembered Dante ranting on about how his cousins were not nearly as tall as he was and how they were proud of him for getting away from his mother. I remembered Dante at first having mixed feelings about being around them, but I also remembered hearing Dante on the phone for hours at a time talking about his father and his childhood. I never weighed in heavily on Dante's familial relationships because I knew they were personal for him.

I recalled the one time that Dante had cracked a joke in front of Paola, thinking it would be funny. Paola ran back and told me because she was offended and concerned. I remembered like it was yesterday.

She came in the room, quiet but furious.

"Rilei, Dante... Well, has he ever said anything kind of... you know... racist?"

I remembered it as if it were yesterday. Dante had asked Paola if she knew what FUBU stood for. Paola had told him it meant "For Us, By Us." Dante started to laugh and then told Paola, "No, it means "Farmers Used to Beat Us."

Paola told me that she couldn't even crack a fake smile. She said she asked Dante if he knew that she too was black. Dante told her that she wasn't black; she was Columbian. Paola then went into a long rant about how she was Latina, but she was indeed black, and so was every other person of color whose ancestors descended from Africa.

I wasn't there for the conversation, but I was there for the aftermath. Paola stormed into the bedroom spouting off a lesson in history as if I had been the one who cracked the joke. I could hear Dante's laughter from the living room and when Paola first told the story, I too, laughed with Dante. I found no harm in the joke.

That's what G and Marvy were trying to teach me. I had no idea at the time that where there is smoke, there is fire. I thought I knew Dante enough to know that the joke was not harmful, but I didn't know enough about life or myself to know that the thought process behind Dante even feeling like it was appropriate was harmful. Now, I had to accept that I was the undoing in my own fate and Dante's because all I had to do was read the signs.

I thought back to when Paola was explaining the African Diaspora. I thought about how much pride she had in being black and how much pride she had in being Latina.

"Rilei, we all left from the same continent, some of us migrated willfully, and some of us were forced. The lucky ones, they got to stay. What he said to me was disrespectful because one, he thought he had the right just because he thought that being Latina meant that I wasn't black. And two, because he thought it was funny. My people were slaves, they were taken from Africa and enslaved in South America. Your people were taken from

Africa and enslaved in America. The difference between us is the culture that we rebuilt for ourselves based on what we learned from our conquerors, who made us believe that we were inferior and not worth anything because we were black. Nigga in America, Negro in Spanish lands, but we are all of the diaspora, and we are one. Out of one, there are many. He is disrespectful.

He is nothing but a faded black person. He comes from people who migrated to colder regions, lost their way, and convinced themselves that they were better because they didn't know any better. It is our own people, in that sense, that oppress, dehumanize, humiliate, and downgrade us. But you tell me this Rilei, how great is the fruit that rolls too far from its tree. We maintain our greatness; it's laced in our melanin. Farmers used to beat us... The fucking nerve."

I could remember her rant almost verbatim. I remembered cracking up with laughter when she told Dante that he was a "faded black person." It was an idea that she had taken from her hero Jane Elliot. I remembered Dante getting angry and storming out, but I didn't pay it any attention because it was not that serious to me.

I should have known then that Dante was going through some things. I had never met his dad's family. Dante never invited me, and he never brought them to the house. I didn't question it. I was happy that he was happy. I ignored that he was changing. I missed the signs that could have saved my life and his.

Now, he was gone. Now all I had left were memories, and they were all tainted with overwhelming speculation and me questioning what I had missed. Even memories from the playground in kindergarten, when Dante jumped on fat joey. I never questioned how Dante had gotten us out of trouble. Now, I knew. Dante, with his problematic behavior, still appeared to be the poor little innocent white kid. Dante played on that. I was too young, too dumb, too naïve to realize then, but I could see it now.

Unc was on to something, he was just too ignorant to convey it. Unc could see what I couldn't see in Dante. Everyone could see what I couldn't see in Dante. I continued to stare in the direction of the TV, and while my mind ran wild, I busted into tears.

Once back into the cell, I ripped through my pillowcase and recovered all the letters I had stashed there. I separated them into piles and focused. I had letters from Ollie, Paola, Jairo, Mrs. Donaldson, and Helena.

I stared at Helena's letter as if it would jump out of the envelope. I wanted to open it and read it, but I feared what the content would be. The thought of reading it gave me a headache, so I stuck it back in the pillowcase. I started to pick up one of the many letters from Paola, but I couldn't get my mind off the letter from Helena.

I threw all the letters back into the pillowcase and laid down. I laid still, once again, staring at the ceiling, begging for sleep.

Chapter 23

Nothing Happens to the Wicked

Rilei,

I hope you get this. You know how Helena is. I left this with her and told her to send it to you. I got your letter. I know you got questions. I don't know how to answer them. A lot is going on. Everything is just fucked up.

It's people on my ass, people want me dead. I violated probation; I know I probably have a warrant out. I am out of places to turn.

I know it's wrong of me to ask you for anything, but I need help. You are the only person I could ever count on. Maybe if you could ask Jairo if I could borrow some money to get out of town, or if I could borrow from Paola.

I would come see you, but I can't walk into a prison with warrants.

Rilei, this is going to sound like bullshit to you. Everything that was wrong with me was because of my dad. Being with his family made me feel like I had a piece of him again. They loved me, and they told me like Teigen use to tell me, they hugged me, they welcomed me with open arms. They taught me a lot about my father and who he was.

They wanted me to do shit for them too, though. I read Mein Kampf because I was in a different place. You had left on your adventures with Jairo. You didn't need me anymore. You had traded me in for Paola a long time ago. I knew it was only a matter of time before you left like Helena. My cousins were there. They taught me how to love myself. I used to think I was so worthless, I would never have your luck, but my cousins convinced me that I was better than you.

I got involved with their shit. I don't disagree with it all, but some of it made me think of you and Teigen. I knew some of it wasn't true. After Mr. Donaldson passed, we held counter-rallies. I felt guilty the whole time. I know that doesn't mean much, but I want you to know that.

I know that the officer who killed him didn't get indicted. I know that hurts you. I know Mr. Donaldson didn't like me, but I know he wasn't the type of man to do what they said he did. I am sorry. I been fucking up and I am so sorry.

For initiation, I was supposed to have you set up and killed. I was supposed to have the house raided, and you killed on the backside. I was angry with you. I was going to do it, and at the last minute, I couldn't. You had been busting my balls about using. You went with Jairo to profit off the shit that took my mom from me. You were turning on me, and I wanted to do it, but I couldn't.

Instead, I put the coke in your car. I figured it was the next best thing. I know I been doing a lot of shady shit, but the coke was to save you. No matter what, no matter how I show it, I love you, man. You are my brother.

I am going to get away for a while, and once I get my mind right, I am going to write again. If Helena is worth anything, she will at least put this in the mail for me. I gotta stay low-key. You know how this shit go. I am going to get back to you, and I'll answer whatever you want.

Oh, sorry to hear 'bout your pops, man.

Rilei, I am sorry.

Signed—
You Know

~ ~ ~

I closed the letter and held it. There were no feelings. Just numbness.

Mike.

Sorry to hear about your pops.

I had no idea what he was talking about. Unsure of how to feel about the letter or Dante, I balled the letter up and tossed it in the corner. G stared at me.

"Did it make everything go away? Does it change anything? If not, let it go," G spoke softly.

G was getting worse. His illness was getting the best of him, and he did little to change his circumstance.

"He said something about the man who raped my mom. He said, '*Sorry to hear about your pops.*' I don't know what he means by that," I said to G, knowing that he wouldn't have any answers for me.

"Nothing," G answered, "do what makes you sleep better at night, but I wouldn't do nothing."

I was too curious not to do anything. I wanted to know what Dante was referring to. It was odd enough to be receiving a letter post-death from Dante, but to hear him tell me so many things and not be able to confront them drove me insane. I couldn't ask any more questions about why he did the things he did, but I could at least find out what he meant about Mike. If any good news was to come of it, then Mike was dead.

I waited until it was time to use the phones, and I contacted Paola. She was like her father in the fact that she followed all the news channels and was up on current events. I told her about the letter from Dante and the comment he made regarding Mike. I asked what Dante could possibly be referring to.

"Have you not read any of my letters, Rilei. Seriously. What is going on with you, I don't hear from you in weeks. You removed me from your visitors, and now you call me, and the first thing you ask about is Mike, not even Ramon?"

I apologized. I didn't want to argue, and there wasn't a lot of phone time left. I told her I would make sure to add her back and then repeated my question about Mike.

"Read the fucking letters, Rilei. Bye."

She hung up on me.

I rushed back to my cell and emptied my pillowcase. I pulled out each of Paola's letters and read through them.

Mike was sentenced to prison. He was given 5 years but no rape charge. The rape charge was pleaded down and used the verbiage 'sexual assault' instead of rape. Mike's influences were working for him again. I was relieved that he was at least charged.

I told G. I couldn't wait to tell G that Mike would possibly be in prison with us.

"They don't usually put the perverts with gen pop. We ain't gone see him. I don't know what you all happy for. That just goes to show you the system failing you once again."

I wasn't sure of G's logic, but I knew he had logic behind how he felt. He always did.

"Why you say that G?"

"He raped your mother. Nothing. No justice. Because a powerful white man raped an irrelevant black girl. Now, this white woman, let you tell it, you said she was younger but willing. Right? Correct me if I am wrong. This is a case of her not getting what she wants and taking vengeance, right? You said she got a child, your brother, correct? Well, you tell me how that's not statutory rape; sexual assault was a favor. Honestly, I would have felt better if he got away with raping that young girl. At least then we wouldn't have to ask if race had anything to do with it. This just goes to show, like I always said, the price of a black life ain't much."

I begged him to explain more. I wanted him to drill the point home to where I could no longer question if he was just pushing an agenda that made all blacks sound like victims.

"A black man kills a black man, he may go to jail if they take the time to investigate properly, but he don't do much time. A white man kills a black man, and well, George Zimmerman. He like some sort of fucking hero or something. Just like the man who killed the boys about the bike. It's always a 'good enough' reason for them to do it so that no time is needed. We are three/fifths of a human to them, to that damn constitution they wrote up, so you gotta kill more of us to get the time you would for killing just one of them. Dylan Roof, you see what I am saying. He killed nine of us for that life sentence, and even then, it had to be written as a hate crime, and maybe the fact that it was a church helped a little – but he took out nine of us and lived to talk about it.

I know you tired of hearing this race shit Rilei. I say to you, do your research. Race, classism, inequality, the powerful and the powerless, that's what this country thrives off. If you think they not still lynching niggas, then look into the lady in Ferguson, look at what they did to her son. I am not telling you we are not capable of overcoming this shit. What I been trying to get you to do is realize that this shit ain't new. It's the same thing just a different way of doing it. Here's the kicker Rilei, you ready? We know how to beat this shit. We got a cheat sheet, we seen it done with Toussaint Louverture and the likes. And, we seen why it failed. Unite. Learn more about you, educate your people, teach your kids, and soon – greatness will return. It can't stay away from home too long."

After listening to G, I knew what I had to do. I knew what was next for me. I knew what I needed to do for my appeal. Not my appeal to crime, because I hadn't committed the crime I was charged with; but, my appeal to myself, my appeal to my people.

PART 3

Chapter 24

Voiced

"There comes a point when silence is betrayal." —
Unknown

Dear Judge Neal,

As you have read my story, you have read my truth. Sentencing me was the easy part. It was words and a gavel bang. Knowing me, having read my enclosed book, will be the hard part.

When you slammed that gavel, you didn't see Rilei sitting in front of you. You saw a criminal. Now, if you can remember my face from the hundreds that you passed judgments on, you know me, and you know my story.

I am the criminal that you practiced law for. Before you knew me, you knew that the law said I was guilty. I get it. I look guilty. I understand how that works now. Long lessons from G and Marvy taught me that, as you have read by now. Now I ask you, am I still the criminal you practice law for?

I am making it a point to let you know that I forgive you. I did not know me, so how could I expect you to know me? Self-discovery is a beautiful thing. When our *vision of ourselves is no longer dependent on what someone else drew, it's enlightening.*

Who drew for you, your vision of me? Does it look anything like what I have described for you? I am a man, a black man, but I can own up to my guilt, and I can accept my faults as a man. I am a fatherless son, abandoned by a man who could do everything society said he wasn't couldn't. I no longer live with the pain of knowing, but will you?

There is no way you can bang your gavel as often as you do and get every case right, but do you try? Do you see criminals as those who break the law or those who look like they break the law? I struggled with my image when I thought of that question. I, undoubtedly, fit the description of someone who breaks the law. I learned that from Unc. That is why Dante was his scrambler. Dante was damned good at it too, because he didn't fit the description of a lawbreaker.

Now I ask you, who had the official say so when it came to pinning down a description of a criminal?

I do not send you this letter or my life story, hoping for sympathy. I send this hoping for a voice. I hope I am that voice that rings through your head when you gather with other judges.

I hope that I am that voice that you hear when you watch one of your fellow judges unfairly sentence a man for a crime.

I hope that I can be that voice that bursts through your lips when you sit and watch an officer of the law walk free, knowing that he shouldn't.

I hope I am the voice that causes people to reevaluate who patrols our neighborhoods and if they are equipped with the right morals and traits to serve.

See, I hope to be the voice that ends the George Zimmermans. I see people tremor at the stand your ground law because they know that it means that the majority has the right to stand their ground against the minority. Not the other way around.

I hope to be the voice that lives on though Botham Jean, Stephon Clark, and Jemel Roberson. The voice that says, I am black, not a criminal, and I do not deserve to have the justice system continue to justify my death. I do not deserve the speculation on my personal habits to be brought into question because you have searched and searched but cannot find my criminal record.

I hope to be the voice for Oscar Grant, Alton Sterling, and Michael Brown that says whatever you think I did, let's take it to court, not to the morgue.

Tamir Rice, Freddie Gray, Eric Gardner, I hope to be the voice that says 'I can't breathe' in this current design, let's change it.

I want Paola and I to talk to our son about how to be a great father and how to open car doors for a lady. I want to teach him about the birds and the bees. I want to teach him about how to be a man, not a coward. I want him to learn how to be a scholar and provider through legal means, not like me. I want to have those conversations with him, without having to teach him about how to dim his light in the presence of white people, or how to mute his voice and tread lighter than

Jesus on water when interacting with police. I do not want to teach him how to bow in the presence of his white counterparts because any sign of advancement or progression is a possible threat. I do not want to teach my son to fear the police, to fear his greatness, or to fear himself. I do not want to teach my son fear.

I want to be the voice that teaches him light. I don't believe anyone's light is greater than another's. But I do believe we all have a light and they all shine differently. That's ok. One light is not inferior to the other, but they all play a part in making the path to our future brighter. Every light is necessary, important, needed, and valuable. I want to be that voice.

Your gavel silenced me for a while, but now, with my pen as my gavel, I order my own path.

Geronimo Pratt, Barney Brown, Anthony Graves and so many more, I hope to be the voice that says, 'stop wrongful convictions.'

I hope to be the voice for myself. I forgive you for sentencing me to 15 years. I know that you know that it was a lengthy and undeserved sentence and I forgive you.

You did what you were taught to do. You followed the design. I hope to be the voice that says, 'change the design.'

I hope that you hear my voice saying loud and clear, that the racial disparities in prison sentences are obvious. We notice this new form of captivity and slavery. We notice this new form of inequality and containment. We notice.

We notice when we are dragged on the media and our ways of expressing emotions are criticized. When we lose a black man to police, we are met with criticism of what we do to each other. When we protest or destroy things in an emotional rage, we are animals, savages, and our behavior is typical.

Yet when our white counterparts' favorite football team lose a game, their poor display of behavior, their rioting, their destroying of property is simply charged to their favorite team losing a game.

We are supposed to behave non-violently in a country that seeks to control and maintain its control through violence.

I hope that my voice brings awareness. I hope that my voice brings change. I hope that my voice causes people to kneel with Kaepernick and stand with Black Lives Matter.

I hope my voice brings attention to anti-black campaigns that turn a blind eye to black injustices. I hope that it explains that all lives do not matter if black lives are not included. I hope that it explains that being pro-black is not being anti-white or anti-police but being proud of being black.

I hope that it makes people aware.

I hope that my story helped you to see the human in me. I am not a criminal. I am more than that. I am a man. I am a king. I am a descendant from the great continent of Africa, and although I have bent many times, I am not broken.

I hope this shows you that we do not break.

In closing, should this letter read nothing else, I hope it reads "We will prevail. We will survive. We will unite. We will rise. The choice will be given, stand in a glorious and colorful unity as one race of humans, or....

What does your voice tell you?

I hope that you see that justice seems only to be serving Just Us.

I forgive you, and I thank you for placing me in a circumstance that forced me to learn and educate myself beyond what I thought was education.

AmeriKKKan JustUS,

—Rilei

~ ~ ~

After reading Rilei's story and letter, the former judge, Maryann Neal, inserted the thick manuscript back in the envelope from which it came. Her tired hands shook as she fiddled with the pen on her desk. Her glasses slid halfway down her nose as she thought back to the day that she called out "15 years."

A tear slid down her face as she looked onto her desk at the picture of her perfect daughter, holding her mixed-raced grandson who she could not help but love.

She remembered a time when her daughter wasn't so perfect, and her choices impacted her family greatly. She remembered her daughter coming into her bedroom that she once shared with her husband. Her daughter, Sage's eyes were bloodshot, red with cheeks to match. She could remember Sage stammering while trying to deliver the message that broke her marriage apart. The message that she was pregnant.

It wasn't as big a shock as Sage thought that it would be. Sage was young, but she was out of school, and she had parents who loved her.

It was indeed the next bit of news that caused Sage to exit the bed, the home, and the family in a rage. It was the news that Sage was carrying a baby that indicated she had no respect for the purity of her family and what they stood for. Her father could never accept a child conceived in such a way, regardless of the biological ties.

Maryann thought back to the conversation she had with her daughter that day. She regretted how she spoke. She had accused her daughter of trying to ruin their family and ruin their name. She didn't know how to handle the information.

She vividly remembered the look on Sage's face when she said, "I would rather you be gay than to bring a black man into this home, let alone, having you tell me that you are carrying his seed. Have you thought about what this could mean Sage? It's re-election year for crying out loud."

Maryann recalled the guilt that had consumed her when Sage left home. She remembered the moment she found out that Sage had started using drugs. She was disgusted. Not only was Sage pregnant with a bi-racial child, but she was using drugs. She remembered the embarrassment and wondering if the news was getting around the courthouse. She blamed the young man who impregnated Sage; it was his fault that her daughter had forsaken her with pregnancy and drugs. However, in her heart, she knew the fault was her own. She had turned her daughter away time and time again and ignored every sign of needing help that her daughter displayed.

Maryann had developed a deep resentment for Sage; but with her name and reputation being of utmost importance to her, she relented and sought the best and most private drug treatment centers that the country had to offer. She monitored Sage closely for all the wrong reasons. She had a lot to lose, and unlike her husband, Sage's father—she would not let Sage destroy her reputation.

Maryann looked at the picture again with a tear in her eye. She remembered talking with Sage while she was in rehab. It was as if she were getting to know her daughter all over again. But it was the delivery room that had the greatest impact on her heart. Watching her daughter give birth was miraculous, and all the resentment she once held turned into love. As she watched Sage deliver the most beautiful child she had ever seen, she felt a protective feeling come over her, and she knew she would defend Sage's mixed mistake with her own life.

Maryann recounted the evening six months after her grandson Charles was born. Sage dropped another bombshell on her and announced that she was indeed a bi-sexual woman with a stronger preference for women than for men.

Maryann remembered the feeling of heartbreak all over again. She felt as if she had finally come to terms with the fact that she had a mixed-race grandson whose father was actively involved. It was hard adjusting to having her grandson's father visit her home to pick up Charles. She soon learned that Charles' father was different. He wasn't like the other black men she had been coached about or had sentenced in all her years on the bench. Charles' father was proper, ambitious, and educated. He was well-spoken and maintained a proper image, and although he would have never been Maryann's pick for Sage, he was a tolerable option since she had no other choice.

The thought of Sage being gay was different. Maryann couldn't help but think that not only would her daughter be parading around with a woman, but given her daughter's previous choice, it might be a black woman.

The love Maryann had for Charles kept her silent. She couldn't fathom Sage running away again with Charles at her hip. She unwillingly accepted Sage's admission and only asked that she not parade it around town. Although she knew that her request hurt Sage, she knew that Sage understood.

When Sage introduced her to her female lover, Maryann was relieved to see that it was a white woman but disgusted all the same. Once she spoke and got to know Sage's girlfriend, she took a liking to her as she had with Charles' father. She was smart and came from an elite family, much like herself. In fact, she reminded Maryann of herself. After learning more about her,

Maryann discovered that she wanted to be a judge. It was a proud moment for Maryann. Maryann could not have been more excited if the words had come from Sage's lips.

"What do you stand for?" Maryann remembered asking Sage's girlfriend, Melissa.

"I stand for the voiceless. Being a lesbian woman today is hard. We are either sexualized as if our preference is strictly for male entertainment, or we are criticized. It is hard to be a part of the LGBT community these days. The hate committed against my community is scary. I just want to protect those who can't protect themselves. I will be hard on hate crimes."

Maryann asked, "how do you feel about the black community?"

"I don't mind them. Entitled, but it doesn't bother me much. I'll be fair. It's hard, though because they blame everything on race. It's not always about race. Sometimes it's just them. I love Charles, though, and I know and respect how Sage feels."

Maryann knew how Sage felt as well. She could never forget when Sage busted into tears having to defend Charles' father to her own father. Her message had not resonated with her father, but it had with Maryann.

Sage had repeated to her father the example that Charles' father had given her. She made an emotional plea for her father to be in her life and in his grandson's life. She wanted him to accept her sexuality, her son, and her son's father. She wanted him to be what she considered a better man."

Maryann thought of Sage's example. It brought tears to her eyes. She couldn't deny the accuracy.

Sage had said to her father: "Do you love me?" Her father answered as expected.

"With everything I have, that is why I cannot understand why you do the things you do."

"I am not doing anything except living and trying to be happy. You have poisoned me with your views, and I hate to tell you, Dad, they are so wrong. Have you ever spent a day with a black person, so you know what you're talking about? It makes me ashamed to know that I once laughed at your jokes around the dinner table. I don't blame you. You are what you were raised to be. I do hold you accountable, though, because you can choose to be different."

Her father answered again with arrogance, "Ashamed of me? I am ashamed. Look at what you're doing. I am ashamed. I am the joke at the table now. You did all of this to spite me, and, how your mother came around, I will never know. You tried to ruin us when all we ever did was love you. Your mother can do as she will, but I will never..."

Sage cut him off and said, "Dad, I am the same as those blacks you hate so much. Your grandson will have to deal with scrutiny in this world because of people who think like you. I made the mistake of telling Charles' father that my struggles were just like his because I was bi-sexual, and do you know what he said to my dad?"

At those words, Maryann remembered without flaw all that Sage had said.

"He said if he and I were to walk into a restaurant, and a gunman said that he is going to kill everyone who is either lesbian, bi-sexual or gay, that I would have the option to live because I can act as if I am straight. He, on the other hand, if the gunman says he will kill every black, there's nothing he can do to change the fact that he is black. He cannot pretend. It wasn't until he said that – that I realized, I am and have always been at an advantage. I thought I could feel his pain because of the pain that I felt from this family as a result of having Charles and being gay, but I can't. His can be so much worse than mine sometimes because of people like you. Now that I know how it feels to be judged and condemned, belittled, and degraded, and to face adversity, I would never want it done to Charles because now I know, it could be so much worse for him."

~ ~ ~

Maryann continued looking at the picture as she thought about her painful, yet meaningful memories.

She had long ago hung up her robe and put down her gavel. She traded in her long days in the courtroom for long days with her family instead.

Nothing she had done caused her any regret, except for reading Rilei's long story and realizing that she was the gunman in the restaurant that Sage had spoken of so long ago. She couldn't help but feel the weight of his words. She was worried about the injustice done to Rilei, not because she was the cause; that wasn't what bothered her. She was worried about the reality of Rilei's words and whether her grandson that she had grown fond of would suffer or be a victim to the same reality or similar. She knew how people thought, and she knew the ways of the courts. She was worried.

'Suffer,' she thought. She chuckled slightly and wiped her face as the tears continued to fall. Grabbing the pen from the desk and pulling out a larger envelope from her desk drawer, she stuck Rilei's envelope inside. She scribbled a message on top and licked one of her many liberty stamps to place in the corner.

She rushed outside to catch the mailman before he could get too far down the street. Handing the envelope to him, she told him, "make sure this gets there safely."

Once back inside, the former judge, Maryann Neal, grabbed several copies of Rilei's story that she had made earlier. She looked in the corner at her robe and at her new campaign sign.

"Vote Melissa Morehall, the judge who can hear the voices of the voiceless."

She wasn't sure about the campaign slogan but looking at her grandson's photo, she was sure that it was the right message.

Rilei's story would be the motivation. She had given specific instruction that the story was to be passed through the Courthouse to any Judge who would take it. She would title it the same way he signed his letter, 'Amerikkkan Justus,' and she would take the chance, the risk, that she would make the unpopular decision to recognize the reality. She would do it for her grandson. She would do it because no matter how she was raised to feel, she had had enough of denying what she knew was the reality. She would do it as a reformed racist who knew she was shedding light on a system whose design she knew all too well.

When she looked at her grandson, she saw nothing inferior. She saw nothing criminal. She saw only love. She knew the world around him would not see him through her eyes, so she had to see the world through his. She was thankful to Rilei for that.

A *ding* sound shot out from her computer, notifying her of a new email. The mailman had done as she said. She may have ruffled a few feathers, but it was ok.

She opened the email, and across the screen, as she knew it would, it read...

"They're just niggers, Maryann. Who cares if it's true?" It was what she would expect from the appeals court judge, and all she needed to give to Rilei's attorney to ask that he be recused from Rilei's appeal.

She printed the email and forwarded a copy of it to Rilei's attorney who set up to file the appeal. She went back into her sent messages where she had once before conversed with the DA and Public Defender on Rilei's case.

After reviewing it carefully, she sent a follow-up email to Rilei's lawyer for his appeal simply letting him know that she would like to have Officer Brown investigated and to use the grounds of illegal search and seizure, and fruit of a poisonous tree to argue Rilei's appeal.

Maryann knew that she had not allowed certain evidence into court, she knew that her practices were less than ethical, but she was ready to make it right. There was nothing more she could do to apologize to Rilei, but there was so much more she could do to save her grandson.

As she prepared a list for who she wanted to receive copies of Rilei's story, she started to cough. Hurriedly, she continued to write out all the names that she hoped to send copies to.

Once finished, she moved back across the room to her computer and pulled up the scanned copy of Rilei's story. She navigated to her email and selected as many names as she could from her contact list, *'send.'*

She started to cough again. It felt like she had something stuck in her throat, but she could not get it out. She chose to ignore it while she completed what was most important to her.

After sending the last of her emails, she grabbed the picture of her daughter holding her grandson. She stared at it long and hard. After growing tired of staring and growing more tired of wondering, she picked up the phone.

"Sage, let me speak to Melissa. It's about the campaign and her brother."

No sooner had Melissa made it to the phone did Maryann begin to ramble off about Rilei.

"If you love my daughter and her son like you say you do, then do right by your own brother. I won't back your campaign unless you do. You should shed light on the truth about your father and fix what I did so many years ago to your brother. A voice for the voiceless, right? What you did to that Teigen gal all those years ago is quite shameful, but we have all done things of which we should not be proud. I have a book for you. You read it, and you make things right while you can. Don't let me down."

She hung up. Maryann wasn't one for back and forth. Just then her email dinged again. It was what she was waiting on. Officer Brown's jacket at her disposal. She clicked the button to forward the email to Rilei's attorney as a sharp pain shot across her chest.

Determined to get the letter to its destination, she started typing his name in the address bar. With her instructions to Sage and Melissa, a copy of the book and her will stacked neatly at the edge of her desk, Maryann grabbed the picture of her grandson once more, and, while she stared at his face, she hit send.

She opened up a YouTube video that Charles' father had once sent her in her less-accepting days. *'A revolutionary that boy was,'* she thought to herself. She forwarded the video to Sage's father's email address, along with Rilei's story. She knew the chance of it doing any good would be slim, but she hoped for the best. She left a small message in the email stating:

I know what we thought all these years, but we have to examine the part we play. I listened to a guy, Minister Farrakhan. I can't help but ask if he is right. Do we only see violence because that is what we inflicted, and we feel the guilt of that? Are we really fearful of them, or are we fearful of what we have done in the past and what we continue to allow to this day, coming back to bite us? I know that this is not the popular consensus, but is it the truth? There is just so much more to the story. At least look into it, for your grandson, because regardless, he is YOUR grandson.

With Love,

Maryann Neal

"I'll make sure they hear your voice," Maryann uttered as she took her last glance at her grandson and last breath of life.

~ The End ~

About the Author

DaLena Slayton

DaLena Slayton was born in Akron, OH and currently resides in Dallas, TX. She served in the US Army and holds a Bachelor's of Science in Criminal Justice from the University of North Texas. Her love of writing stemmed from poetry and its ability to make the darkest things sound the most beautiful. Obsessed with the Criminal Justice system and its effect on different cultures, her poetry began to take a more political tone. With growing interest, an idea for her first novel popped into her mind, and so, AmeriKKKan JustUS was born.